AF522124

BY JANA CASALE

The Girl Who Never Read Noam Chomsky

How to Fall Out of Love Madly

HOW TO FALL OUT *of* LOVE MADLY

HOW TO FALL OUT *of* LOVE MADLY

A NOVEL

JANA CASALE

SIMON & SCHUSTER

London · New York · Sydney · Toronto · New Delhi

PARAMOUNT

This edition published in India by Simon & Schuster India, 2023

Simon & Schuster India
818, Indraprakash Building,
21, Barakhamba Road,
New Delhi 110001.

www.simonandschuster.co.in

Paperback ISBN: 978-93-92099-71-7
eBook ISBN: 978-93-92099-72-4

Grateful acknowledgment is made to W. W. Norton & Company, Inc. and Russell & Volkening, Inc., a member of Massie & McQuilkin Literary Agents, for permission to reprint "To the Woman Crying Uncontrollably in the Next Stall" from *Now We're Getting Somewhere: Poems* by Kim Addonizio, copyright © 2021 by Kim Addonizio. Audio rights are controlled by Russell & Volkening, Inc., a member of Massie & McQuilkin Literary Agents. Used by permission of W. W. Norton & Company, Inc. and Russell & Volkening, Inc., a member of Massie & McQuilkin Literary Agents.

Printed and bound in India by Replika Press Pvt. Ltd.

1 3 5 7 9 10 8 6 4 2

This book is dedicated to all the women in my life.

To the Woman Crying Uncontrollably in the Next Stall

If you ever woke in your dress at 4am ever
closed your legs to a man you loved opened
them for one you didn't moved against
a pillow in the dark stood miserably on a beach
seaweed clinging to your ankles paid
good money for a bad haircut backed away
from a mirror that wanted to kill you bled
into the back seat for lack of a tampon
if you swam across a river under rain sang
using a dildo for a microphone stayed up
to watch the moon eat the sun entire
ripped out the stitches in your heart
because why not if you think nothing &
no one can / listen I love you joy is coming

—KIM ADDONIZIO

PART ONE

JOY

Let me tell you something about my stomach. It's big and I hate it. I think about it all the time. I think about the way it looks in shirts and dresses, the way it sits over my jeans and hangs over the edge. When I'm sitting, it juts out in the most hideous way with big folds. There's no flattering way for me to sit with it so I think about ways to not sit, and I think about sucking it in whenever it is that I am sitting. I think about what other people think about it, and what they think of me because of it. I never want to look at it, but I can't stop staring at it in the mirror whenever I get the chance. I would love to tell you that it doesn't define how I think of myself, but those are just words and they're not making me feel what it is I want to feel and what it is that I want to feel is thinner. I cry about it a lot, mostly to myself and sometimes to my mom. She usually tells me I'm crazy and that I should stop obsessing. One time, just once, when I'd called and started in on the same conversation about my weight and how fat I am, she said as I was sobbing,

"Jenny Craig, maybe?"

And that moment I think about all the time. I'll hear her voice as I wait at a stoplight or even when I pee.

"Jenny Craig, maybe?"

I know it would kill her to think that even though she's told me I am thin ten thousand times over, the only thing I think about is the one time she said, "Jenny Craig, maybe?" I know it would kill her so I don't tell her; I just think it and wonder what motion there was in her heart the moment she said it and I fear whatever that motion was is not part of me like I want to believe everything about my mom is part of me. And then I feel as vast and big as anything else. *Empty* is the word for it. So I sit down and suck in my stomach and just keep on going, Jenny Craig, forever.

Joy was put on birth control at thirteen years old by her doctor, who was a man. He was old and had been her doctor since she was a baby. When her mother had told him in private that her daughter had very painful, heavy periods, he suggested it, and without question they put her on a small dose of hormones. From the age of thirteen until now, at nearly thirty years old, Joy had not ovulated.

At first she immediately felt superior to everyone else in her eighth-grade class. *If I wanted to have sex right now I totally could, and I wouldn't get pregnant,* she often thought. But the thought such as it was was useless because no one had sex with Joy until she was twenty-four. Besides that, the birth control did help with her cramps, which had been so violent that she'd once thrown up from the pain. Her mom and she had been at the movies seeing Disney's *Tarzan,* and she'd been trying desperately to keep from having to go home. She even took off her shoes and tucked her feet up under herself trying to find a position comfortable enough to stop the pain. But nothing worked, and she found herself running to the bathroom nearly doubled over. She could vividly remember throwing up completely undigested Sno-Caps to the sound of a little kid's voice outside the bathroom stall saying, "I think someone is throwing up."

It was a godsend when the cramps eased up and she didn't have a ton of side effects from the hormones either, as her mother had feared she might.

"If you feel bad at all let me know because there are other options that might help just as much," she'd say, but Joy was fine and felt better. What she didn't know and wouldn't know was that the minute she started the pills her brain's response, besides stopping ovulation, was to change the way it perceived other people's pheromones, and because of this, Joy wasn't attracted to the men to whom she would have been if she'd never gone on the pills to begin with. Instead she found herself attracted to many of the wrong types of men and every relationship she'd pursue would end badly. She dated a guy named Felix and a guy name Cory and then a guy named Guy. Her only real relationship was four and a half months long. His name was Ryder and he thought extremely highly of himself. Joy knew very early on that she wasn't in love with Ryder, and that he was at best an inappropriate choice for her and at worst a damage to her self-esteem, but she didn't let herself acknowledge even one of those thoughts. Instead, she tried desperately to convince herself that she was in love with him, even telling friends, "I think I'm falling in love with him," something she could text and almost believe, but the second she said it out loud, she felt foolish and instantly regretted it. Ryder broke up with her just shy of their five-month anniversary (a date he would likely forget and she would likely make excuses for him for forgetting), because he wanted to "live in a tiny home in Alaska." When he told her this she didn't cry, but when she got home she cried a lot, and it made her wonder what was it that was making her feel this devastated if it wasn't love and the best she could come up with was that it was loneliness and the second best she could come up with was disappointment and the third, rejection. She wouldn't know much more than that; she wouldn't know that even though she'd told herself for ages that she didn't mind being single and that she didn't want children anyway and that turning thirty very soon meant nothing, somewhere it terrified her that at this age she'd never been in love with anyone and that no one loved her, no one at all, and coming off of this state, not too much later, she would meet Theo.

MOVING IN TOGETHER

Joy and Annie had become roommates even though they were also good friends, a risky decision that in most contexts could be cataclysmic, but as it was they bought a couch split fifty-fifty and although he was Annie's cat, Joy would feed Simon in the mornings and Annie would feed him at night. They rented a three-bedroom in the trendy part of town with the hope that they'd keep the spare bedroom as a guest room.

"I've got my friend Sophie from Paris," Annie said. "Maybe she'll invite me to stay with her in Paris if she comes here first."

"I thought you hated her," Joy said.

Annie shrugged. "I don't hate her more than I hate any of my other friends."

Joy nodded. "My mom could stay with us too."

But not more than three months into the lease, both women became frustrated by their monthly expenses: the landlord had gone up a hundred dollars in rent, the heat was costing them a fortune—in the end they decided the smartest thing for them would be to rent out the third bedroom.

They put up an ad on Craigslist that read:

Two young women professionals looking for a third roommate. We're neat but not crazy neat. We are respectful, yes, crazy respectful, and we have a cat.

"We sound awful," Annie said.

"Do we?"

"Isn't there a less pithy way of writing this? It's obnoxious."

"Should we mention our ages?" Joy said.

"Why would we do that?"

"So we don't end up living with someone who is too young or too old."

"You think an old person is going to move into this shitty-ass apartment with us?"

Joy hated the way Annie would rip into the apartment like that. It made Joy feel like Annie was just throwing everything away, or more accurately clearing it away like you would a dirty glass or a fogged windowpane. A blistering transparency of their little home would flash through Joy's thoughts: the matching teacup and teakettle from a flea market they'd bought together, uselessly cheerful. The potted plant garden they'd spent entirely too much time planting. The blinds left half down in the dining room, suddenly with menacing abandon. Joy shook it from her mind.

"Well, what about too young? Do we really want to live with a college student?"

"You're overthinking this. I think everyone knows 'young professional' is code for early thirties anyway," Annie said.

They took a picture of the empty guest room, soon to be the home of a stranger, and posted it alongside the description.

Annie was silent for a moment as she reread the post. "Let's make a pact that no matter who moves in here, this is still our home and we're not going to be pushed out by them," she said.

"I don't want things to change just because someone new comes in."

It may have been unnecessarily fretful or even a little mean, but Joy was happy to hear Annie say it. With all the apartment bashing Annie had done, it was nice to indulge in the idea that it would be them against the world as they chose the dish soap scent and reorganized the refrigerator magnets.

"Agreed. We won't let them touch a damn thing," Joy said. And they both laughed at how bitchy and lovely the world could be.

They got fourteen emails within hours of posting. Half were from college students so they immediately discarded those. Of the seven remaining, five were from women and two were from men.

"I'd definitely prefer a woman," Joy said.

"I totally agree. I don't need to worry about rape as I'm, like, trying to eat a bowl of cereal," Annie said.

"I just don't want to be self-conscious wearing my sweats."

"You're so crazy. You look like literally everyone else in sweatpants."

Joy was very certain that you could see the pockmarks of cellulite on the backs of her thighs whenever she wore sweatpants. She'd confided it to Annie and literally no one else, which she nearly regretted because Annie was the kind of skinny a person would jealously try to attribute to an eating disorder.

"Okay, but I just don't want to have to worry about it," Joy said. She ran her hand along her thigh and sucked in her stomach. *Jenny Craig, maybe?*

They emailed everyone back (including the men, just in case) and set up appointments with each of them for that Saturday.

That morning they cleaned the apartment enough to look decent but not too much to look too decent. "The last thing we need is some asshole counting the frozen bagels every damn day. Remember that girl Lauren I lived with in college? She actually told me not to wear slippers because she thought they marked up the floorboards," Annie said. "Frickin psycho."

Joy remembered Lauren. Most particularly a story Annie had told about how one time when she and her boyfriend were having sex they could hear Lauren in the next room crying her eyes out.

"We were doing it from behind and then all of a sudden we hear her on the phone going 'I can't do it. I can't,' and she was, like, hysterically crying."

"What did you do?" Joy had asked her.

"Nothing, we kept having sex. We weren't, like, friends so it wasn't like I could go comfort her or something."

For whatever reason that story stuck with Joy and any time Annie brought up Lauren in the context of being an awful roommate and a "mega bitch," Joy found herself only feeling sorry for her. *I wish I knew you, Lauren,* she'd think, and maybe to some extent she felt like she did.

On Saturday three of the women didn't show up. One emailed and said she'd decided to move in with her boyfriend instead.

"Dumb bitch," Annie said when she read the email.

The other two asked to reschedule.

"Jeez, I hope that one girl that's coming is good," Joy said.

But she was not good. Her name was Claire and she was dressed better than both Annie and Joy were even though all three of them were wearing slight variations of T-shirt-with-jeans combinations. When she passed by the potted plant window she said, "I love it. So earthy," which neither woman knew how to respond to. After checking out the bedroom that was meant to be hers, she asked if she could possibly see the other two bedrooms. Joy and Annie looked at each other but both agreed and led her to their respective bedrooms.

"Nice," Claire said. "Could I possibly switch with one of you? It's just, I noticed that my bedroom has the least light and I have a thing about sunshine."

Though neither Annie nor Joy wanted to switch rooms with Claire, they found themselves discussing the possibility, a charade that seemed easier to oblige to than being straightforward and saying, "Actually no. That's a totally unreasonable request."

"Who the fuck *doesn't* have a thing about sunshine?" Annie asked after Claire left. "Does she think anyone ever wants to be, like, living in darkness? We all want the lightest rooms, Claire, you aren't special."

"I don't even think that room is any darker than our rooms are," Joy said.

"Now what? We have to live with a man?"

"Let's wait for another woman," Joy said.

"They're coming anyway. Let's at least give them a chance," Annie said. "Apart from rape, how much worse can they be than Claire?"

The first guy showed up and walked around fast and didn't say much. He was in his late thirties. Shorter, balding.

Right before he left he turned around and said, "I do potluck dinners once a week. Would that be an issue at all?"

"Oh fun," Annie said. "I don't think so."

Joy knew no one in this home would have tolerance for potluck dinners once a week, but she nodded along anyway. She considered saying, *"As long as you invite us!"* which is what someone might say in a context that didn't involve a roommate relationship, where such a statement could be read as a dangerous obligation more than anything else.

"Jesus Christ," Annie said after he left. "I'm so glad I don't have to have sex with that man."

"When's that other guy getting here?"

"In an hour."

The women went their separate ways for the hour they waited. Joy wasn't sure what to do with herself alone in her room. It seemed like not enough time to even do nothing. *Should I read?* she thought, but the book she'd been reading had been slow and the last chapter involved a sex scene that made her feel worse about herself than virtually anything else had in recent memory. Sex scenes often did. Something she'd feared about herself was that she simply wasn't sexy and that's why she'd never had a serious relationship. It wasn't as if you could ask someone if you were sexy. Sexy was something you were anointed, like being a princess or winning the Nobel Prize. She remembered one time asking Ryder what he thought of Annie. "She's sexy," he'd said, and that response made Joy instantly furious and paranoid and just generally depressed, but rather than say anything to him about it, she had sex with him twice that night, which was, in the catalogue of all their terrible sex together, the absolute worst sex of all. She almost cried after the second time, but she didn't. She sat there in bed and tried to remember the names of all the kids from *Jon & Kate Plus 8* in the hopes of forcing herself to fall asleep.

Instead of reading, Joy went on Facebook and was happy to see she'd gotten more "likes" on her picture of oatmeal from that morning.

"Blueberries are fabulous," she'd written, which she thought was a pretty clever caption to a picture of oatmeal with blueberries on it, and it turned out seventeen people agreed. She scrolled through a former co-worker's beach pictures before searching Ryder's page (something she did mindlessly nearly daily). His name didn't come up right away as she typed "Ry" and she ended up having to fully type out his name. Had she taken a moment to consider why this might be the case, she would have realized it was wisest to stop dead there and then and do something else, anything at all, but she forged ahead and typed it all in and found his page and when she did, she came to the halting realization: he'd unfriended her.

Why would he do that?? Why would he do that?? Does he hate me that much that he doesn't even want to know me in the absolute most superficial way possible? She checked her Instagram. Unfollowed there as well. That was all the social media she had besides a Twitter page she was too intimidated to use.

Her first instinct was to text him.

"I had your penis in my mouth and you don't even want to know me anymore?" But she of course didn't do that. She felt herself start to shake a bit. Her stomach felt like someone had rattled a bell inside of it. She thought to go tell Annie but was unsure. Sometimes Annie could be the best to talk to, but other times she seemed to have little patience for Joy's sensitivities. The last thing Joy needed right now was a catty remark tossed her way. She knew she couldn't call her mom over it either. Her mom would say something like "What's unfriending mean?" and that conversation would likely be so incredibly aggravating that it would only make everything a million times worse. It was now that Joy felt a feeling she had never felt before. She felt that here was something in her life that was hurting her, and she absolutely could not express it to anyone at all. *I'm all alone,* she thought. And then she heard the doorbell.

"He's early," Annie said as she came out of her bedroom and started down the hall. "I hate early people."

Joy walked behind, still so shaken up that she touched the wall on occasion to keep herself fully upright. She wasn't sure how she'd act together enough to engage socially, but she also didn't care.

Now there was a second, a breath, a pause: here was the doorway, here was the door handle, here was Annie, and here was their apartment. What could move and switch in a little life? So many things and so quickly.

The door opened, and he came inside. He was instantly effervescent.

"Hi, I'm Theo," he said. And, really, that was it.

THEO IS HOT

He had salt-and-pepper hair and his hands were nice. He wasn't exceptionally attractive, but he was more attractive than most men and so that felt exceptional. Annie kept making swooning faces behind his back.

"Love your wallpaper," Theo said, referencing the very out-of-date wallpaper in the kitchen.

"Thank you. We're all about 1972 and stains," Annie said.

To which Theo laughed a balanced laugh that was neither too loud nor too quiet.

"What do you do for a living?" Annie asked.

"I'm a graphic designer."

"Oh cool."

"It's okay, yeah. Pays the bills, sort of. What do you guys do?"

"I'm a producer on the Kathy Willis show. NPR," Annie said.

"Oh, wow," Theo said. "That's incredibly impressive. That's like a dream job."

"Thanks, yeah, it's been a long haul."

Up until this point Joy hadn't said anything at all. She'd

laughed a few times, but now was the time for her to speak. Her job wasn't sexy or exciting, but actually, she liked it a lot. She felt it was worthy and helpful and people needed her. She wished she could somehow say it in a way that would make this gorgeous man understand every single thing about how much it meant to her to do what she did.

"I'm in HR," Joy said.

"Nice," Theo said.

They walked around a little longer before Theo caught sight of Simon, who was sprawled out in the windowsill.

"Oh my god, and who is this guy?"

He walked over and crouched down to be eye level with the cat.

"That's Simon," Annie said.

"I love him more than you guys, no offense."

"As you should," Annie said.

Simon rolled over on his back.

"Aw, what happened to his eye?" Theo said.

"He was a feral kitten, and it was badly infected so they had to remove it. Doesn't slow him down a bit."

"He's a stunner," Theo said.

After that they said their goodbyes at the door and Joy managed to say, "If you walk down the road that way there's an amazing bakery and a really good pizza place. Just to give you an idea about the neighborhood."

"I love pizza and baked goods so I will definitely be checking both of those out," he said. "Thanks again, guys. I'll be in touch." And then he walked off in the direction she had pointed and it made her think it was likely he was going to get a banana nut loaf right then and there.

"Oh my god," Annie said as she shut the door. "He is so insanely gorgeous. Hot Theo. That's what we're calling him."

Joy wasn't sure what to say, but the memory of Ryder unfriending her had withered.

"Well, what do you think? If he wants to move in, are you good with him?" Annie added.

"I think so. I mean he seemed really nice, and he liked Simon," Joy said.

Annie sat down on the sofa. For a second she looked sad.

"Are you okay?" Joy asked.

"Just tired," Annie said.

"Should we email him and tell him the room is his?"

"Shouldn't we wait? We don't want to seem too eager, right?"

"Does a rule like that apply to roommates?"

"I think it applies to men."

Joy agreed, but she was already silently drafting what she'd say in the email.

"Theo, we adored you, Simon did too. Please say yes to the apartment!"

ANNIE

I hate my breasts. They aren't just small, although they are that too, they're, like, weirdly flabby and my nipples are too big. It's like my breasts are all nipples, which, why is it like that? Who has breasts like that? I knew I was going to hate my breasts even before I had breasts because they took way too long to come. It really felt like I couldn't possibly be waiting that long for anything that would actually be good. And they're not good. I'm so embarrassed by them. I don't mind it in my clothes so much because a good bra helps a lot, but when I'm naked I really feel like I look like a freak. I've never had a boyfriend say anything to me about it, but I've been worried they would my whole life. TV, movies, things I read in magazines, I don't know, it's just all there—breasts aren't supposed to look like that, breasts aren't supposed to look like yours. One time I had a friend say that if a man says something mean to you about your body it's like a hate crime. At first, I thought that was stupid, reckless even, but I know what she meant. Saying something like that isn't like a normal insult because we've been made to feel bad about our bodies since forever in all these ways. I care about my body because I really feel like it means something about who I am as a person. I know it shouldn't and that it actually doesn't mean anything, but I don't *feel* it. What I feel is sad; what I feel is that I hope I'm the only one who has to ever see my breasts again. And I hope that when I see them, I see myself as I really am, who I really am, but I know that I won't. I know that all I'll see is my failure. A viciousness that I can't change. A fear that I can't shake.

When Annie moved in with Joy she felt devastated and pissed off. It wasn't what she wanted. She loved Joy, but she wanted to live with her boyfriend, and the fact that she couldn't made the whole experience feel sour and frantic. When they went furniture shopping, she'd tried to feel happy as Joy excitedly pointed out a lamp, but she didn't give a damn about a lamp, not at all. What was worse was Joy was so incredibly thrilled by it all, and so Annie felt much of the time that she had to fake her enthusiasm to give her friend some sense of shared experience.

"Let's do movie nights!" Joy would say and Annie would respond, "That'd be fun." But the charade often caused her to become unnecessarily sharp with Joy to the point where she was sure her friend noticed, and she felt bad about it, but at the same time, she was frustrated by Joy, who very often seemed childish to her. They were in their thirties now. Living together wasn't fun, it was sad. The fact that neither of them could afford their own apartment at their age didn't seem right.

"Do you ever feel like we're stuck in perpetual childhood?" she'd asked Joy once as they made cupcakes.

"Cause of the cupcakes?"

"No, cause we're in our thirties and we live the same way we did when we were twenty-three."

"When I was twenty-three I was still living off of student loans."

"True," Annie said, but she didn't really feel it was true.

Joy was single and that divided them also. She'd dated some guy she met online. His name was Turner or something like that, but he broke up with her to move to Alaska. The whole thing was stupid, and Annie hated hearing about it because she knew Joy was about as in love with Turner as Annie was happy to live in this apartment. Whenever she told Joy about her relationship—about her and Jason, and their love together—she knew Joy couldn't relate and wouldn't understand. Joy would look at her vacantly and say things like "Well, why don't you just tell him that's how you feel?" She didn't know what it was like to be so painfully in love with someone that you could hardly function. And so that along with how old they both were, that along with the rattle of the broken furnace, and the lamp they bought, which was the beacon to a living room she hated, that was why Annie wanted to punch herself free from it all. Living with her friend was just a feeling of explosion kept in her stomach, and so she'd snap at Joy during movie nights and pay her half of the rent on time.

She and Jason had been dating now for nearly two years. What did she love about Jason? His hair and how it curled by his ear. The way he sat on a bus seat. How he quoted an old poem about a boat whenever they'd take a shower together. How everyone who knew him liked him and how he was so magnetic that it felt like you were more alive beside him than when you were anywhere else. But he hadn't asked her to move in with him. Even though he knew that her lease was up and he knew that he was thirty-two and that she was thirty and this was how things usually went, and somewhere too he must have known how much she wanted to, although she certainly never expressed it. She did try to bring it up once; it was at dinner, it was casual. "I wonder what it would be like if we shared an apartment." She'd meant to be more direct about it, but she didn't want to seem clingy or needy. Even as it was she already felt like she wanted to pull the words back into herself as soon as she said them.

"You mean like roommates?" Jason said.

Here in this moment she may have changed much of the direction of her life if she'd said, "No, not like roommates, we're in a relationship and I have sex with you so not like roommates at all." But she would have never even thought to say something like that to Jason because she knew Jason was not a man who did well with expectations, and so she said, "Yeah exactly."

And Jason laughed. "I think we'd kill each other." And that was it. They went home. They had sex and then it was the next day. And the next, and the next.

She was hoping the second she started packing up her old place he'd feel bad about it and offer for them to move in. Something she knew wasn't even at all possible, and yet still she found herself inviting him over to help her pack. She was sure to leave all their couply things for last so she could pack them in front of him. A scheme that she'd not given much thought to and yet spent far too much time preparing for, each thing laid out on the bed with care.

"Aw, remember when we went to Coney Island?" she said, holding up a sweatshirt that read CONEY ISLAND on the front.

"Yeah, that was fun," Jason said, and he genuinely looked happy, but the sweatshirt did not incite eternal love in him in the way she'd hoped.

At the end of a long day of bubble-wrapping coffee mugs

and pulling tape off her fingertips, she felt so exhausted and sad that she could hardly bring herself to pretend she wasn't.

"So what's the story with Michelle? Why aren't you guys staying roommates?" Jason asked her.

"Are you kidding?" she snapped. She'd told him a thousand times what the story with Michelle was. Telling him about Michelle had been the earliest hope she'd had that he'd know what it was that she wanted without actually saying it.

"She's moving in with her boyfriend. She and Ivan are engaged, remember?"

Jason looked at her and shrugged. "Why are you upset?"

"Because I've told you this like a million times." She picked up a box and needlessly moved it to another spot on the floor in an effort to look less pissed off than she actually was.

"So? Is it that big a deal if I forgot?"

For a brief second Annie thought of herself as a child. She'd once gotten stung by a bee running in her backyard. A feeling like this one, pinpricked, shook. No, a bee sting doesn't matter. No, neither did this. But either way here it was. Ice pressed up against her until her skin was numb.

"Did you forget or did you never know to begin with?" she asked him.

"What do you mean?"

"Can you just tell me?"

"I don't know what you're asking me."

Now she looked out her bedroom window. There was a tree she'd seen for over two years. She and this tree had slept side by side. It was unmoved but constantly changing. Each season different, each year older. There would have been an intimacy between them if such things existed, and maybe such things did. She felt sorry that soon she'd never see it again. You certainly couldn't go visit an old apartment. You couldn't say, "I used to live here. Can I go and see the tree? I want to see if it's the same. I want to know if it remembers me." And then she thought, *I'm getting old,* and this thought, as much as it was not a thought that was reasonable for someone her age to think, was as true a thought for her as it was for anyone. A baby fresh from birth, still bruised on a hand from the birth canal, could think the same exact thing and be just as right.

"Jason," she said. And that was it. Her voice was heard and then nothing at all.

FALLING BADLY

The first sign of it was that Joy was constantly looking for excuses to be around Theo. She'd see him heading into the kitchen to put groceries away, and she'd go in and get a snack.

He'd be walking out of the apartment, and she'd say, "Oh, hang on, I'm headed out too," and she'd grab her coat and walk out with him, but once outside, she'd have nowhere to go, and he'd head off in his direction, and she'd have to invent a destination. Usually, she found herself walking to the bakery to get a scone, but pretty soon the people in there started to recognize her.

"One lemon scone, right?" the guy at the counter would say, pointing to her and then emphatically packing her scone up.

"Here you go, miss!" He'd hand it to her with a big smile and the whole thing made her feel so wildly transparent, as if he could see this entire charade: her walking out with Theo and the way Theo said, "See ya," and waved and how happy that wave made her feel. She stopped going to the bakery after that.

Annie called him Hot Theo and would constantly say things like "If I were single, I would be all over him." Joy loved every second of it. Annie's approval thrilled her of course, but she also just liked to talk about him.

"We should make him come to movie nights," Annie said.

"We should." Joy was beaming just thinking about it. "Do you know he plays viola?"

"That's so sexy."

"I know."

"Is he single?"

Joy had social-media-stalked the hell out of him the second he moved in (and even before he had if she was being totally honest with herself), and she was pretty certain he was in fact single.

"No idea," she said.

Before Joy had a chance to invite Theo to movie night Annie had already done it. Joy had planned on saying something snappy, although she couldn't think of anything that seemed quite right. A line from *Scarface* passed through her mind, but it didn't really make sense in the context; either way, it didn't matter because Annie just said, "Hey, Theo, are you up for a movie night with us tonight?" To which Theo said: "Definitely."

Joy wanted to sit next to him, but she found herself seated on the floor in front of the couch where he was seated. What propelled her to sit down on the floor in front of him rather than to sit down beside him? It was something small. Likely something that was intrinsic to her nature to some degree, a passivity inherited, but there were also many little buildups in her life that led to this as well. A teacher who said, "Who made you the boss?" as Joy directed a schoolyard game. A friend who disappeared from her life with no real explanation. *Susan, where did you go?* she'd write in a notebook to console herself. And maybe her first job, where for no reason she was not promoted and a more attractive, but considerably less experienced co-worker was. "Skill set" was what she heard that day, but that night she skipped dinner and did eighty sit-ups. There were many more of these kinds of things. Another person might have not cared, might have buried them below small victories and compliments, but Joy would not or could not, and so they built up in a little stack of space below her breast. She carried them around with her, and she'd sit on the floor rather than take up the space on the couch. *Internalized* is the word, and terror was the feeling.

Nevertheless, she could smell his cologne or soap or whatever it was from where she was sitting, and it was a rich earthy smell that reminded her of what she'd imagined sex was before she'd actually had sex.

"I'm so sick of superhero movies," Annie said as she pressed play. "Wonder Woman, go fuck yourself," and then *Wonder Woman* began playing.

Theo was as delightful to spend time with as Joy had imagined he would be. He laughed just at the right points. His comments were insightful but not verbose. And he had an endearing habit of passing the popcorn bowl around. Joy didn't even like popcorn, but she found herself eating so much of it that night that she was certain she'd end up with some kind of blockage. Annie laughed a lot and seemed less troubled than she had in ages. She'd been fighting with Jason lately, or whatever it was, maybe not fighting as much as feeling continuously injured. When the movie ended Theo stretched his arms up in a big stretch.

"That was great, you guys. How often do you do movie nights?"

Every single night, Joy wanted to say.

"Once a week usually," Annie said. "It varies."

"Well, if you're doing it, I'm there," Theo said.

"Fridays," Joy blurted out. "Let's make it Fridays each week."

"Fridays I see Jason sometimes," Annie said.

"Thursdays then?" Joy said.

"I'd be down with that," Theo said.

"Okay, great," Joy said, and she couldn't help but smile and eat another handful of popcorn.

"Well, I'm off to bed. I'm old now, and I need to be asleep by eleven-thirty or I can't function. Have a good night, guys," Theo said as he got up from the couch.

"Good night," Joy said.

"Good night," Annie said.

Once Theo was gone, Annie shook her head. "Movie nights every Thursday? Won't that be a bit much? We hardly know him."

"What? He's great."

"Yeah, but, still, I can hardly stand you once a week."

"Shut up," Joy said and tossed a pillow at Annie.

"Why don't you go out with him?"

"What?" Joy felt heat rise and fall through her body in one swift motion.

"Yeah, I mean he's gorgeous, and he seems totally sweet."

Joy wasn't sure what to say. She felt exhilarated and panicked.

"I doubt he'd go out with me."

"Why?"

"I don't know. He's so hot."

"So what? You can't date someone hot? You're hot too."

Joy was never sure if Annie was serious whenever she'd compliment her like that, but either way it made her feel a little pinch of sadness. She didn't know why, but it was likely for the same reason she'd sat on the floor rather than the couch.

"I think it's a bad idea. I mean we live together. How would that go?"

"True," Annie said, and she began texting on her phone. "I'm going to bed. I'll see you tomorrow."

"See you."

Joy sat there for quite a while longer. The room was quiet and empty and the popcorn was gone. Her back was pressed up to the couch and her bare feet were against the rug. It was silent, but not in any kind of menacing way. Maybe she could hear the traffic or a person on the street. Maybe the sound of herself taking in a breath. The world was alive around her and many things were going on very brilliantly, close by and far away, and all that energy seemed to be as present as she was, as she sat there alone in their little living room. *I feel happy,* she thought.

JELLIED

Annie was frantic that morning. Jason hadn't texted her all night. A thing he did very often for no reason that would be discernible to anyone on earth but Jason. At the beginning of their relationship, she would hear from him so sporadically that she was continuously sure that he would just disappear from her forever, but then just like that he'd be there in her life again like magic. It would be his magnanimous self in front of her, beside her; he'd spend the day with her, and she'd feel like the only person, the absolute only person in the whole world, and with Jason that was not a bad feeling, not a lonely feeling, it was an impenetrable one because he, a man who chose what he did, and how he did it, and where he did it, and when, was choosing *her*. It felt, above all else, pristine.

Now that they'd been together longer, Annie found herself accepting lesser and lesser forms of magic. If she hadn't heard from him, she didn't need a whole day with him, just waking up to a text the next morning with a "how are you, gorgeous?" was enough for her to move on and to be propelled back into euphoria (though certainly a more tepid euphoria). In reality she didn't even need that to move on. Just a "hey" or a smiley face would suffice. She knew somewhere too that even if he'd sent her a text with nothing written on it, just pressed send with a blank text, she'd likely have found at least some kind of reassurance in that and really that's what she was looking for: affirmation of being cared about by the person she cared about.

This morning she'd woken up to nothing. Not even a smiley, which was her least favorite. "Why are you smiling?" she'd once texted back when she was extra-exhausted and angry. All day she imagined what he might say in response. "Smiling cause I love you," "smiling cause I can't stop thinking about you," but he never responded to the text, and out of anxiety she texted him. "How's work?" which he did respond to with "fine." This morning the silence was making her crazy, and she raced around the kitchen trying to convince herself of some kind of sanity. *Here's the fridge. And here's my hand opening the fridge. And here's a butter knife and an apple core,* she'd think as she moved with a haste that was directed at a destination she couldn't have verbally expressed even to herself.

She packed a quick lunch for work. She'd been trying to save money so she'd bring a sandwich from home. Somewhere she'd read of a woman who supposedly got a down payment for a house together this way. Eating sandwiches from home and skipping Starbucks. So far she hated it, but she had saved seventeen dollars.

Joy came in the kitchen, still beaming from movie night.

"Good morning," Joy said. "I'm warning you now if you haven't eaten the last donut, I'm eating it."

"Eat it," Annie said. "I'm sick of those donuts anyway. I feel like crap after I eat them."

Joy didn't say much after that. She ate her donut and made herself coffee and left for work.

One time Annie had heard Oprah say "Charming is something you do, it's not something you are," and that quote bothered her a lot because Jason above all else was charming.

When they first met at a sunny backyard party, he went across the street to buy her a lemonade after the hostess informed her they'd just run out.

"You didn't need to do that," Annie had said as he put the cool drink in her palm.

Once they'd been on a hiking trail and he'd climbed a tree to grab her a branch of orange blossoms.

"Here," he said, sweat droplets pooled tightly on his forearm.

Then there was last summer when they'd binge-watched *Better Call Saul* and she'd swooned over the scene when Saul sings to Kim on a voicemail. All week long he called her phone and left her song messages.

"Sometimes all I need is the air that I breathe and to love you," he sang, and she felt hot and sick and so in love.

His charm was, or at least it felt like, the lifeblood that ran through their relationship, and sometimes Annie feared that without it there was nothing there. She did love him though. So much so that she wasn't sure anything else really mattered, which was cliché, but sometimes things were just cliché and in some ways that was comforting because it made her feel like she was a part of something big. The big painful love that you hear so much about. *Sleepless in Seattle* love, she thought, although she knew that wasn't the right reference because she was fairly sure Tom Hanks was actually pretty nice in that movie.

She checked her phone quickly. Still no text. She could hear Theo stirring in his room. There was some kind of maleness in it, a heavy motion that was inconsiderate and sexy—she didn't want to deal with it so she grabbed her sad-sack lunch and headed out the door.

Work she mostly liked. It was a job others could easily romanticize and so everyone in her life admired her for it, which was probably the best perk of the job considering it didn't pay that great. She wasn't super into radio to begin with. At one time she'd wanted to be a writer, but as she was getting her MFA, she'd found the literary scene so bloodsuckily depressing she kind of gave up. What moment that was she wasn't entirely sure, but she thought it might have had to do with the day she and her classmates were all standing around about to go into a meet-and-greet with agents and one of them said something to the effect of "well she knows Meg Wolitzer so I know she can," and although Annie hadn't heard what it was that that person who knew Meg Wolitzer would supposedly be able to do, she could feel in her hand the first quarter of a manuscript she had printed out, through much of which she had overused the word *likely,* but she likely hadn't noticed, and all her little-girl dreams were right there squishing in her hand and there was a desperation that manifested in a muscle in her thumb which was pressed up against a sentence that read: "She'd likely only do that for a little while longer," and soon she'd be in a room where she'd be trying so hard to sell something that was almost as intimate to her as sex or the back of her own earlobe, and she felt exhausted all at once, and so she turned to the girl who'd said that thing about Meg Wolitzer and she said, "Well, Lorrie Moore is my mom." But of course Lorrie Moore was not her mom and soon after she quit writing.

Radio was a better career choice for her because she didn't care as much. It wasn't her love, and so it couldn't hurt her. Instead, it fulfilled some of her desire for a creative outlet and gave her a paycheck in hand each week, something writing would never be able to guarantee. And what was more, she was good at her job. People liked her at work. They respected her. She felt needed and competent, and she worked hard. Once in a meeting her boss said to her, "Annie, where would we be without you?" And everyone else started clapping right then and there for her, and that triumph, as it was, became part of why she could stand straight, look forward, why when she talked, people listened, and if they didn't, she made sure they would hear her whether they listened or not.

She typed out an email and answered another. It was nearing lunch now, and she still hadn't heard from him. Her phone was on her desk and although she wasn't checking it, she found herself eyeing it and every time she did, she felt like screaming or crying but the feeling wasn't urgent enough to warrant screaming or crying. *I'm so used to it,* she thought so she grabbed her phone and threw it in her bag so at least she wouldn't have to look at it anymore.

"Did you get the invite?" Patrice, her co-worker, said.

"To what?"

"Beth's wedding."

"Oh no, I haven't yet."

"It's rustic chic but without the chic."

"Is it?" Annie smiled trying to walk the line between acknowledging the gossipy nature of the whole thing without indulging. She really liked Patrice, but she had high aspirations and there was a level of professionalism that she felt was required for that kind of ambition; that aside, she was completely depressed at the idea of Beth's wedding.

"Her fiancé is ugly as hell," Patrice said. "Look." And she turned her computer screen around so that Annie could see a picture of Beth and her ugly fiancé. They were embracing in a selfie with a cliffside behind them. The guy had a big goofy grin. Beth looked happy. It was heavily filtered.

"They're going to have ugly kids. If I've learned anything

from social media it's that babies look like their dads. Stop settling for ugly-ass guys, ladies!" Patrice turned her screen back around. "Beth is pretty. She could do better."

Annie laughed a little but still didn't say much. She wouldn't let her mind even wander to where it might strike on what her and Jason's children would look like. Having children was something she wanted in a part of her soul that was so sacred that she dared not go there like this.

Her phone buzzed in her bag. Without worry about looking frantic she grabbed it quick, but infuriatingly it was a text from Joy about Theo.

"He's playing viola," she wrote.

"Don't you have work?" Annie typed back.

"I came home for lunch."

"Doesn't he work?"

"Yeah, but he has today off he told me . . ." and then the text went on into this long explanation that Annie was not about to read.

"Do you want to get lunch? A bunch of us are going to that new Thai place," Patrice asked.

"It sounds great, but actually I brought my own lunch. Trying to save up some extra money," Annie said, but she felt depressed even saying it.

Not too much later she was alone at her desk pulling out her brown-paper-bag lunch. Everyone at the office had left. Really truly everyone, even her boss's new assistant, who usually worked through lunch. Certainly they all hadn't gone for Thai food, but everyone besides herself was somewhere else. She took out her Saran-wrapped sandwich. At one time she'd told herself that she was going to be making quinoa salads to bring to work. That lie was short-lived and soon it was peanut butter and jelly every day. She unwrapped her sandwich and took a bite. It didn't taste right. It was slimy and cold and there was hardly any taste besides the bread, which wasn't good in the best of circumstances. She pulled the slices apart and saw that there was only jelly. In her intense haste to nowhere this morning she'd forgotten the peanut butter. *This is all your fault, Jason,* she thought. She grabbed her sandwich and threw it in the trash. She wasn't about to eat jelly for Jason. She sat back down and picked up her phone. He still hadn't texted. She held it in her hand and looked at it and looked at it and looked at it, and she felt like she would almost be able to will it to explode right there in her hand, burst her body parts into a million pieces. The thought scared her. She dropped it fast, and it landed loudly against the desk, but she was alone and it didn't matter. Now she wasn't moving but was just waiting for something. *I'm not happy,* she thought.

YOU DON'T IN LOVE

Two and a half months had passed and rather than getting sick of Theo who like all roommates was imperfect and in constant close proximity, Joy found herself thinking of him more and more often, which wasn't hard to do considering that they were spending more and more time together. There were movie nights of course, but there were also the days he worked from home when she found herself always leaving late for work or coming home for lunch. But unlike before, when she would have to invent ways to hang out around him, now Theo was very much a participant in all of it. He'd make her coffee or see her on the couch and come sit by her. He laughed at her jokes and would ask her questions about who she was.

"Did you grow up around here?" he'd ask or "What's your favorite color?"

She loved how he seemed genuinely interested in hearing her answers. Something she'd noticed about many other men she'd been around was that they rarely seemed to want to know her. They'd make conversation and nod along, but a genuine interest never seemed to be part of their motivations. It was easy to internalize, but one time she had someone bring her a complaint about two co-workers.

"I overheard these two guys say that they feel bad about it, but whenever a woman talks in a meeting, they assume she just doesn't know what she's talking about. They said they don't mean to, but they just don't respect women as much as men. How can I complain about it?" the woman said. She'd come to Joy's office, which almost no one ever did. Usually people just sent emails.

"You can absolutely lodge a formal complaint. I'll send you a link to fill it out yourself, or if you like, you can just email me the incident and I'll do the rest," Joy said. "It'll be totally anonymous, so no worries there."

"But what will happen to them?" the woman asked. She seemed distraught.

"I can't say what will happen to them unfortunately," Joy said.

"But I don't want to work with someone who doesn't respect me."

"Totally understandable. It's definitely within the company's policy to take note of something like this, so I'm sure the appropriate action will be taken."

"Are you sure?" The woman narrowed her eyes. Between the two of them there was a soft switch of energy. Joy felt jolted by it.

"I'm sorry. I wish I could tell you more," she said.

"I don't want it to be anonymous. I want them to know." And the woman walked off not waiting to hear Joy's response.

After that there wasn't much Joy could do other than forward the complaint. She flagged it for urgency even though it really did not fall within the guidelines of what could be considered urgent. Ever since that incident though, she often found herself considering what men thought of her as she spoke. Sometimes it got to her so much she just wouldn't say anything. She'd just be quiet when really she should have been speaking.

Theo, it seemed to her, was not one of these men, and when he asked her something she'd answer, and she'd expect that what she was saying mattered. It made her find him infinitely worth considering, and so she considered him a lot: what he was doing, what he was thinking, why he'd leave the butter out, but rarely anything else. When she was at work she thought about him, and when she was at home she was often spending time with him. She and Annie were spending less and less time together as a result, which didn't seem to matter all that much to Annie, and, if Joy was being honest with herself, it didn't really matter all that much to her either. Over time too she noticed that Annie joked less about Theo being hot and complained more about how he left the bathroom messy. She'd started to treat him the way you'd treat any other roommate living a deft and distant life in the home you shared together.

One Sunday, Annie and she cleaned out the pantry. It was the first thing they'd done together in weeks.

"Yuck, we're disgusting," Annie said as she threw out a loaf of bread that had molded. "This is like the third loaf like this."

"We should coordinate what we buy. It's not like we don't share. Hot Theo would probably be fine with it."

"Jesus, are you still calling him Hot Theo? Who really cares about him anymore and his dumb salt-and-pepper hair," Annie said as she tossed an old box of muffins away. "I'm totally over him."

"Yeah, I can see that." Joy was trying hard to figure out what to say back, but she couldn't think of anything.

"What do you think about this pasta?" Annie held up a box that looked like it had gotten wet at one point.

"Did it really get wet or is it just the box?"

Annie opened the box up, took a look, and then chucked it out.

Joy looked through the assortment of half-eaten granola and tried to organize them. The cluttered smell of the pantry reminded her of something familiar, and for a second she found herself feeling like she was not around anyone but herself and so she said, "You know Theo told me—"

"Theo again?" Annie said. Then she stopped dead and turned to Joy. "You're in love with him."

Joy felt like someone had slapped her. "What? No, I'm not."

"You totally are. You're in love with him."

"No, I don't in love with him."

"No, you *don't* in love with him? You're totally in love with him."

Joy didn't know what to say and so she laughed out of being uncomfortable. Annie dropped it for the most part before adding, "You better watch yourself with him or you'll be a goner soon, girl." After that they continued to throw out food and organize cans and whatnot. Joy could not for the life of her process anything that Annie was saying or anything that she herself was doing. At one point she threw out an unopened box of Oreos without even thinking about it. She just watched herself as if she were watching someone else's hands pick up and mindlessly toss out perfectly good cookies. It was lucky Annie was so busy, otherwise so much of the private hell Joy was living through might have been exposed. *You don't in love with him* kept repeating in her mind, and Theo and his face and salt-and-pepper hair seemed overly present also. It was like he was watching her.

Annie and he could see something that she couldn't even see to begin with, and what was she now? Nothing but a frantic woman holding old breadstuffs.

Annie grabbed the recycling and the garbage and headed to the door.

"I got this," she said. But Joy was so preoccupied that she wouldn't have offered anyway.

Joy went to her room. She shut the door behind herself but stayed stock-still for a moment, the vision of her room a strict and suddenly unforgiving vantage point. Was this it? Was this what it was to be in love with someone? She hadn't even allowed herself the thought that she had a crush on Theo. She'd been telling herself that it was just something she joked about with Annie. A bit of fun they were having. But god knows she spent twenty minutes putting on makeup before she'd think to leave her room. That wasn't normal. That certainly wasn't *not* a crush. *The unexamined life is not worth living,* she thought and tried to place where the saying was from. A self-help book she'd read in college? For about seven months of her sophomore year she'd gone on a huge self-help-book kick at the advice of a friend who told her it "changed my life." Joy felt like her life needed changing even though she wasn't sure how. She read all kinds of books and even started a bullet journal, which lasted three bullets: Hopes: Dreams: Making It Happen. She had a few lines for "Hopes" and a few lines for "Dreams" but on "Making It Happen" she felt stuck. The only thing that came to mind was "be lucky," and that thought, as soon as she thought it, ruined every single self-help book she tried to read after that. Whenever she'd take luck out of the equation, there was nothing left. She tried to tell her friend about it, but her friend was really bothered.

"That's not true," she'd said. "If you work hard things can happen."

"But what makes you work hard?" Joy had said. "Even the will or ability to work or to work hard is being lucky."

"I just don't agree with that," her friend said, "I just don't." And then she got up and walked over to the watercooler, but she forgot to bring her cup so she had to walk back to the table where they were sitting, and when she walked back, Joy saw her friend's face and she looked like she'd been emptied out. Like the air was depleted and the oxygen was gone, and so after that Joy didn't say another thing to her about luck anymore. But as it was, everything that had seemed controllable before didn't seem so controllable now. It was the first time in her life she'd understood what the word meant when people said "bitter." She tried hard not to internalize it, not to let it define how she lived, but she knew deep down that "be lucky" was fundamentally right and far more so than anything she'd read in a book.

Now Joy sat on her bed. She took a few deep breaths and tried to consider what everything that had happened in the pantry meant. A moth flew in front of her bedroom window and then fluttered like a shadow behind her curtain. She could see the silhouette of its wings flapping before she lost sight of it entirely. Then she closed her eyes for a second. Then she opened them again. And then she heard Theo cough a door down from where she was and the sound, even in the midst of everything, felt reassuring. And when she'd look back on it months from then, this is when Joy would remember herself first being in love with Theo, but what she did not know was that it had happened when she was sleeping. A little ripple was created in her life at that moment, and she wasn't even conscious for it. What kind of luck that was hadn't yet been determined.

MAN

Annie had no patience for the three men she worked with most closely. There was Carl, who was smart but lazy. Brett, who was not good at anything and never took responsibility for whatever he did wrong, which was everything. And Reid, who was—well, Reid was mean. Each of them was young and loud, and they spent time talking to each other and thinking highly of each other and trying hard to win the affections of each other.

"Not gay, but something else," Patrice once said. "I mean, it *is* like they want to have sex with one another."

"Not sex," Annie shot back, "I think something more intimate than sex. Maybe something we can't even know what it is." It was the closest she ever came to fully indulging in office gossip with Patrice.

"More intimate than sex," Patrice said, "that's exactly right."

Annie worked on the Kathy Willis show, one of the few political talk shows at the station hosted solely by a woman, but she didn't work directly with Kathy; instead she worked most closely with her male boss, who was the go-between with Kathy and everyone else. His name was Arly, a nickname that came from nothing but perfectly suited him. He was one of those people in radio who everyone knew from his first name.

"I spoke with Arly about it" was all it took for things to change, to move, to become real. Annie knew something about the world better than a lot of people: most things were run by a few people. It was a lesson she'd learned back when she'd been trying to be a writer.

"Did you know the *New York Times* bestseller list is actually not just the bestselling books?" her classmate Sandy had said one time as she sank a spoon into some flan. "It's something that a handful of people in New York, like, decide on, or something." Annie hadn't known. She hadn't known at all. She looked at Sandy eating her flan, and she felt a shift. She didn't plan to stop doing what she was doing, going to class, writing a novel, but she did feel something calcify in her bones: she didn't want to be one of the people who was decided on, she wanted to be one of the people who decided. She didn't say that then to Sandy or even to herself. She'd just hold on to it and when she met Arly it was there in her bone marrow, growing blood to bring air to her body. Sandy would go on to write a short story collection. It was good, but it was no *New York Times* bestseller.

Annie got along well with Arly. He took to her right away and started her on a path to move up. Sometimes when she talked to him he'd smile and hold his chin and then shake his head and say, "Another great one, Annie. Another great one." Annie was never entirely sure what he was referring to when he said "one" (Her idea? The point she was making?), but, regardless, it felt incredibly good.

"He, like, adores you," Patrice would say. And Annie would say no and try to be humble, but she agreed. It was nice to be adored; it was nice to feel like this chosen person was choosing her.

The men in her office had all taken notice. Reid was the most outspoken about it. "The golden child," he'd call her at lunch or as they walked to a meeting or pushed an elevator button, and she'd laugh, but she wasn't doing it out of discomfort or nerves, not to appease him or to get his affection like Brett or Carl might. She laughed because she was waiting for the right opportunity. And now, on this day, here it was, and she was ready.

In meetings Reid talked as much as possible. He asked questions that he likely knew the answers to or that he probably didn't care about. He spoke over people, mostly Annie and Patrice and sometimes Beth, who rarely spoke in meetings in general, which made it even more egregious in those instances. Annie loathed it, but she was used to it. It was a part of dealing with men that had been ingrained in her early and often.

When she was in the fifth grade her class had gone on an overnight field trip to a place called Nature's Classroom. She hadn't wanted to go, and her mom bribed her with a trip to her favorite toy store with the promise of "I'll let you pick out whatever you want if you don't have a good time." Well, she didn't have a good time. She chipped her tooth the first night and a fight about hygiene that she was not a part of but was witness to left one girl sobbing and begging to go home after the other kids laughed when she declined to add her name to the shower schedule. "I showered this morning and we'll be home tomorrow night" seemed reasonable enough, but not to this prepubescent group, who had established an ardent culture of cleanliness that was likely linked to early menstruation and a misunderstanding of what sex was. Beyond that there was a counselor who allowed mosquitoes to suck blood from him because he believed that "they need to eat too" and another counselor who obviously was hired because of his love of clipboards and his ability to read lists of names off of clipboards, which he did at every interval possible.

"Sarah."

"Jacob."

"Leda."

"Aidan"

"Maeve."

But what Annie would think of most often whenever she did think of Nature's Classroom, which was surprisingly quite frequently, was an incident with a dead bird. She and a small group of kids, none of whom she knew all that well even though they'd all gone up through all of elementary school together, were doing an exercise where they had to "get lost" in the woods. "The woods" were nothing that anyone could get really lost in, but for ten- and eleven-year-olds, it felt perilous enough to take seriously. Instantly, one of the boys took over the compass and started calling out directions of where to go and what to do. Annie couldn't remember much about him other than that he was shorter and had dark hair that was cut close. He was someone's child, a man's child mostly.

As they meandered along someone took notice of a dead bird that was lying in some brush.

"A dead bird!" that someone called out.

All the other kids gathered around and many of them instantly started poking at it with sticks or kicking at it with their shoes. For whatever reason it made Annie feel bad to see them mistreating the animal's body. She loved animals, and even though this one was dead, the tenor of the way the kids behaved seemed too close to how they might have behaved towards something alive. It didn't seem like much of a step from desecration of something that had stopped breathing to torture of something that hadn't, and so she said loudly to the group, "We should bury it." Everyone was quiet for a moment, but then the boy who'd been barking orders said, "She's right. We should bury it." And just like that every single one of them agreed. Annie was thrilled. She was powerful all of a sudden. Sure, it was power filtered through a penis, but standing there in the fake woods without any compass in hand, it felt like it was enough.

As she got older that culture persisted. In college over and over again the boys would speak up and the girls would fall back. It was depressing, but she found herself going along with it, stepping in line, waiting for a penis to tell her what was what. Slowly over time though, something changed for her. Courage kicked in and a vitality manifested.

She'd been in a fiction workshop where a small group of male students had banded together. They were nasty and snarky and would back each other up. There was one in particular who Annie was certain had never slept with anyone. *There's no way anyone has touched his penis,* she thought. Annie, for whatever reason, got the absolute worst of it. With every story she'd bring in, he'd make dismissive comment after dismissive comment to the point where she actually left the class in tears. The professor was well meaning enough, but he couldn't call it out for what it was. Annie would later reflect, *We don't have the language to say what this is. There aren't words to explain why one group of people think they should be loud and the other is quiet, willingly quiet.* But then she'd later think, *Willingly?* And soon after she didn't think of it at all. Too busy in her life to think of it more broadly than that. She focused on herself and what she needed. Someone would call that being "a good businesswoman," someone would call that being "a bad bitch," but really she didn't want to think about it too hard because anger felt more like a solution than anything else. At the time though, she was desperate for a feeling of something more, something greater. She wanted vindication.

Annie knew that she couldn't start yelling or just stand up and say, "You're not more than I am," so instead she sat down and she wrote a story about masturbation that emasculated the hell out of all of them. The story was the stream of consciousness of a woman bringing herself to orgasm and she wrote each boy from class in as the barrier to climax her protagonist had to overcome. She called it "The Mental Processes of the Female Orgasm." When she brought it to class, everyone loved it, and the boys did not dare say a word against it. Her professor was beaming as they went over her notes, and when she got back his copy, she saw that he'd written "This is very funny . . ." in the margins as each one of them was referenced. But what was more, what was most, was what that boy had written in his notes to her: "My girlfriend says female orgasm is nothing like this," and the minute she read that, she felt an enormous sense of calm. She wasn't the grateful girl standing by the dead bird. She was holding the compass and it felt good, it felt great, and without realizing it, that moment became the catalyst for this moment with Reid, which was maybe not as vindicating but no less satisfying.

It had been a long week and a Friday meeting, which was unusual, was unfortunately necessary. They were expecting a congresswoman as the guest of next week's show, and Arly thought it best that they go over everything as soon as possible. Annie had done most of the preparation for the meeting, and it was she who had booked the congresswoman to begin with, so she felt an enormous sense of responsibility in the show's execution. She knew Reid was jealous of the whole thing, but Annie had done what she always did and ignored it. The day of the meeting she made sure everything was perfect. She looked down at her binder, and felt a wave of pride at the beauty of paper and the sharp inherent organizational quality of typeface. Sometimes hard work felt good even without anything else besides it. *Sometimes you don't need a reward to feel rewarded,* she thought.

When she got to the conference room Reid was already there, seated before anyone else. His chair was directly in front of where she would be standing. Normally she would try to keep him out of her line of sight during meetings, but clearly he was not about to allow that.

"Hi, Reid," she said.

"Annie," Reid said.

It threw her at first as the meeting started. She could feel her body tense up as she'd catch sight of him staring directly at her with a smirk on his face. Her hands were sweating, and she knew her voice sounded jittery.

Don't let him now, don't let him ever, she thought, as she saw him texting on his phone.

She thought of her mother and she thought of the feeling she felt the first time she'd mastered walking in high heels.

"Progress, that's the theme we really want to focus on for the show. That's the note we want to strike," she said boldly as Reid yawned and then smirked again. She kept going and going, elegant, strong. When they came to the end of it all, Arly was impressed and the rest of the room followed along with that, and then Reid did what he often did as they came to the end of a meeting and started to talk just to be sure Arly heard him speak.

"Such a fan of the congresswoman," he said.

And Annie, without even trying to, without even needing much of a pull, snapped up this opportunity.

"Actually, Reid, what's her name? No peeking!" And she flipped off the PowerPoint.

Reid turned bright red. He breathed in hard and everyone

was silent. Between them was the opposite of chemistry. Electricity, not as it lights something up, but as it sets something on fire.

"Just kidding, I know you know her name. Sorry, been a long week," Annie said.

Arly laughed knowingly, and the rest of the room picked up on that same energy. "It's been a long week for all of us, Annie, but this was another great one," he said.

After the meeting Patrice ran over and squeezed Annie's hand with a devilish grin, and a few other people said how great she was, and then she watched as Reid left the room quickly and the way his body moved made her think this phrase: *things that are alive and things that are dead*. And then her phone buzzed and she looked down to see a text from Jason, which said: "Hey my lease is up on my apartment. Want to move in together?" And she felt so thrilled by herself and the way she had moved so much in her little world that in that moment she might have been able to tell herself that somehow she'd willed her boyfriend to move in with her. But, of course, the truth was, she had not.

UNDERNEATH

"Joy, do you hear that?"

"What?"

"That guy downstairs. He's drumming."

"Is that what that is?"

"Yeah, it's 2:00 A.M."

Theo was talking through the wall between their bedrooms. He knew she was still awake because they'd been up late watching Netflix. Movie nights were basically every night now, although Annie almost never joined. She was mostly at Jason's or in her own room. She'd work late too. Joy didn't care. If anything, she preferred the way things were. Usually it was her, Theo, and Simon, who often sat between them on the couch sprawled out with his paws reaching forward.

At first, she had felt nervous to see Theo the morning after the day Annie and she had cleaned out the pantry. She'd avoided him the night before, sitting in her room by herself and googling makeup tutorials endlessly. It was that same night that she'd gotten into a fight online with a woman who wrote "What an ugly bitch" under one of the videos. Joy was not one to respond to anything confrontational ever, but the day had left her rattled and in so many ways "ugly bitch" could have been something she might have said to herself that night.

Her hands were shaking as she typed, but she just couldn't help herself and she commented back: "We're women. We're supposed to support one another," which she thought was the best thing to say in response to someone like this. The woman answered almost immediately: "Are you an ugly bitch too? Ugly bitches unite!" To which Joy wrote back without much consideration: "You're incredibly rude." She was trying to elevate the conversation. She was getting older, and it felt immature not to speak to people the way her mom might. She tried to think of what her mom would do in a situation like this, but the only thing she could imagine was her mom looking straight at the girl and shaking her head. "She's probably been hurt somewhere in life," she would have said. "Hurt people hurt people." And while Joy admired her mom's judiciousness, in this moment the image of her mom essentially taking the "ugly bitch" girl's side made her sad, but even so, she tried to respond accordingly.

The girl shot back. "I went on your Facebook. You're ugly as fuck."

Joy felt her stomach drop as she read the words "You're ugly as fuck," each one hitting her harder than the last. She laughed at first, a conditioned response that you might have if you were in public, which would in no way be reflective of what you were really feeling. She went on Facebook and quickly clicked through her profile pictures. Her in sunglasses making a scrunchy face (it was a selfie but who could tell?). Then her at the beach (not in a bathing suit, Jesus Christ, no way) with some friends where the flash had washed out all of their features, a.k.a she thought she looked nicer when her nose blended in with the rest of her face. And then another one of her holding up a book where you could only see her forehead and eyes (it was another selfie, but again, who could tell?). The rest were all old and she'd already made them private so she knew the girl couldn't have seen them. *These aren't that bad. I don't look that bad, right?* Joy thought. *I'm not really ugly as fuck, am I?* She wished she wasn't thinking these thoughts. She wished she could just laugh them away. Be an adult, a thing that she imagined would lift her above it somehow. *I've been marching forward towards nothing,* she thought. She felt sad and she did feel ugly as fuck. She clicked back to the YouTube video. She thought of a few bitchy comments to respond with and one really long-winded one that she actually typed out, which read:

> You know you don't know what another person is going through in life. You shouldn't insult someone like that. It could be the thing that pushes them over the edge. What if their mom died that day or they just found out they had cancer and then you're calling them ugly? You should always treat everyone like they just found out they had cancer.

But she thought better of it and erased it. Instead she reported the girl's comment to YouTube and changed her privacy settings on Facebook so all of her photos were private.

After that she felt restless. *Why did this have to happen the day I had this thing happen?* she wondered and she stayed up all night thinking of Annie in the pantry and this unknown stranger on YouTube, and she was sure that the next morning when she saw Theo everything would be different, everything would be worse. But the next morning he was in the kitchen making himself toast, and when he saw her he looked up at her and smiled and said, "Good morning, toast for you?" and she didn't feel worse. Instead she instantly felt happier, instantly lighter, the comments from the night before vanished and everything that had happened with Annie in the pantry, as present as it was, felt almost like a godsend. *Okay, I have feelings for Theo, but things aren't different* was the thought. But things were different. They were better.

"I'm not going to be able to sleep like this," Theo had said. "Who the hell drums in an apartment building at fucking 2:00 A.M.?"

Joy took a breath in. She wanted to answer something back that was witty or charming, but nothing came to her so she was just quiet, which normally if she were with another person would be fine. In fact, silence was something that worked well for Joy. When something stressful was happening, and everyone around her was upset or fretting or asking each other for answers, she would usually just get quiet and serious and stand there not seeming nearly as upset as everyone else. People assumed she was stoic. They assumed this was part of some kind of silent genius when in reality she was stressed out of her mind and unsure of what to do. But as it was, Theo couldn't see her being serious and looking stoic, and so she searched hard for something to say, but absolutely nothing was coming to mind, and she started to panic. *Say something! Say something! Say something!* she thought. But before she could, mercifully, there was a knock at her door.

"Joy?" Theo said, his voice beautiful.

"Yeah." She sat up in bed. As far as she could think he'd never seen her lying down, and the potential of the intimacy from that was startling and warranted no other response than to sit up. She even thought of standing, but there was no time. Theo cracked the door open and peeked in.

"I have an idea," he said, smiling.

"What?"

He held up something in his hand.

"What is that?" she said.

"Harmonicas."

"What?"

"Yes, let's go down there."

"Down where?"

"In front of his door."

"Are you crazy?"

"A little bit, maybe."

"We can't."

"Why not?"

"Cause it's crazy."

"Come on, please."

Joy couldn't help but smile. The whole exchange was electrifying. This was what she'd been missing in her life: a man who would drag her out of bed at 2:00 A.M. to harass a neighbor with harmonicas.

"Come, on," he said.

In one big swooping motion he leapt to her bed and grabbed hold of her arm. That feeling of his skin on her skin, she felt so incredibly out of control. Oh, she got up, she went with him.

Now they were running down the hall. Now they were opening the apartment door. Both of them were laughing under their breath. There was a warmth between them in their quiet frenzy as they moved in a fervored mass. He made sure she didn't trip on the wobbly step. He made sure not to let her go.

"Shhhhh," he said as they went down the stairwell.

They could still hear the neighbor's drumming. It hadn't stopped or slowed at all. Joy listened to it. The sound of it as they grew closer and it grew louder broke her from her stupor.

The giggling stopped, but Theo was still smiling as he handed her a harmonica. Boom, boom, boom, she looked at his eyes. Boom, boom, boom, he held his harmonica up to his lips. Boom, boom, boom, she held hers up to hers. Boom, boom, boom, for a second they were both totally still. Boom, boom, boom, they blew hard into the harmonicas. Boom, boom, boom, the sound to her sound.

PART TWO

JOY

I'll be honest, I nearly quit my job for him. I know that sounds so silly, but he was sick for two weeks with a really bad flu, and I really felt like I needed to be there for him. I'm not totally insane, it was really bad. He texted me he went to the hospital, but I can't check my phone when I'm in meetings, so I had no idea what was going on, and I felt awful about it because he really needed me, and I just felt like I had totally failed him. When I told my boss my roommate was sick, he just looked at me like he had no idea what that meant. He had no idea who Theo was to me. I guess people can't see with words the way you wish they could sometimes. He wouldn't be able to hear the word *roommate* and know anything about our relationship or my life. And really, I guess so much of everything is wanting someone to see you for what you are. Isn't that what language is? We've invented so many words not to feel so invisible. I wanted to say, "I quit, asshole!" I almost said it. I really did, but the second I thought about it, even had that thought, I felt really scared because I just knew that somewhere in me I was ready to leave my job just for Theo and that's absurd, obviously.

Who would quit their job for their roommate? And then the language, it's there again, you know. "Roommate" means something even to me. So I just took a sick day instead. And then I got home, and he was already back from the hospital, and I felt kind of stupid standing there. I thought back about my panic at work and it seemed crazy all of a sudden. But I made him soup and he loved it, and let me tell you what, I felt happy after that. And that's what I feel mostly these days, happy, and that other feeling, being ready to snap your fingers and break your life right apart.

When Annie told Joy she was leaving it was rude as hell. She said, "Guess what, Jason wants me to move in. I'm out of this dump for good!" It was Annie being nasty and glib and trying to be above it all. Joy couldn't prevent herself from being hurt by it, but she knew too that it wasn't really Annie being her deepest self in those moments. Joy knew Annie's deeper self was actually very lovely. One time she caught her friend laughing really hard at a YouTube video. Joy was passing by Annie's bedroom and her door was open, and she could hear her laugh in a way that was superloud and free, sounds she'd never heard Annie make. If ever Annie laughed it was always silent and a bit cynical. She'd often say, "That's funny," rather than really laugh. But this was really laughing. She was lying across her bed on her stomach, and to Joy's luck, she was facing the other way so Joy could stop and really watch for a moment. The video was of a baby laughing at her dad ripping up a piece of paper. The baby was hysterical and squealed with high-pitched laughter every time the paper was ripped up. It wasn't that funny, honestly, but the whole thing was so endearing that

Joy indulged in every second of it and she thought: *Annie, you're lovely.*

And so when Annie was being a little nasty about moving out, Joy did her part to make the friendship work in the way that their friendship did work.

"You'll miss me," she said.

And Annie, free for a moment from whatever it was that made her plow through life rage-filled and ready to kill, brightened up and walked over to Joy and hugged her hard.

"Yes, I will," she said.

That was it. A few weeks later she was moving out. She offered to pay for another month or to help them find a third roommate, but Theo and Joy mutually decided things were fine as they were.

"I think the place would feel better with just us, don't you think? More space to move around. I'm happy to split the remainder of the rent if you're up for it?" Theo said.

"I think that's perfect," Joy said, ready as ever to let their little bubble grow smaller and smaller even if it meant stretching her paycheck even further. Whatever had felt impossible about the empty third bedroom before suddenly felt doable in the glow of the potential of what this could become.

Annie took half of the furniture since most of it she and Joy had bought together anyway, and it was what seemed most fair given the circumstance. The apartment looked funny half empty. Each room gave off an aura that indisputably showed its loss. Joy was surprised how sad she felt seeing it like that. It was almost as if those things that reminded Joy so much of Annie—that their absence, the empty spaces they left—made Annie feel even more present than if she'd just left them all behind. Simon though, him leaving was what really made everything real. Joy hugged him tight and kissed his head ten times.

"You can visit him every day if you like," Annie said. "And he'll visit you if I go on vacation."

It's not the same, Joy thought, but she couldn't bring herself to say it because she was fighting back tears. The minute the door closed behind Annie and Simon, Joy felt instantly sorry about so much. *This is my life, this is my life,* she thought, but not more than an hour later she and Theo were on Ethanallen.com picking out a sofa and everything was restored instantly to what it was: she and Theo and their little home, which now was just theirs and no one else's.

Not long after, the two of them had settled into a completely domestic life together. They'd cook together, and eat together, and they'd organize, and decorate. They shared every space of the house and rarely weren't in the same room. Everything had homogenized into a dynamic that in no way resembled how roommates were meant to live. It happened so instantaneously that it seemed almost absurd that they'd ever lived differently. It was clear that Annie living there, even with as little presence as she'd had towards the end, had kept the dynamic what it was originally intended to be. Back then, Joy would force herself into her room just because she felt that's what roommates were meant to do. Shared space needed time to breathe so that it could be shared properly. These were the rules she'd known since she was twenty and moved into her first apartment. Her roommates were Zoe and Claudia, and none of the three of them ever spent time together. They'd say "hi" as they passed in the halls or would have a short conversation when rent was due, but that was it. Then one night Zoe knocked on Joy's door. It must have been midnight or one in the morning, but Joy was still awake. She'd been reading a book for school. The first thing she thought when she heard the knock was that there had to have been a fire or maybe the rent check bounced.

"Yes?" she said.

"Joy?" Zoe said. "Is this yours?"

Joy opened the door, not sure what to expect, not expecting anything really, and there was Zoe standing there holding a bloody tampon by its string with a piece of tissue.

"Is this yours?" she repeated. It might have been a long time between the second she saw the tampon and the time Zoe repeated the question "Is this yours?" It was impossible not to be transfixed by the scene in front of her: a woman who had been a nod hello in her life holding the blood of another woman in her hands like it was nothing.

"No, it's not," Joy said.

"Okay, it must be Claudia's then. She left it in the middle of the bathroom floor."

Joy didn't know what to say to that. "Oh" was all she managed to mangle out of herself.

"She's disgusting," Zoe said, and she turned and headed to Claudia's room.

Joy probably should have immediately shut the door, but she couldn't help it, the whole thing was so bizarre, so inhumane, she found herself just standing there ready to watch the horror about to unfold. But Claudia wasn't home, thank god for that. Zoe mumbled "sloppy bitch" and walked away.

After that who knows what happened. Joy wasn't about to go up to Claudia and say, "So whatever happened to your bloody tampon? You know, the one Zoe was carrying around? Oh yeah, she showed it to me. I've seen your blood. I've seen your period. Your body is much more real to me than my body is real to you." And she sure as hell wasn't about to ask Zoe—who from that moment on she thought of as being as disgusting a person as anyone she'd ever known. Vaguely she'd associate her with every man in her life who'd ever said anything derogatory about women's bodies, anything that made clear that the mechanisms of living and all their inherent gore were only permissibly male.

"My girlfriend hardly ever poops," a guy in her college chemistry class had once said.

"She's hairless, right?" she heard her friend's boyfriend say.

"Cellulite, ewww," a classmate in sixth grade had said.

Joy tucked all of these moments away in her mind and even as rarely as she thought of them, they were ingrained in almost every second of her day, every motion of her life. She hated her stomach. She hated to see her body fold the way a body folds when it sits. Some days those men and Zoe would be the reason she'd be standing.

Claudia, Zoe, and Joy only lived together for one year. They moved out one by one and away from that place. Joy kept no contact with either of them, and on some level, that seemed strange. She knew them so intimately and yet not at all. It felt unhealthy that anyone should be so close and yet remain untouched by the other person. Maybe, in so many ways, even beyond her feelings for him, that was why it felt so good the way things were going with Theo. It felt like life was opening up as it was always meant to be opened up. When you're a child you're born into the arms of other people. And other people are your family and you see them every day and every second there is someone close by to you that you can cry to or can hug, but then you grow up and only if you're lucky do you have that with someone. It isn't an easy thing to ask of a stranger. It isn't easy to say to them: "Love me, be with me, hold me." Only a small number of strangers in your life will ever care to know you, let alone to love you, and so now with how things were with Theo, it felt like she was back in a family again. She felt like a little girl, and she felt so grown up. And Theo would say one morning:

"It's Saturday, let's lie around and do nothing all day and get fat." And they would do exactly that. They shared spaces and they didn't need to let those spaces breathe.

And not too many days later she'd be in the bathroom and Theo's wet towel would be on the floor and she'd accidentally graze it with her bare foot and between that and the steam that was still in the room, she felt like she'd seen his blood. And god, was she hoping he'd somehow see hers too.

ANNIE

I am so fucking happy to be getting away from Joy. I feel bad saying that, but she is so in love with Theo, and honestly it's sad to watch. At first I thought it was a crush, but it's not a crush. She is totally insanely in love with him. She talks about him 24/7. She stays home to hang around with him. All weekend she'll just be home. If he's home, she's with him, and if he's not, she's waiting for him. She won't say that's what she's doing, but that's exactly what she's doing. I asked her to go hang out like a million times, and every time she'd do the same thing: check her phone and then would be like, "Why don't we stay in? I'm kind of tired." That's what really pisses me off more than anything. It's like, be honest, say: I'm obsessed with Theo, and I don't want to miss even one second of a chance to be around him. I could respect that in a way, but instead she's just lying. And I see what he's doing. He's enjoying everything that anyone would love about Joy. She's smart, she's so kind it's almost unreasonable, and she's fun to be around. It's easy to be yourself with her, and I know Theo loves it. He loves all of it, and what is she getting? Nothing. But I don't know. Maybe I don't know what she wants. One time I remember looking at her face, and I felt, for a very small moment, afraid in a way because I thought maybe I don't know her at all. Maybe everything she's thinking is not at all what she's showing me. It's easy to feel that way about Joy because of how in control she always seems. One time I read this article about conjoined twins, and in it they were talking about how people always want to know how conjoined twins have sex, and they were suggesting that maybe conjoined twins don't need sex in the way that not-conjoined people need sex. The idea was that maybe being connected to another person like that your whole life gives you a feeling of intimacy that makes you need a partner less or maybe even not at all. I think about that all the time: the idea that there are people getting something that I want in a way that I couldn't begin to understand. It makes me feel stupid when I say anything definitive about anyone. Who am I to assume I know what other people need? Who am I to assume I know what Joy needs? Maybe she's a separated conjoined twin and her other twin is out there in the world so maybe she only needs half of it all. Maybe she doesn't need Theo to hold her and to love her and to fuck her. But the truth is, I don't want to believe that. I want to believe that in my friend are the same things that are inside of me, and maybe whatever those conjoined twins have is what we're all searching for. Maybe we're all just separated before birth from the realest love we'll ever know. My point is: I'm thrilled to be moving in with Jason.

Her first night living with Jason was like a slow-moving nightmare. Annie hadn't realized it until about eighteen hours into their move, but apparently she'd never been relaxed around her boyfriend before. Sure they'd had many nights at each other's places and had gone away for weekends, but for whatever reason, this wasn't that. This was real life, and real life wasn't as easy to do around him as she'd thought it would be. The first thing she noticed was that she was constantly overlaughing at his jokes.

"Fuck that guy," he said, referencing some guy who had parked poorly on their street.

"Ahahahahahahahaha." She heard herself laughing in this big loud way that sounded like every person whose laugh she ever hated. *What the hell am I doing?* she thought. *Is this what I always do?* And when she thought about it, she realized that it was exactly what she always did. Without meaning to she'd been laughing like a freak at every one of Jason's jokes for the last two years like they were on some never-ending bad first date.

The next thing she noticed was how she ate. They took a break from unpacking and got Chipotle for dinner. She ordered a burrito bowl and as she was picking out what she wanted, she saw herself asking for all kinds of healthy things she rarely if ever ate when she wasn't around Jason.

"No, no cheese," she heard herself say. *Am I going to live my whole life without cheese?* she thought as she watched the woman dump a pile of lettuce in her bowl.

She found herself covering her mouth as she chewed and being obsessive about making sure there wasn't anything on her face. She always did that on dates, but this wasn't a date. She was going to be living with this man now. Could she not eat like herself in front of him? She liked to lick ice cream off the back of her spoon or eat three crackers at once. When she ate salsa she'd dip her chips over and over and over until all that was left was a tiny little chip, and even that she'd dip into the salsa too.

Was that going by the wayside along with cheese? She felt panicked.

"I have to pee," she said and got up to use the bathroom. She made a point to say *pee,* a word that she didn't feel embarrassed to associate with herself when she talked to Jason. Peeing was fine. It was cute enough to verbalize. She thought now was the time to whip out anything vaguely crude that didn't terrify her—anything that could ease them into disgusting humanity together.

When she got in the bathroom she didn't know what to do. She remembered the bathroom at this Chipotle as having one stall, but it didn't. She wouldn't be alone like she'd hoped. An older middle-aged woman was by the sink fixing her makeup. She took notice of Annie just standing there.

"Oh sorry, hun, do you need the sink?" she asked. "I can scooch over."

"No, sorry," Annie said. She saw the woman's wedding band and for a brief second she had the impulse to say, "Do you eat cheese?" but instead she walked into a stall, forced herself to pee, and then headed back to Jason.

When they got back to the apartment they brought in the last of the boxes from the U-Haul, and the whole time she took note of everything she was doing and everything she was doing was not herself. She caught herself saying "wowza" twice, and more than once sucking in her stomach when she'd lean over to lift a box up. Even the way she walked when she really scrutinized it seemed to be fake as hell. She was walking with a kind of peppy step, like she was a lot happier than she actually was or had ever been. When she tried to make herself stop, she just couldn't bring herself to do it. Her body would not relax in the same way it would have when she was alone. Every attempt she made became more and more awkward. Finally Jason said, "Did you hurt your back?" And she stopped the fake not-fake walking and went back to her normal fake walking.

Once they were inside she changed into the pj's she'd bought especially for living with Jason. That act alone had been something she'd willingly participated in without even a moment's reflection. She'd gone to a high-end store, asked the sales associate for help, picked out these very expensive nice pajamas. She even threw out an old sweatshirt she'd formerly loved, all in the name of whatever person this was that she was trying to be. She sat next to Jason and tried to listen to him speak, but all she could think about was what tomorrow would be like and the next day and the next day after that. She looked over at Simon, who sat primly watching her. He'd been stressed out the first couple of hours in the new place, but now he was acting exactly like himself. *Don't judge,* she thought. Would he notice this better self she had created? He'd only ever seen her as her worse self. He loved her worse self.

"Simon," she called. "Come here."

But he didn't walk over. He just watched her from his corner, judging her or at least looking like he was.

The rest of the night muddled on like this. She had many frantic thoughts and noticed many frantic things. She tried to imagine herself as a child and the way it had felt to be inarguably her freest self. She used to do an impression of Mae West when she was little. She'd do it for adults at the command of her parents. Only a free person is happy and excited to do an impression of Mae West on command. All of it seemed like it blurred into the person she was now, and then into the person she was in front of Jason. She thought of her old apartment and the pile of dirty laundry she lazily kept on the floor. *There is joy in not doing things,* she thought and then laughed again at something she heard Jason say because she couldn't help herself. It was all building in her life and in her and now in their new home together. She felt scared and crazy, but then she felt her phone buzz. A new email. She opened it. It was a save the date for Beth's wedding. Seeing it interrupted the existential crisis at hand and not too much later she felt less crazy and less scared. She'd take out her laptop and begin searching dresses to wear to the wedding. It functioned as a welcome distraction, this she knew, and that's also where she left it. She wasn't about to turn the soil and see what else was there, that she'd felt a sense of grief that it was not her wedding and soon after that, a sense of relief that there was a man, a man she loved, who had chosen to sit beside her and only her, and now he was living with her and only her and they were moving forward in life. Annie wasn't alone. And so, who cared how she walked. New pajamas were nice. And not too many minutes later she'd go to bed still wearing makeup, and she'd post a picture of herself and Jason cuddling on the couch with the caption: "First night in the new place together! <3 <3 <3."

The next morning she wouldn't poop till Jason went to work and the next evening she'd say "wowza" two more times. It was a little bit of hell, but so was anything. Annie would manage it, and as the days passed, she'd be more like her real self and less like her fake self, but that real self was also becoming more like the fake self and so where she was was somewhere in the middle. People would say one of two things about that, they'd say dormant or they'd say dead.

BURNT

Joy didn't know what to say to her mom about Theo, but she resolved that today was the day she was going to say something. She called her mom almost every day and while they rarely had anything to update each other on, they always managed to have plenty to say. This day was no different. Joy didn't want to blurt out what was going on first thing so she waited until it felt right. She was nervous.

"I've been adding chives to almost all my meals," her mom said.

"Adding what?" Joy said.

"Chives."

"Really?"

"Yes, they're so flavorful. I find almost everything tastes better with them added. Even pizza."

"Frozen pizza?" Joy asked. She could feel herself reaching for questions, procrastinating with as much inanity as she could.

"No, even real pizza."

"I'll have to try that." Joy thought hard of something else to say but nothing was coming to mind. She could feel herself panicking. Her mom would surely direct the conversation to her within the silence between them.

"So, how are things with you?"

"Oh, okay." Joy stalled. "Was thinking of going for a hike today."

"Oh nice, where?"

"Somewhere nearby." Joy knew literally nowhere to go for a hike.

"How is Annie? I've been meaning to ask."

This felt like the moment she'd been looking for and dreading since they'd gotten on the phone together.

"Actually, Mom, Annie moved out. I've been meaning to tell you." Here was where Joy imagined that her mom would be totally shocked. *"You didn't tell me that Annie moved out????? Annie is your best friend!!! We speak every day and not one mention????"* was how she'd envisioned it, but her mom just said: "Oh wow, when?"

"Three months ago," Joy said. She took a breath in, waiting hard for the response.

"Where'd she move?" her mom said.

"She moved in with Jason."

"Oh, that's nice."

That's nice? Where was the outrage that she'd been keeping this secret? This was the first thing like this she'd ever really kept from her mom. They told each other everything. They'd been that way her whole life. The summer Joy was thirteen they went out for ice cream every single Friday night together. It was the way she envisioned their relationship in totality: the two of them sitting in her mom's car laughing and gossiping as they ate moose tracks ice cream with marshmallow and hot fudge. What this was now seemed like two women. Two very separate women.

"I thought you'd be upset," Joy said.

"About what?" her mom said.

"That I hadn't told you," Joy said.

"Why would I be upset?"

"I don't know." Joy had no way to put this feeling into words.

"What about your other roommate there? The guy."

Joy felt her heart shake. "Theo," she said.

"Yes, Theo. Are you still living with him?"

"Yes," Joy said, her own voice sounding sheepish and stupid as she said it.

"You're not looking for a third roommate?" her mom asked.

"No, we've decided to keep it just us two."

"Oh, really."

"He and I, we"—Joy steadied herself—"we really get along well."

"That's great," her mom said.

"Yeah, we spend a lot of time together."

"That's really nice. It's always a plus when you get along well with a roommate. Hey, you know what? I have coupons from Trader Joe's for you. I was going to send them to my sister, but you know how she is. She'll forget about them or accidentally throw them out or something. I don't want them to go to waste."

And that was it. That's as far as the conversation went. Joy felt alone in a way she never had before. Her mom was married to a man and had kids and a whole life like you're supposed to have. She'd been married at twenty-six. Engaged in Paris like some kind of fantasy. Joy would know the phrase "engaged in Paris" before she even knew what Paris was. Her mom at thirty was, by all accounts, a more successful person than Joy was at thirty. Her mom owned a home. Had a family. Was a manager at her office. Joy couldn't say, "I'm so in love with this man that I'm the happiest I've ever been in my life right now." That wouldn't make sense to a woman like her mother. She couldn't say, "We burned cookies last night and laughed and I never want to be anywhere else."

She couldn't say, "Two nights ago he lay down in my bed beside me to watch a movie, and I was so turned on that I wanted nothing more than to lean over and kiss him, but I stopped myself because I am so afraid of what this is. I'm so afraid of every little piece of happiness falling away because I make one little mistake and try to be closer to him than I'm allowed to be. I'm your daughter and you know what, for whatever reason, it's not in the cards for me to be close to this man or maybe any man right now, but that's okay. I'm happy. Even right now we're going to spend Saturday night here making paella and drinking wine. I've already chopped zucchini for it. He calls me 'Joyous.' That's his nickname for me that he created. Every inch of me is riddled and brittle and here is this man, Theo, and I am a woman in his life and in his home. *Together,* what a concept."

Two nights before, the same night that she lay in bed beside him, Joy would kiss the back of her hand. It was after he left. After she shut off the light and lay under the covers. As a girl, she'd kissed the back of her hand a million times, imagining what it must be like to kiss a boy, but after she did finally kiss a boy, she stopped. She no longer had the need to wonder. But now she kissed her hand and thought of Theo, and rather than fill any kind of fantasy, rather than find Paris or the smell of burnt cookies, she found this: her hand felt older. Her hand felt old.

SIXTEEN

Jason worked Sundays now that they had moved in together. Annie was hoping that he'd be able to at least work from home, but he explained how he couldn't access some certain thing from his computer unless he was in the office, so most Sundays she spent the day alone in the apartment. Sometimes she'd go over to her parents' or she'd get together with friends. She even saw Joy once in a great while, but more often than not she just wanted to be home. Weekdays she worked long hours and Saturdays would be busy, so the thought of doing anything that required energy on Sunday just wasn't appealing. Alone at home she'd read or watch TV. She had an ambition to start scrapbooking, but the second she started she realized scrapbooking was not at all something that was for her in any respect so why had she gripped on to it like that? A childhood memory of putting together a scrapbook of Devon Sawa photos in 1998 did not come to mind, but really that had been the catalyst. She was in love with him at ages ten, eleven, and twelve. His non-threatening good looks and expert haircut were irresistible to her prepubescent self, and the crush would remain the strongest, most hard-felt crush of her lifetime. It was the foundation for the way in which Annie would learn to love later, when the man in her life did more than smile back at her as she gently cut his photo from a magazine, careful never to crop any of his beloved hair.

Nevertheless, she wouldn't consider Devon Sawa as she started sorting through old photos of her and Jason. Her plan had been to create a scrapbook of their early dating days and to give it to him for Valentine's Day, but even if she hadn't instantly hated scrapbooking, she wouldn't have been able to complete the task because she only had a dozen photos of them from those first few months, and in eight of them she hated the way she looked, and in two others Jason had his eyes closed. But looking at the photos of herself from two years ago, just two years, she could see very clearly that she looked younger because in not one of the photos could she see her forehead wrinkles. She'd first noticed them around twenty-six, but only in direct sunlight or with the magnified mirror of a makeup compact. But recently she was sure they were visible always, even in pictures. The first time she noticed it she texted a picture to Joy. "You can see my forehead wrinkles in selfies now," she wrote, hoping to god that her dear friend would know exactly what to say.

"I can't see them!" Joy texted, which was good, but what would have been better would have been "You always had those."

"You always had those" is exactly what anyone wants to think about anything changing on their body. If there's a bump or a blemish or a breast looks saggier or even just a gray root appearing, if you can tell yourself that it was always that way, you can still be happy. This is something Annie knew, and so she would look for forehead wrinkles on everyone everywhere. Even on babies. If babies had forehead wrinkles there was hope. But here looking at these twelve pictures of herself at twenty-eight she could not find one forehead wrinkle, and now every selfie she frantically took of herself that day revealed forehead wrinkle after forehead wrinkle.

She felt out of control and didn't know what to do. She got up and made herself a salad, but salad would not stop her from aging. Then she took a shower, and then put on makeup, a bold lip, a smoky eye, lots of foundation, but all of it was useless to these forehead wrinkles. At one time she'd read an article in which a young woman was mortified that her hair was going gray and her sister said, "Dye it or shut up about it." Annie found the sentiment of the sister very comforting, especially considering that she had stumbled on the article at twenty-three, when she found her first gray hair. But wrinkles you couldn't dye and looking older was its own death. The death of power. People could tell you whatever politically correct garbage they wanted to, but youth meant something in this world and it especially meant something for a woman. What would life be to leave sexiness behind? To no longer be the age that mattered? Movies were about young people. Songs were about young people. Sex was about young people. All of it was slipping away. She'd been blindsided by this feeling. In her twenties she never gave aging a real thought, but now that she was thirty, she had a hard time placing herself. From childhood on everything had been such forward motion: marching into adulthood, and then on to college with the prospect of a career, then leaving college and starting life. But now it felt like all of it was behind her, and she was just moving towards death. And, what was more, her body was reflecting that. She sometimes would catch herself thinking, *Well, what does it matter, I'll be dead one day,* when she'd struggle to get some kind of menial task done or when she burned toast or sliced her finger on the edge of an envelope. Life felt so different now that her youth was draining, and so a photo of a wrinkled forehead on a Sunday afternoon alone in her apartment sent her teetering, and without even giving much thought to it, she found herself obsessively searching through the photos of random famous teenagers on Instagram.

Most of them were former reality stars from this dance show she used to watch on Lifetime. Others were celebrities' children or an odd musician she'd vaguely heard of. They were beautiful and young and not one of them was afraid to be in a bikini publicly. Annie googled them and watched their YouTube makeup tutorials. They were exactly as Annie remembered teenagers being. So much had changed since she was younger, with the internet and social media, and yet it seemed like nothing had changed at all. There was in them power and flash and vapidity. Annie wasn't popular as a teenager, and she remembered feeling in awe of girls with the perfect hair and boyfriends. The girls who were chewing gum and giving blow jobs. She felt so small in comparison back then, but the nice thing was that thanks to social media she knew where many of them had ended up, and without question she was more successful than most of them, and oftentimes prettier, which was at least as, if not more, important. And so this is how Annie spent a lot of time on Sundays as Jason was at work: cyberstalking these people and loathing them for everything they were, the teenagers because they were young and didn't have love handles and were having sex—which just seemed unfair for whatever reason—or the people she used to know, searching for any excuse to feel superior.

She clicked through pictures of one of the reality stars she followed most. A girl who had posted so many sexual photos of herself that Annie had actually reported one of them to Instagram. *She's sixteen,* Annie had thought at the time. *Just because she's doing it to herself doesn't mean it's not exploitation.* She tapped open a recently posted selfie. The girl had her hair up in a bun and a soft expression. Annie mindlessly read through the comments.

"You are so pretty!"

"I love your hair! Please follow me!"

"I wish I was you!"

Kristin Stottier, Annie thought. Something about the post, the comments, herself sitting there in a full face of makeup, made her think of her. Kristin wasn't the most popular of the popular girls, but she was really pretty, and at one point she'd had a clear backpack that in sixth grade everyone was envious of. At sixteen Kristin wore a short skirt to class, and someone Annie knew joked Kristin's tampon was showing. Annie thought of the way Kristin laughed or the time she and Kristin did a project about whales. Kristin did less work on the project than Annie, but wasn't that what Annie wanted? At the time she'd been really angry that she was having to do the bulk of the work, but looking back, it seemed a little unfair of her. She wanted to be the star and to get the good grade and to be sure there was perfection. Certainly Kristin didn't care about perfection regarding the migration patterns of humpback whales, in fact she'd wanted to pick puffins for the project, but Annie had insisted. Kristin was a woman who gave Annie power, and Annie had nonsensically hated her for it. *I could have given her a break,* Annie thought. *She had such nice hair too.* And then Annie searched her on Facebook and Kristin did come up quite easily since they had many mutual friends. She clicked her profile, a shining picture of Kristin smiling on the beach, but when she got to her page, it wasn't the friends or the parties or a marriage or a career or a new baby or a family or a vacation or a meal or a pet or a new home or even a selfie of this beautiful girl, no, Kristin was dead. She'd died at twenty-six. It didn't say how, and even after googling around Annie couldn't find much out. She read through all the eulogy posts by friends and family. Their sentiment mirrored love in her own heart, although she didn't know Kristin enough to love her. Annie felt herself welling up with tears. She thought to text Jason or Joy. She thought to reach out to one of her old high school friends to see what happened, but she decided not to. Instead she felt herself typing out a eulogy for the page also, but of course she would not post it. You could not express love for love's sake. You could not want or cry or share pain when you had no business doing so. A clear backpack, a short skirt, puffins flying into the sky, Kristin was not hers. But Annie typed it anyway and read it silently to herself before she deleted it:

Kristin, you were beautiful. I wished I was you.

BIKINI

That morning Joy had eaten an orange for breakfast. She felt good about that choice. She'd eaten nothing but garbage the week before and so the fact that she didn't grab something sugary or carb-filled felt motivating. She'd even think, *Wow, I'm doing so good,* as she tossed a piece of peel down the garbage disposal. This was the frame of mind she was in, focus on that: she was thrilled with herself for having eaten an orange.

Theo had stayed out late and Joy didn't really notice. She'd been tired and wanted an easy night anyway. They'd texted about the rent earlier that day. There'd been an increase. Joy had to deal with it because her name was on the lease (hers and Annie's). Theo just lived there unofficially. The landlord didn't care as long as he got paid, but Joy was sorry she always had to deal with him. Annie had been the one who usually dealt with anything related to the apartment. If there was a leaky sink or a heater needed work, she was the one who called Joe.

"I'll call Joe," Annie would say, and Joy knew it would be taken care of. Life could go on magically carefree, almost like it had when she was a child and meals were presented whenever you were hungry and folded clothing was always in your drawer.

But now that was over and she had to provide the magic of their home. She didn't care for Joe. He was a rough person with a harsh voice. Whenever he was around she felt uneasy. It wasn't that she worried that he'd rape her, it didn't seem likely that he'd rape someone paying him so much money every month, but it did feel like he could have raped somebody somewhere. She hated being alone with him. Whenever it was just the two of them in the apartment, she felt like she couldn't take a full breath. Sometimes rather than call, he'd just show up unannounced. She'd hear a bang at the door, violent and unapologetic. Seconds later his face, scary and real, would be in her doorway.

"The heat's broken," he'd say. "I'll send someone out tomorrow."

Then before she'd have a moment to answer he'd be turning and walking away, and she'd be standing alone in the empty air he'd left behind.

At least this morning he'd sent a text rather than just turn up like that.

"Rents going up 100 next month," it said.

She was never entirely sure if it was legal for him to raise the rent without some kind of formal documentation, but she wasn't about to question it.

"Okay, thanks, Joe!" was what she wrote back.

She texted Theo about it, and he sent back a series of disconcerted-looking emojis. She sent a few more back and that was all the talking the two of them had really done that day. Joy had been busy at work dealing with complaints about the temperature in the office.

"I can't focus. I need cool," an email had said.

She got home and made herself a sandwich for supper. Chips on the side because she still felt good about that orange. She settled onto the couch and turned on the TV. Theo wasn't home, but she didn't think much of it even as it was nearing 9 P.M. The lock on the front door turned, but it was not remarkable. Nothing jolted her. Not even the brief second as she heard the sound of footsteps on the hardwood floor, the commanding click of high heels shattering time as they stepped forward into her reality.

Joy sat up sharply as her thoughts came together and it was clear that Theo was not alone. *What exactly . . .* she thought before he appeared in the doorway. "Hey, Joy," he said, stepping aside to reveal her, "this is Celine."

There were many women who Joy knew in her life that she thought of as pretty or prettier than she was. In fact most of the time she thought the women she met were prettier than she was. It wasn't hard to be envious of someone's fit legs, or skinny arms. It wasn't hard to feel bad about yourself in relation to other people. But even so, every woman she'd known bore some level of imperfection that was visible and humanizing and that would make it possible for Joy to continue on in her own imperfection. But that is not what Celine was. Celine was so unreasonably, inexcusably, inimitably beautiful that Joy instantly felt her own existence being chipped away just by being near her. *No,* she thought. *No.*

"Hi," Celine said.

"Hi," Joy said.

Now Joy wasn't sure what to do. She didn't want to stand up. She was wearing her good pajamas because she only ever wore good clothes around Theo, but she wasn't about to stand around in lounge clothes next to Celine. Sitting while the two of them stood wasn't helping things either. She could not find a way to place her body successfully next to Celine's body so she just stayed as things were, a status quo of her stupid reality. *Is this real?* she thought, watching Celine reach up and push a piece of hair back from her face revealing a perfect cheekbone, a perfect corner of her eye.

"We went to that new pizza place," Theo said.

"Oh, really?" Joy answered. She didn't take her eyes off Celine the entire time she spoke.

"Yeah, it was great," Theo said.

"Hawaiian," Celine said with a hand to her chest like she could not believe how delicious the damn pizza had been.

Joy just stared. She wasn't even searching for a response.

"Well, I should probably show Celine my room," Theo said, and he started to walk off with her right by his side. "Good night, Joy."

Joy still didn't really respond, but it didn't matter. Celine waved as she was ushered away; Theo was already headed to his bedroom, led by his penis. And then Joy was alone in the living room with her good pajamas and little else. She sat there for a second feeling her hands grow numb. She wanted to jump up immediately and head to her room, but she felt like they might hear her eagerness or her panic. She looked down at her thighs, which pressed together against the couch looked massive. *I take up so much space,* she thought, and she pulled a nearby blanket over them so she didn't have to look at them anymore. After what felt like an appropriate amount of time sitting there in a stupor, she got up and walked down the hall. As she passed his bedroom she could hear him laugh the deep continuous laugh she loved, a sound that now ravaged her. She walked faster, and when she got to her room she locked the door behind her. It was needless, but it felt good to hear that click.

The first thing she did was start to frantically search the name Celine on all of Theo's social media accounts. It didn't take long before she found Celine's Instagram. She clicked through the scores of pictures, each one more astounding than the last. How was this person real? Her body was everything a body was meant to be. Her face was sexy and elegant. There was a reckless number of bikini pictures. Joy had tried counting but quit halfway through to spare herself from a point that lost its meaning as she saw Celine giggling in the sand with perfect breasts and a perfect butt and the crème de la crème, that perfect tight flat stomach that was so far from everything Joy was or could offer. Joy had quit going to the beach at around the age of twelve as most of her peers switched from one-piece swimsuits to bikinis. She knew even then with her preteen weight gain that she definitely would not be able to wear something midriff baring. A pool party early that year when she had suffered the nickname Old Lady during an excruciating game of Marco Polo would be the last time she'd wear a bathing suit in public. Joy clicked one of the pictures and focused in on the way Celine's rib cage poked out, her waist dove in, her belly button sat fully open rather than slumped shut. In it she was sitting on a beach towel, and rather than rolls of fat, her stomach concaved in, defying the laws of physics.

This is where Joy could have spared herself. She could have gone to bed and tried to sleep, but there was in her something vile to herself. This same thing made her cry after she was weighed at the doctor's office or chastised her for eating bread. This same thing would push for spurts of jumping jacks at 1:00 A.M. or would tell her to stand rather than sit when in company. And so here was Joy alone in her room, vulnerable as she'd ever been, and now watch her take off her shirt and stare at her stomach in her reflection in the full-length mirror. Watch her hand move over her body and feel its form. Watch her push down on fat pockets. Watch her wrap her arms around her waist. Watch her suck in her stomach and watch her push it out as far as it will go. Watch her squint, watch her pinch, and watch her start crying, our dear Joy.

The rest of the night she wouldn't sleep much. She tried not to listen to any sounds coming from next door and mercifully there weren't many. At one point she heard the sound of someone in the hallway walking to the bathroom, but she was pretty certain it was Theo. *Does she even use the bathroom?* Joy wondered as she fell into a hazy sleep where she dreamed about Hawaiian pizza and the loud steps of high-heel shoes against concrete. When she woke the next morning, she got up quickly and got ready for work. Theo's door was still shut. She could beat them out of the apartment and not have to deal with any of it. She skipped breakfast and grabbed her coat. She walked quietly to the door and opened it carefully and silently, but as she was about to take a step out, she was stopped. Joe was standing there. He was seconds away from knocking.

"Oh hi," she said, catching herself from saying, "You startled me." It was jarring to see him unexpectedly in all his roughness. His breath steamed in the air. His face looked as unshaven as always, but it was morning so it seemed even more unkempt.

"The gutters are being cleaned tomorrow," he said as he turned to leave before her response in the oblivious way he always did.

"Joe," she called after him.

He turned around to face her.

"What time?" she said.

"Eleven-thirty."

"Okay, thanks," she said.

Joe turned back around and walked off, but he also seemed to nod a goodbye. It was an acknowledgment and sometimes in the violence of life an acknowledgment was as meaningful as anything.

On her walk to the train station she texted Theo: "Joe stopped by. The gutters are being cleaned tomorrow at 11:30 just FYI." She didn't expect he'd respond for a while, all things considered, so it was a pleasant surprise to feel the vibration in her pocket just seconds later. She swiped open the text to find a disconcerted-looking emoji. She smiled. Sometimes that's all it took.

FRIENDSHIPPED

"Holy fucking Jesus Christ," Annie said.

Joy had texted her about Celine but refused to send the link to her Instagram. She told Annie to come over. This was, in the span of female friendships, cause for the most alarm possible. She'd texted Annie simply, "Theo is seeing someone. She's gorgeous. Can you come over tonight?" And Annie, despite any estrangement between them, didn't have to think about it. She responded instantly with "Of course! What time?" Now they were sitting in Joy's bedroom. Theo was still out, but they knew it was best to keep the door closed either way.

When Annie got to the apartment Joy had her iPad in hand.

"Is that her Instagram?" Annie asked.

"Yes, she's gorgeous," Joy said.

"Oh come on," Annie said, stepping out of her shoes. She tossed her coat on the same chair by the door she used to toss it on, even though above the chair was now a set of hooks that Joy and Theo had added at some point since she moved out. It felt strange to be in her old home, and her remedy to that discomfort was to treat the space like it was still her own. She didn't mind doing that in front of Joy. That's what was nice, she feared no judgment from her. It would never be Joy who would point out the hooks in her life. It would never be Joy who would say, "Hang your coat, Annie."

Annie reached for the iPad.

"No." Joy shook her head. "Not here."

They walked towards the bedroom. Joy was moving fast. Annie noticed there was sweat on the back of her neck like she'd just been working out. Joy never worked out as far as Annie knew. She thought to ask her, but she stopped herself.

As soon as Joy shut the bedroom door, she handed Annie the iPad.

"Holy fucking Jesus Christ," Annie blurted out. She hadn't meant to respond like that. The best thing she could have done was say something to the effect of "You think she's pretty? I don't" or "You're way prettier than she is." But she couldn't help herself. There was no pretending about this girl in her hands. She was as close to the standard of perfection as Annie had ever seen.

"I told you," Joy said.

"There's no way she really looks like this."

"I met her. She does."

Annie shook her head.

"She does," Joy said.

Annie looked at her friend, who now it seemed so clearly had been working out and maybe even crying. "No offense to Theo, but how is this possible?" she said.

She wasn't sure if this was the right thing to say. Even though Joy had never acknowledged her feelings for Theo, Annie had begun treating the situation as if, in so many ways, he was her boyfriend.

Joy shrugged. "Well, he is a great guy."

"Joy, I mean come on, this girl is ridiculously beautiful. Even if he is a great guy, this is crazy." She still wasn't sure if this was the right direction to go with the whole thing; she certainly didn't want to hurt her friend, but there was also always a part of her there that wanted to reach out and pinch Joy. Pinch her arm or her face. Make blood vessels snap under her skin so that maybe she'd feel oxygen running blue and warm and would feel alive enough to see how absurd all of this was.

"Okay, I know what you mean. I've never seen anyone like her," Joy said. "You know, supposedly she's related to Emily Ratajkowski."

"Who's that?"

"Remember that girl from the 'Blurred Lines' video?"

"You're joking, right?"

"No."

"How did you find this out?"

"From a comment on her Instagram." Joy grabbed the iPad and scrolled through the photos. Annie could see in the fast way she moved the intimacy her friend had already developed between herself and this Instagram page. It struck her because years ago she remembered Joy chastising her for an obsession she'd had with Jason's ex-girlfriend. It was a few months after she and Jason had first started seeing each other. His ex-girlfriend had commented on a photo that Annie had tagged Jason in of the two of them sitting banally side by side at dinner.

"Cute!" his ex had written.

"Who is that?" Annie had asked Jason, expecting an answer that would be less upsetting than "my ex," which is exactly what he said.

The whole thing: Jason casually saying, "my ex," the "cute!" the nerve of his ex to write "cute!" and most of all, herself, who sat silently beside him, unable to say what she wanted, which was "Why don't you feel you have to consider my feelings when you answer me? And why won't you like the photo?" sent Annie on a spiral of manically cyberstalking the hell out of his ex-girlfriend.

After about a week of confiding in Joy all the many things she'd uncovered (the ex's name was Shai, she'd worked at a restaurant in college, at some point she'd visited Thailand, she stuck out her tongue a lot), Joy said, "Honestly, Annie, why do you care? He's with you now, isn't that what matters?" But Annie could not verbalize why she'd felt so betrayed at the existence of this girl and of their former love together. Maybe something like *I want to be a part of every part of him, and I don't want her to have even what was before* or *it hurts to love and there are no reasons why* would have sufficed, but instead she just shrugged and said, "I don't care." And from then on she kept the stalking to herself and didn't show Joy the picture she found of the two of them kissing on his birthday from the year before, even though when she saw it, her heart sank in her chest a little, which, just like all things, brought her a little closer to death. Now she could see in Joy the same frenzy, the same pain, the same precious seconds of her life wasted as she scrambled herself around.

"Here." Joy showed her comments on a picture of Celine wearing a big hat and drinking out of a coconut.

There were a lot of comments, so Annie just scanned through them quickly. Was it evidence of Celine being related to Emily Ratajkowski? Maybe, it was unclear, but looking at the girl with her tight waist and large perfect breasts she did feel there was a good chance that it was true.

"You know what, Joy?" she said.

"What?"

"I would bet you anything that he just slept with her, and he'll have nothing to do with her after that. I mean, I know that sucks, but I highly doubt you're ever going to see this girl again. What are the chances that she would really want to date Theo, and what are the chances that she's this gorgeous and isn't as dumb as a box of rocks? Theo wouldn't want to date a girl like that."

"You think they slept together?" Joy asked, wide-eyed and still sweaty from whatever she'd done before Annie got there.

"Well, I mean, I don't know, I just meant I don't think it's serious."

And then like some kind of scene out of a horror movie, they could hear the front door click open, and they could hear the clopping of two people walking down the hall, and they could hear Theo's voice and then a voice that said freshly, "Oh right, Sunday." And then Annie looked at Joy and Joy shook her head, but Annie did it anyway, she walked over to the door and swung it open and caught them as they passed in front of Joy's room.

"Oh, hey, Annie," Theo said, but Annie was fixated on Celine, who stood in front of her. She was exactly like every picture Annie had just seen only real. Annie didn't want to believe that they made women like that, but here it was. There was no more lying.

"This is Celine," Theo said, and then with a final plunge, "my girlfriend."

Not too many hours later Joy would be sobbing and doing jumping jacks alone in her room. And Annie would feel two things that night: the first, and she was not proud of it, was a sense of superiority to her friend Joy because at least Jason was here, and anyone who hurt her was called "ex" and not "girlfriend"; and the other thing she would feel that night would be her own breasts. She would pinch them in her palm. Nipple to her hand, her pulse not far away. She'd do this for a few seconds and then a few seconds more. Oh what it was to let time tick towards death like that.

PART THREE

CELINE

There are about a hundred things wrong with my body. My knees have these weird fatty folds over them. My elbows have these rigid bumps at the ends. I've never liked how my nostrils look. I once had a doctor say I had an incredibly small nose when he looked at my nostrils, and I don't know what that means, but it didn't sound like a compliment. My butt sags. I once asked a boyfriend about it. He didn't answer so I know he wanted to say yes. He was mean like that. He was never kind enough to lie.

I know most women think I'm crazy. They tell me as much whenever I complain about anything. It's been this way for a long time. When I was twelve I was a C cup already, which, on my skinny kid frame, looked pretty big. I went to a pool party for my friend Becca's birthday. I jumped in the pool, and when I came up for air, rather than a bunch of screaming kids around me I was alone. All of the other girls were standing on the side looking down at me in the water. I'll never forget their faces. Each one of them had the same expression. It was as if something had been revealed to them about me, about themselves. I just stayed bobbing there and a few minutes later Becca would swim over to me in the pool and say something like "Celine, you know you're gorgeous." And I remember her just swimming away after that, her feet splashing hard against the water and her kid body moving away from my kid body.

I started thinking of my body then as something separate from myself. It was powerful. It meant something just by being the way it was. Does that change me being so hard on myself all the time? Not at all. If anything it makes me more hard on myself.

One time the big sister of my best friend in high school said to me, "When you're so close to perfect it's easier to obsess about perfect." She was putting on lipstick and looking in the mirror. Maybe it's that. Or maybe it's just that once you can see the awesome power of what this is, you're scared to death of losing it. I don't know. But I do know that my body makes my life a certain way that has nothing to do with me.

I remember one time complaining to this girl I knew my sophomore year of college about this boy in class who kept hitting on me. We were in the library working on this project for class.

"He sent me flowers. Can you believe that?" I said.

"What's so wrong with that?" she said. I remember she was wearing a sweatshirt that had PENN STATE written on it even though we didn't go to Penn State.

"I don't want flowers from him. I'm not with him."

"Yeah, it is a little creepy."

"Oh my god, and remember that guy from the bagel place that was like weirdly flirting with me?"

"Yeah."

"He did ask me for my number, but it was so awkward because he tried to pretend it was, like, for the bagel."

"What do you mean?"

"I could not even begin to explain it if I tried. Why do guys always do that?"

"Do what?"

"Like they're too scared to just be straightforward with you because they don't want to feel hurt from rejection."

"I don't know."

"I just wish when they asked you out, they'd be vulnerable. I mean we're vulnerable all the time, right?"

Then I remember she looked shaken up all of a sudden and she only ever looked one way, calm and busy with herself, so I was surprised by her looking like that and then she just turns to me and looks at me and says, "None of that happens to me."

"What do you mean?" I said.

"I never have guys hit on me or flirt with me. No one has ever asked for my number. No one has ever asked me out. I've been on three dates. Two were set up by my cousin and one was from online."

And then I shut the hell up because I realized something: my body was defining my life and her body was defining her life, and it was reckless and absurd of me to pretend we were living the same life.

And I'll tell you the second part of that story, which is this: that bagel guy sent me seven dick pics from three different numbers to the point that I had to change my number. Worst of all was that I'd never get to go to that bagel shop again, which had been so convenient for me when I walked to school.

Let me make that more clear: I was enjoying a lunch spot on my way to school and that was taken away from me by a man who had the expectation that I should be sexual with him.

And even more so this: every time for months when I heard my phone go off I was nervous. When someone does that to you, you have a feeling about yourself like your body, which you already know to be separate from yourself, is not your own at all. Some man somewhere is touching it in his mind. Some man somewhere is taking food out of my mouth.

And so don't be mad at me when I feel fat or worry about my elbows, my butt, the folds above my knees.

Celine was named after a purse. Her mom had bought a Celine bag when she turned thirty years old to celebrate a big promotion, something she'd described to Celine often as "I was the only woman in the office, and I was outperforming all of the men." Her mom had a beautiful bag collection that she'd add to a couple of times a year. They weren't rich or anything; it wasn't easy for them to afford luxury handbags like that, but it meant something to her mom.

"Don't ever let anyone make you feel bad for spending money on fashion," she'd said once. "Do men apologize for nice cars? Boats? A watch collection? Never. It's sexist bullshit used to make women feel like what they love is less worthy. There is no difference between a nice bag and a nice car, remember that."

It wasn't exactly that Celine was named after the bag so much as her mom just liked the name, or that was how her mom had explained it. But when Celine was a child it felt precious to be named after something her mom held so dear, and so she liked to believe it was both. Very often when she was little she'd go inside her mom's closet and try on her bags or stand in her shoes. In the privacy of the small space Celine felt closer to her mom than she did anywhere else. She could smell the sweet smell of her perfume. She could see the wear and tear of her mother's life in a tangible way. Here was a sandal that was nicked on a train track. Here was a thread pulled loose by the hug of a stranger. She was too young to understand it then, but what it was was intimacy, something children seek out and cling to with their parents harder and more voraciously than to anything else they will in their lifetime. Celine looked back on herself as a child and only ever saw some level of desperation. Not because there was any kind of deficit, but because in her, as in all children, there was a violent need for a family unit to exist and be upheld and to spin love and comfort in long spools of thread among them all. And so she found herself always wanting, always trying, always stepping into shoes and wrapping silk scarves in her hands. As she got older though, those feelings, that need, that desperation, diminished and she became resentful. She hated the bags. Hated the clothes. Hated how her mom talked and the way she thought she knew so much about life and love and the way time unfolded.

"Because I don't care!!" she'd screamed at her mom on Valentine's Day one year.

"Celine, what is this anger?" her mom had asked. She was standing at the bottom of the staircase; her face looked elegant and exhausted. Celine didn't know what to say, but she was still angry so she said, "You only care about yourself!" And then she stormed off and slammed her door hard and she listened for her mom's footsteps but they didn't come.

This was how it was and how it stayed for all of her teenage years and a touch into her early twenties. It was what most people would write off as hormones or a childish desire for maturation, but Celine looked back on it as what it really was, and what it really was was accepting mortality. She couldn't be that child in the closet breathing in perfume and fumbling through wool for a sense of forever. Forever wasn't forever and death was coming and so it was necessary to say to oneself, *Mom, I have to hate everything you are so that I can live here without you. Please understand that's why I'm angry. Please understand that's why I hate my name.*

Now Celine was thirty. She and her mom talked all the time and she took note of everything her mom said. But when it came to her name she felt indifferent. Did she feel she was named after a purse? Maybe. She wasn't sure that mattered one way or the other. She and her mom were different people, yes, and she loved her very much as different as they were. It's hard to accept death, that too. A family should be together, that as well. All of it was important to her conception of self. All of it circled in her mind in simultaneous ways, an equilibrium for her to live off of. That was adulthood. That was a way for her to feel in control and separate enough to stand alone when the time would come to stand alone.

But on her thirtieth birthday her mom said, "Celine, I want to get you a Chanel bag. That would mean a lot to me." And Celine, even though purses did not matter to her, and certainly they did not mean to her at all what they meant to her mom, could not help but feel her blood pump in her body just a little faster. And when your blood moves through your veins faster it creates more energy and energy creates heat. And who is to say what is love and what is warmth?

"I'd like that," Celine said. And what is most important here is that she meant it.

JOY

I did fifty-five jumping jacks this morning, and I plan to do just as many when I get home from work. I know it doesn't mean much, but it gives me a sense of control over the whole thing, which I need because I haven't slept more than three hours a night for the last two weeks. I'm drinking four cups of coffee a day. I've switched to vanilla lattes. I don't even like them all that much, but I just need a change. Celine has slept over three times in those two weeks. I can't hear them having sex, but I did hear her say one time, "There's no way I'm doing that." And I can't help but wonder what it is she doesn't want to do. Is it give him a blow job? Anal? Maybe something fetishy? I have run through every sexual scenario I've ever heard of in my mind, and every single one of them seems like something either she'd do or he wouldn't ask for. And if she won't do it, would I? I don't think so, but when she said that I wanted to scream out and say, "I'll do it!" And it scares me that I'm ready to sign up for something without even being able to imagine what it is. I don't know, I'm just so exhausted. I once watched this documentary about a man who only slept one day a week. The doctors were so worried he'd have a heart attack they were doing all this heart monitoring stuff with him with wires. I was hoping by the end of the movie he'd have found a solution and would be sleeping, but instead he was just walking around living his life like a zombie. What is it with our bodies and sleep? You're exhausted and yet your mind won't let you rest. It forces you awake. I once met a hairdresser who had a theory about it. I'd gone to get my hair cut the day I had this big presentation to do at work, and I was really nervous about it and couldn't sleep hardly at all the night before. I told him I was worried I'd be sluggish for the presentation. And he said, "No, it's a good thing. It's nature's Valium. It levels off your anxiety and you end up at the perfect energy level." I'm trying very hard to tell myself that this is true. I'm trying to tell myself that because I'm so exhausted, Theo won't see me as miserable as I am. I also tell myself that this could end any day now. People break up. That's what I say. But who knows what is right. I can't say why I'm doing anything I'm doing. I just feel an intensity in my heart like everything that matters is between him and me, and without it, there's nothing. I won't say that out loud or scream it through a wall so I'm trying not to think so hard, and I would like to lose some weight.

Annie agreed to come to movie night that week. The last two weeks with Celine around there hadn't been any movie nights, but it was because Joy had opted out.

"I'm tired."

"I'm sick."

That was what she told him, but really she was just afraid

he'd bring Celine, and she could not fathom what that would be like. So far the most Celine and she had ever spoken was when Celine had said "Hawaiian" that first day they met. That image of Celine gripping her chest in mock euphoria over pizza saying "Hawaiian" would pop up in Joy's mind day in and day out. She'd be at work stapling with a stapler and then boom, "Hawaiian." Or when she'd wake up and pull the covers off herself just before her foot would meet the floorboard, "Hawaiian." Or opening a letter, "Hawaiian," or brushing her teeth, "Hawaiian," or on the toilet, "Hawaiian." "Hawaiian," "Hawaiian," "Hawaiian." She did not want to put herself through the hell of having a hundred more images of Celine like that saying whatever other stupid thing she would say, and so she'd been avoiding movie night like the plague. Funnily enough, Theo had brought it up both weeks. Since the second he'd introduced Celine as his girlfriend, Joy had just assumed that would be the end of their movie nights together. In fact over the last few months for one reason or another they'd fallen off schedule with movie nights and had missed more than they'd made. They still hung out all the time, but the actual planned sit-down of "movie nights" just hadn't happened, so when Theo stopped her on her way out the door that first week and said, "Movie night tomorrow, right?" she just about fell over.

First she said "yes," out of the pure excitement that he'd asked, but moments later she regretted it. She was absolutely certain that Celine would be invited and there was no way she could possibly ask him if that was indeed his plan. She fretted about it all day at work and hardly slept at all that night. Alone in her room, as the sun rose, streaking over her through her blinds, she thought, *There is no way in fucking hell I'm doing this.* And so she said she was tired and suggested the next week with the hope that by next week he'd let it go, but next week he asked again and the next and so because three excuses in a row didn't seem reasonable, she asked if Annie would bear the burden of a movie night with Celine looking perfect and saying "Hawaiian" as she clutched her chest.

Joy was nervous all day. She ate salad for lunch and even though she had a lot to get done she found herself clicking through Pinterest photos of ponchos (she'd recently begun to believe a poncho might make her more confident). At around three her mom called and she stepped out to answer.

"Sorry to bother you at work," her mom said. "But I heard from your aunt and she said she never got the email about the reunion this spring, which honestly I know she got it but would you mind forwarding yours to her? I'm out all day, and I can never find emails on my phone."

"Sure." Joy was barely listening.

"She's always got to have something extra done for her, doesn't she? I'm so sick of it."

The last thing Joy wanted was to hear her mom complain about her aunt. Her aunt was alone. Childless. She lived in the middle of nowhere with nothing. Movie night with Celine was the only depressing thing Joy had room for right now.

"Mom, I have to go, but I'll forward the email."

"Okay, sorry, honey. You okay?"

"Yeah I'm good."

"Call me later tonight."

"I will." But Joy knew she wouldn't.

At around five she shut down her computer and headed home. She took the long walk to her train stop. She was in no rush to get there and face the misery. The nice thing was that it was getting darker earlier now. For whatever reason there was comfort in that. It felt almost like Christmastime or her birthday, which also fell in winter. She had a flash of a memory of

herself at eleven standing in the parking lot of the Italian restaurant that she and her family went to for most of her birthdays. She didn't care for parties all that much, so apart from a few she had when she was little, she'd celebrate her birthday at home with her family. Her mom made her a cake. There were presents and the same set of noisemakers every year. Chicken Parmesan and ravioli was the dish and if they didn't get takeout, they would go to the old family-style restaurant and request the booth in the back corner under a painting of Robert De Niro that Joy had always loved. One time the waiter had mistaken her for a boy. It was during her tomboy phase when she only wore sweatshirts and a tight ponytail.

"What can I get you, young man?" he said.

Her mom corrected him, and when he left, she and her family laughed it off, but Joy felt embarrassed and went to the bathroom, where she pulled down her hair, but it had been in a ponytail for so long that it looked like it had never not been in one. Something about it made her feel more empty and older than she ever had. When she got back to the table she was extra-nice to the waiter as he put her chicken Parmesan on the table. A few weeks later she'd wear a dress to school. A boy would make a kiss face at her, and she would feel a different but similar feeling. That night she'd lie in bed thinking of the boy and a thought not very different from this would strike through her mind: *Sleep is the only time I'm myself.*

When Joy got to her apartment building she could see the kitchen light was on. Above the rooftop through the darkening sky a shooting star flickered past. She watched it go, illuminating, brief, but she felt too distracted to make a wish. She took a deep breath before heading inside.

It smelled good instantly, warm like cookies or cupcakes or

some mix of both. Before she could even get to the kitchen he called out to her, "Joyous!"

She walked towards the kitchen without bothering to take off her shoes. Her steps made loud sounds against the hardwood, but she wasn't listening to that at all. When she got there she saw he was alone, which was the first best part of the night.

"You're home," he said and the word *home* would be the next best part of the night.

"I made dinner," he said. "Eggplant Parmesan."

"You did?"

"We can also order a pizza if you want though." Theo pulled a cookie sheet out of the oven with chocolate chip cookies. "I think we should do this movie night up big. It's been too long, Joyous," he said, and he looked directly into her eyes. Joy felt a hard firm flutter through her body.

"I invited Annie," she said.

Theo looked disappointed. "Did you?"

"Is Celine coming?"

"No, I thought it would be just us . . . But Annie's welcome of course."

"Well, I mean, I'm not sure she's coming. I just invited her, but she hasn't said yet if she was."

"Oh sure, well, whatever, but yeah, I was hoping it would be just us two." He paused a moment. "You know, the way it's meant to be."

Oh those words.

She grabbed her phone and in a frantic loose motion she texted Annie.

"Actually can you ski7 tongight? Celine isn't cominz," she mistyped but sent it all anyway.

"Seriously?? That's awesome!" Annie texted back, but Joy would not respond. She'd eat eggplant, and they'd have cookies, and she'd listen to Theo laugh and talk and crunch through popcorn. They'd stay up till two, and even though they'd part ways to their own bedrooms, Joy wouldn't feel alone as she fell into a deep sleep that was restful and blissful and she'd have many dreams, all of which she would forget by morning. And when she'd wake, she'd dress in happy haste. She'd wash her face and brush her teeth. She'd head to the kitchen and hope to have breakfast with him, but it would be minutes before she'd realize he'd left already and the living room, which was still messy from the night before, would look like something she'd almost imagined. *No bother though, Joy,* she'd think to herself. *Just keep going.*

ANNIE

Bridal showers are the stupidest fucking things. What is the point of having fifty pre-parties for one party? Isn't it enough to make us all suffer for four hours one time instead of ten times? There's the engagement party, and the bridal shower, and the bachelorette party. If I was getting married I'd have a twenty-minute wedding, and then I'd invite everyone out for pizza. I would not make them sit around and suffer celebrating my relationship with this bullshit. I seriously don't want to go, but if I don't, I'll have to hear about it day in and day out because people in offices have nothing to talk about so they'll exhaust the hell out of any one subject that they can. One month we talked about a broken coffee machine twenty-seven times. TWENTY-SEVEN TIMES! I actually counted. Everyone is so unsure of what to say about anything so they'll talk about something boring forever just to avoid revealing anything about themselves. I guess I can't blame them. Work is a strange thing. We're all there so we can have money to eat, but we have to uphold some illusion that that's not why we're there. I guess that isn't true for everyone. Those people whose parents pay for their apartments would probably work no matter what since they've got to have something to base their self-esteem off of. Regardless, I don't want to be the focus of their safety net conversation so I'm going to Beth's fucking bridal shower. The other big part of it is that I really can't afford this right now. Jason and I are hardly making ends meet since we've moved in together. He makes less than I do, and I certainly don't make a lot. I can't afford to buy Beth a cutlery set. I can hardly afford my cellphone bill. But I am cause I have to so I went online to Kitchens Etc to get her her goddamn cutlery. At first I couldn't find Beth's registration. It took me a minute to figure out that she'd registered under his last name, Whitstead. Beth Whitstead she'd be now. And for a second, even though I don't know her that well, and she and I aren't great friends or anything, I felt really sad. It was this feeling like I'd never taken the time to get to know the person that she would no longer be. Her life as the Beth I knew would now be something else, and I'd not known her well enough to know what it was she was giving up to be a Whitstead. I see Beth every day, and yet here she was to me little more than that coffeepot conversation. Maybe that's why I really don't want to go.

Annie could not for the life of her figure out what to wear to the bridal shower. She felt like every dress she owned made her look like an overgrown child on some level. She wanted to look good. She wanted to look enviably pretty. Most of the people there would be strangers or people from work that she knew in passing. She wanted to leave an impression as someone chic and together. Someone who didn't care and could effortlessly eat carbs. Nothing she owned really looked like that though, so in the end she wore a dress from college that was probably too short and was definitely too see-through.

When she walked up to the venue she saw Patrice waiting for her out front next to a chalkboard sign that read LET US SHOWER BETH! in ornate but rustically crafted lettering.

"I wasn't going to go in without you," Patrice said. She looked like she'd had a similar struggle in finding something appropriate to wear for the occasion. Patrice slipped her arm through Annie's and they started walking in together. "By the way her fiancé is in there."

"What?"

"I know."

"I thought bridal showers were supposed to be a woman-only thing."

"I thought so too, but he's in there."

"What's his name again?"

"Benny."

Annie tried to remember what Benny looked like. She remembered Patrice saying he was ugly, but any details beyond that she could not recall.

When they walked in most of the women were seated at a long table. There were balloons and flowers. The back of each chair had a yellow ribbon tied over a light blue ribbon. There were chalkboard signs everywhere.

Beth was leaning over talking to an older relative. She was smiling and laughing. She looked happy and sure of herself, as one would expect a woman would who was about to get so much cutlery. She caught sight of Annie and Patrice and waved a big enthusiastic wave as she walked over.

"Oh my god, so happy you guys could make it!" She first hugged Annie and then Patrice.

"We wouldn't miss it," Patrice said. She was always so snappy and unforgiving that it was almost jarring to see her so polite towards Beth.

"The place looks beautiful," Annie said.

"Doesn't it? My maid of honor did all of it. She's so good with that kind of thing. I'm so blessed."

Blessed. Annie felt the word sitting in the air. It always rubbed her the wrong way how women used it. *Blessed* implied luck, but it never seemed that when women said it they meant luck. It always seemed that what they meant was *better*. Annie once went over an Instagram page of a friend of hers from high school who had three kids and her teeth bleached regularly, and took every single #blessed and turned it into #betterthanyou.

"Took the kids to pick out a Christmas tree #betterthanyou"

"Happy Anniversary, Babe! #betterthanyou"

"Family vacay #betterthanyou"

There was not one time that it didn't work.

Annie and Patrice found their place cards and took their seats. Annie was directly across from a blond girl who looked similar to Beth. She was spreading a piece of bread with butter and looked kind of sad doing so. To the girl's right was another woman, typing out something on her phone. Patrice had started a conversation with the woman to her own right. To Annie's left was an empty chair with the name Ellen placed in front of it. She wasn't sure what to do with herself so she took out her phone. She was hoping Jason had texted her, but he hadn't. She sent him a text: "Ugh so bored." He rarely responded to this kind of text, but she was vaguely hopeful. When they first started dating he'd been working a second job part-time at Zara and she remembered him texting his first day, "On the verge of suicide at Zara." It was so thrilling that he'd texted something that was reflective of himself on any kind of emotional level that she instantly responded with an invitation to hang out, something she usually didn't dare do.

"Oh no! We should get together so you can vent. Maybe sushi?"

Of course he did not respond. In those early days anytime she showed any enthusiasm to see him it was a disaster.

She sat for a moment more before going to text Joy. "This bridal shower is killing me." But before she could press send the girl across from her grabbed her attention.

"Hi, I'm Jordan. Beth's cousin." She stretched out a hand.

"Annie, I work with Beth." *Should I have said "work friend"?* she wondered.

"Oh, nice. Have you met Benny before?"

"No, I haven't actually."

"He's really nice. Beth wanted him here because she knew most of her friends haven't met him yet. He's not staying the whole shower though."

"Oh okay, nice," Annie said.

They sat a second in silence.

"Bread?" Jordan offered.

"Oh thanks!" Annie took a roll.

She chewed a piece of bread and sipped a sip of water from the jam jar in front of her.

"I wonder how she got all these jam jars," Annie said, forcing more conversation. "That's a lot of jam to eat."

"You can buy them now. I think she got them at Target."

"Oh really?" Annie took another bite of bread. "Seems kind of funny when you think about it. I mean aren't jam jars supposed to be something that represents, I don't know, reuse, effortlessness, the opposite of consumerism?"

Jordan just stared at her.

"They're adorable," Annie offered.

Seconds later a jam jar was being chimed. Beth was standing there at the head of the table and to her side was who Annie had to assume was Benny. He looked sloppy. He was oddly shaped, shorter than Beth and worse looking.

"Benny and I would like to thank you all for coming to our bridal shower. We are so blessed to have so many people in our lives who care about us and want to celebrate with us."

"You guys are the fucking best," Benny said.

Everyone laughed like Benny was funny. Then out of the blue he did a funny little dance as Beth continued giving her speech. People laughed again. Seconds later he said something else stupid.

"Babe," Beth said as she touched his shoulder. So much was expressed in that "Babe."

"He's a fucking freak show," Patrice said to Annie under her breath.

Mercifully, the speech wrapped up, and it looked as if Benny was leaving, but before he did, he started making his way around the table to greet everyone.

"Oh, Jesus," Patrice said.

Annie waited and watched as he went from woman to woman making animated appeal after animated appeal. She could feel his insane energy moving closer. It was nerve-racking. *Don't look put off,* Annie thought. *Smile at least.*

"Annie!!!" he said as he finally got to her.

"Hi, so nice to meet you!" she responded as she went to meet his hug.

"You know how I know your name?" he asked her. She waited a second because she assumed the question was rhetorical, but as the silence grew between them it was clear he was waiting for an answer.

"Umm, Beth told you?" she said.

He pointed to the place card and let out a huge laugh.

"Make sure you take some crab cakes home in your purse!" he said, and then he gave her another hug and was on to Patrice.

After that, things quieted down. They played a few games. Then a larger jam jar was passed around where everyone was meant to write down on a piece of paper one thing they felt made for a happy relationship.

"Would it be wrong if I wrote flirting with strangers?" Patrice asked.

Annie shook her head with a smile. "Don't do it."

"But I really think that's true. I know, I'll write, 'Lots of jewelry.' "

When it was Annie's turn she tried to think of what to say in relation to her own relationship, but everything she could think of had a streak of sadness to it.

"Split the bills fifty-fifty."

"Don't fight before bed."

"Set time apart from each other."

Just then she felt her phone vibrate. It was Jason. "Miss you," he wrote, and just like that her heart felt full.

"Surprises make it work," she wrote and stuck her paper in the jar.

The rest of the shower went fine. They ate crab cakes as Benny had mentioned. They had red velvet cupcakes that had BB neatly iced on top. Ellen never turned up, but no one seemed bothered. Beth opened her gifts and made silly faces at lingerie and a whip that Patrice had given her.

"To keep him in line," Patrice shouted out over the crowd.

Beth seemed genuinely grateful for the cutlery that Annie had bought. Soon it was time to say goodbye. Beth hugged her tight, and Patrice and she laughed as they walked out.

"Thank god that's over," Patrice said.

But on the way to her car Annie spotted a loose chrysanthemum that must have fallen out of a flower arrangement during delivery. She picked it up and took it with her to her car. With care she fastened it above her rearview mirror and she felt a sense of calm and maybe even joy. It was a nice day. And here buried deep in much of this was the truth: Annie hadn't wanted to go to the bridal shower because Annie was jealous.

BELOVED

Celine liked Theo. He was nice, and handsome, and he was funny. They both liked going to concerts and trying new trendy restaurants. They'd even had an eerily similar experience in both of their sixth-grade classes' productions of *Wicked*. She'd met him on Tinder. She liked a goofy photo he'd posted of himself standing next to a llama. There was something joyful about the way he looked and what Celine needed in her life right then was joy. She was still in love with her ex-boyfriend. There wasn't hope for that relationship and at this point she knew well enough that there shouldn't be, but even so, she'd have dreams about him all the time. She'd wake up thinking he was beside her. She'd reach for her phone with the hope of seeing his name in bold letters lit up on the screen, and she'd cry sometimes for no reason at all except that she'd thought of something silly to tell him. She was exhausted by all of it and so seeing Theo's face shimmering beside a llama like that, she swiped right. Seconds later, not even full seconds really, they were a match.

The first date went well. Their conversation was easy. She thought they had chemistry. But she found herself bored in spite of it. She checked her phone a few times, and when she excused herself to the ladies' room, she took her time getting back to the table. A waiter winked at her as she passed him, and she smiled. It felt good. A reminder she had options, although kind of gross and very presumptuous.

When she and Theo said their goodbyes it wasn't awkward as they hugged and made tentative plans for another date. She took the train home and all the while she reflected on herself that night sitting there eating pasta and listening to Theo speak. She tried to think of one solid thing he'd said that was memorable and nothing came to mind. She also tried to think of something she'd said. A funny story, an important thought, something banal yet kind, but she couldn't remember anything she'd said either. *Then what even is there?* she thought as the train sped past lights making a blur, a flash, making a memory she would keep: herself riding home in an empty train car thinking about an uneventful first date.

But despite it, when she got home, she felt nervous and worried that Theo wouldn't text her. She checked her phone a few times and even went back to look at his dating profile again, him and his llama. As the night moved on into the next morning, she felt increasingly frantic over the prospect of not hearing from him. The date and her boredom, whatever other melancholy there was, they were draining away. She was seeing him as funny and charming. She so did like his salt-and-pepper hair.

At work she did her best to keep busy. She worked at a company called Loom, which specialized in making women feel that there was a deficit in their lives that could be filled by leather-scented candles and overpriced face creams. Celine had not intended to get a job in the wellness industry. To tell the truth, before she began working at Loom most of the beauty products in her cabinet she'd gotten from a gift bag her cousin gave her a few years before. A casual friend of hers who worked there had emailed and asked her to apply.

"You'd fit right in!" her friend had said, which Celine didn't understand until she got to the interview and saw that all the women in the office were pretty or at least skinny. When Vi, the woman who would be her boss, saw her, she instantly lit up. "Well hello!" she said, and the rest of the interview felt like fluff. "You get it, you really get it," Vi said at one point when Celine had said something marginally impressive.

At first working there had been okay. It was kind of awe inspiring how much there was to know about what a woman could do to be "well." Celine had always assumed it was eat healthy and exercise, but really there was a whole lifestyle that could go along with being your best self. Breathing and meditation and oddly even strategically stacked jewelry could all be part of what was referred to as a "Loom girl." But over time Celine found the whole thing disparaging and often tedious. No one in the office ever seemed aware of how privileged they were to buy seventy-five-dollar healing crystals or to consider alkaline water so thoroughly. "My grandmother once screamed at me because I'd thrown out the excess grease that she was planning on reusing the next day for dinner" was an anecdote that Celine had an impulse to share when they'd called a meeting to put together a list of the best cashmere sweatpants. Everything felt so precious. Her co-workers were as focused and serious about kale-based diets as a person could possibly be. Celine didn't feel like she cared enough about kale, or any of it really.

"For the first time in modern history, women are able to take the health of their minds and bodies seriously on unprecedented levels," Vi had said at a companywide meeting. "It's a new era and we're putting ourselves first."

And so, Celine felt alienated, and to cope she'd watch clips of *Judge Judy* on YouTube throughout the day. It wasn't perfect, but it got her through, and she figured another job would come around or she'd apply to grad school and finally get on the path that was meant for her—something she'd care about, somewhere she'd feel like she could be understood.

Today it was a case where a woman thought she'd scratched up her ex-boyfriend's car with her keys but she'd accidentally scratched up his neighbor's car instead before realizing her mistake and going on to scratch up her ex's car as well. Her ex had claimed that they'd never dated. He said it was a friends-with-benefits situation. "Did she ever once have a glass of water at your place?" Judge Judy had asked him. "Yes," he'd said. "Maybe had a drink with you?" Judge Judy said. "Yes," the man said. "Well then that's kind of dating. Isn't it?" The man begrudgingly agreed.

Celine looked down at her phone; no text from Theo, but there were a bunch of messages from Tinder.

"Fuck me," one of them said. She instantly blocked the guy. She got messages like that pretty much all day long. *It's like they don't even think they have to try,* she thought. She went to put her phone away but not hearing from Theo had made her nervous so instead she swiped through some profiles. Right, instant match, right instant match. It felt good and she was able to move on in the moment.

"I'm not crazy," the woman said to Judge Judy. "You don't understand. I'm not crazy."

Celine got up and headed to the break room to grab something to eat. There were a lot of protein-forward, gluten-free snacks left out for employees to indulge in. Mostly seeds or protein bars from companies with difficult to pronounce names. Celine would have probably stopped in twice as much as she did, but the hall that led there was virtually entirely mirrored, and she hated it. *It's like they're trying to shame you for going to get a snack,* she often thought. But more than that, she hated catching sight of herself throughout the day. She never looked as good as she looked in her mind. Her body seemed oddly shaped, her face always looked tired. She'd suck in her stomach and imagine herself as her best self and curse herself for her real self, or, if she could, she'd avoid looking at anything but her feet marching her towards free hemp seeds.

When she got to the break room she couldn't see anyone but she could hear someone softly crying. Her first impulse was to leave. People who started crying at work usually didn't want the comfort of their co-workers, or at least Celine felt she wasn't close enough to anyone in the office for it to feel appropriate. But before she could make a decision one way or another, the co-worker who was crying saw her. She was sitting in the corner of the room on the floor with her back against the cabinets. She was someone Celine had seen around the office a few times although she didn't know the woman's name. Maybe an intern even? She couldn't have been older than twenty-two. Her face looked like she'd been crying for a long time, but she stopped once they locked stares. Before Celine had the chance to ask if she was okay, she said:

"Do you think I'm basic?"

"What?" Celine said.

"Basic. He said I was basic."

"Cause you work at Loom?" Celine asked.

She nodded. "Do you, do you think that makes a person basic?"

"I—"

"I don't want to be basic."

Celine didn't know what had happened to this girl. Maybe it

was something terrible. Maybe she was just having a bad day. But whatever it was, it felt instantly like the most important thing in Celine's life right then.

"I think, I think, basic is something that only ever gets said to women as a way to make them feel bad about themselves. And really men are the most basic people of all."

It didn't feel like it was all that eloquent as she said it, but it seemed to satisfy the girl, who minutes later was up on her feet and making apologies for crying. She left and Celine ate a packet of seeds before heading back to her desk, where she sent an email about soaps and watched some more *Judge Judy*. For the rest of the day she felt good about herself, even thinking, *I know how to help people,* but by the time it was time to leave, and still she'd gotten no text from Theo, the whole break room thing no longer felt like anything at all. And so that night when she was washing the day off her face with an expensive cleanser that was gifted to her through work from a small company desperate to get on Loom's "Yaasss List," and Theo finally texted: "I had so much fun last night! Dinner again this weekend maybe?" Celine felt immediately relieved, victorious even. She took her time and was sure not to answer right away, finding just the right words to sound excited but not as excited as she was. "I did too! I think I'm free this weekend, so yes! Let me know where and when!"

The next date was nice as well and they did kiss at the end. Yes, she was still a little bored. Yes, there was her at the end of the night, alone on the train thinking of everything inside herself that felt carved out, scraped. But here too she would be still hoping, wishing, praying, that things would move forward. "Let me know where and when!" It was a sign of her times.

EGGNOG PANCAKES

Joy had created a system for dealing with the whole Celine situation. In the morning she'd casually ask Theo, "Plans for tonight?" She worried initially that he would think it was strange, but luckily they'd built such a solid foundation of syncing schedules that the question fit seamlessly into most conversations. If it was a night that he had plans with Celine, she'd be sure to leave work early and get home with enough time to eat dinner before they'd turn up. There she would be: standing by the counter shoving mouthfuls of salad down her throat (she was still hoping to lose weight) and checking the time. As soon as it was eightish, she was in her room with the door shut and music playing or TV on, whatever she could do to block out the sound of them coming home, them in his room. Theo sometimes would knock on her door and ask, "You good, Joyous?" To which she oftentimes would say, "Totally, just tired!" It wasn't perfect, but it worked. She could almost block the whole thing out of her mind, and she could enjoy the days when it was just the two of them.

Maybe then it was a slipup because she *had* been vigilant and aggressive in keeping up the routine. It was a Saturday. Usually

Celine slept over Fridays but would leave early the next morning, or if she didn't leave early, she and Theo would stroll out together late morning to get brunch. The point was, they never stayed home, so Joy was easily able (although it wasn't always pleasant) to spend the morning in her room. This Saturday she'd heard the door click shut and the apartment grow silent. She was relieved because she wasn't in the mood to be locked in her room for hours. She'd slept in her worst sweatpants, which had a big brown stain (a hot fudge mishap from a few years back), and her big Christmas sweatshirt, which was bright red with a big wreath appliquéd across the front. Both articles of clothing very much needed to be thrown away for different but equally valid reasons, but she loved them and the one nice thing about this change in Theo's and her life together was when he was out at brunch with Celine, she would have a blissful morning to herself with no fuss.

She opened her bedroom door and made her way to the bathroom. She'd had to pee for quite a while. She washed her face and brushed her teeth. A flurry of happiness fell through her body as she looked at Theo's toothbrush, which sat proudly beside her own. Something about seeing it always felt reassuring and oddly thrilling. She finished up in the bathroom and headed for the kitchen. There was not a moment between not being in the kitchen and being in the kitchen when she would have or could have suspected anything. Instead she was just thrown in violently, chocolate stained and Christmas ready.

Celine was there.

She was dressed in the shortest shorts Joy had ever seen made out of sweatpant material and a loose-fitting tank top that left her laced bralette visible from the oversized arm openings. She looked flawless.

"Oh my god, hi. Sorry, I hope I'm not in your way. Umm, we were just making pancakes."

For what felt much longer than it likely was, Joy just stood there gawking at this beautiful woman effortlessly moving around the kitchen. Briefly the "Hawaiian" vision came to mind, a vision that had become more and more contorted the longer she'd thought of it. Celine was not as slutty as she remembered her, nor was her voice as stupid sounding. Joy certainly didn't hate her any less, but Celine wasn't who she remembered.

"Where's Theo?" Joy asked. She probably should have responded to something Celine said before asking, but her brain wouldn't have it.

"He went out to get eggs," Celine said. "I love your sweatshirt, by the way."

Joy could feel herself going red faced.

"Oh, yeah, I have to do laundry," she said, still fumbling through the interaction.

"I love Christmas," Celine said. Then it was silent for a moment.

"I was just going to grab a cup of coffee," Joy said.

"Of course, let me know if I'm in your way."

Joy walked over to the counter and started making coffee. The truth of it was she had been planning on eating some frozen waffles too, but she wasn't about to eat carbs in front of someone with a thigh gap who was sleeping with Theo.

"Can I make you a cup?" she asked Celine. She figured it was only right to offer.

"No, I'm fine, thank you though," she said. It was quiet a little longer.

"So, Theo said you work in HR?" Celine asked.

"Yeah, I do." Joy grabbed for a mug from the sink. Neither Theo nor she had done the dishes in a couple of days so she rinsed it out quickly. The mug was faded badly with penguins on it. "What do you do?"

"I'm a purchasing administrator for a wellness company." Celine was pouring pancake mix into a bowl. She hadn't stopped moving since Joy had entered the kitchen. "I like it fine, but everyone who works there pretty much has an eating disorder."

Joy wondered exactly how skinny these women had to be for Celine to be surmising how disordered their eating was.

"And don't tell anyone if you ever get put on antibiotics because they'll tell you to, like, put yogurt in your vagina." Celine pushed the hair back out of her face. "But I used to work in tech so this beats that by a long shot. At least it's women, all women, which I do better with. I find myself weirdly trying too hard when I'm in a group of all men."

"Yeah." Joy held the penguin mug still for a moment. She tried to think of what it would mean for a person like Celine to try hard. She couldn't envision her perfect shape doing anything that didn't seem effortless.

"And I can't really be friends with them. I don't know how it's been in your life, but for me every time I've ever tried being friends with a guy it's not worked out. Someone always ends up in love with the other person. It's never a real friendship."

Joy imagined that in most of these scenarios it was the men who were the "ends up in love" part of the equation.

"I hear you," Joy said. She was about to respond with an example of a guy friend of her own, but she couldn't think of one. She'd been friends with a boy in elementary school, William, but if she was being totally honest with herself, she did have a crush on him. Then in college there was this guy from her speech class, Lloyd, who had helped her fix a printer minutes before a deadline at the start of class. She was so grateful that she was sure to be extra-polite to him when she'd see him in the halls, the act of which slowly evolved into a tentative friendship between them. She didn't particularly love his company, but if they stuck to talking about class, things usually went fine. Then one week before the end of the semester Lloyd said, "Have you ever had a crazy idea?" He was all sweaty as he said it. It was out of the blue, and very strange, even for Lloyd. Joy wasn't sure how to respond so she just said, "No." A few hours later she got a text from him that said, "Want to make out in the darkroom?" Lloyd was a photography major.

Joy didn't respond and Lloyd was suspiciously absent the last day of speech class. From then on when she saw him around campus she would pretend to be looking at her phone or if she didn't have her phone handy she'd just turn in the other direction. She didn't think that Lloyd was in love with her, but obviously he had misunderstood how much she'd valued his fixing the printer for her.

Beyond that, any guys she knew she wouldn't have considered much more than acquaintances.

"I"—she thought of herself with Theo and felt overwhelmed—"I guess that's true," she said.

"Oh my god," Celine said. She was squatted down by the open fridge. "You have eggnog."

Joy just stared.

Celine turned around holding the carton. "What if we make eggnog pancakes?" she said.

"What?" Joy asked.

"You put in eggnog instead of milk." Celine started pouring the eggnog into a measuring cup.

Joy just watched and listened to the clanging of glass, the slide of ceramic bowl against the counter. She was utterly out of place in her own life. Part of her wanted to say something like "Actually, that's my eggnog," but where would that lead? An uncomfortable moment between them and then Theo would come home and correct her that, no, actually he'd bought the eggnog? She didn't even like eggnog.

"Will that be good?" Joy asked, clumsily searching for something to say.

"I don't know, but it sounds good, doesn't it? It sounds like it would work."

Just then the lock in the front door started to rattle. Theo was home.

"We're in here," Celine called out.

"We're?" Joy thought. *What kind of a nightmare is this?*

Theo came into the kitchen with a grocery bag in hand. He seemed startled to see them together.

"Oh, hey."

He looked over at Joy. "Christmas?" he said.

She looked down at her wreath. Her breasts were sticking out. Her stomach too. It was a very specific kind of mortification.

"Actually, yes, it is Christmas because we're making eggnog pancakes," Celine said.

"Nice," Theo said. He walked over to the counter, putting his arm around Celine's waist as he passed her.

Joy turned and left the kitchen without saying anything. She shuffled herself down the hallway. Each footstep made its own creak on the floorboards as she went. Her hand turned the doorknob to her bedroom. She got inside the room, closed the door, and burst out crying. It's hard to cry in silence like that, but she managed.

A few hours later, she joined Tinder.

SNAPPED

They were sitting in their bedroom just after having sex that Sunday morning. It was a rare thing for them to have sex Sundays, most especially in the morning, but they'd woken up and had been having a few giggles in bed. Jason was at his best. He was being silly and funny. She could hardly catch a breath between laughs and somewhere in the folds of that type of intimacy they started kissing. It was much more organic than probably any other sex they'd ever had before, so when he sat up afterwards and started getting dressed, Annie just wanted him back beside her.

"Can't you call in sick today?" she asked him.

He didn't answer but smiled.

"Come on," she said.

"You know I can't," he said.

"Why? It's Sunday, I'm sure they would understand you missing one Sunday."

Jason was by the dresser. He was putting on his watch; then he ran his hands over his head.

"Okay, I'm going to tell you something, but you can't get mad at me," he said.

"Okay, I won't," she said. She couldn't imagine what it was he was about to say, and really in the context of their nice morning together, she wasn't all that worried.

"I don't really go to work on Sundays."

Her mind clattered. "What do you mean?"

"I mean, I just told you that because I knew if I told you the truth you'd be upset about it and I didn't want to hurt your feelings."

Annie sat up. "What are you talking about?"

"I just need time by myself. I love you, but I just need a day where I'm doing my stuff."

"What does that mean? What do you do all day?" She tried to imagine him living this other silent life he had.

"A lot of things. Sometimes I meet up with friends. Sometimes I get stuff done I need to get done. Sometimes I just drive around."

"So you just need to be away from me?"

"No, it's not like that, it's just, we're together a lot, and I just need my space is all. It really has nothing to do with you."

She felt so much of herself being pulled out of place, each fiber separated one by one. She felt anxious, and frenzied. Clarity and more compassion for herself would have led her to the conclusion that really she was just feeling intense loneliness.

"But you lied to me."

"I only lied because I knew if I told you what I needed, you would be hurt."

"Then why are you telling me now?"

"I don't know. I just didn't feel right lying today, and I guess I just hope you'll understand why I need my Sundays."

"*My* Sundays?"

Jason was still for a moment. Annie pulled her legs up to her chest. She suddenly felt very aware of how naked she was.

"You said you wouldn't get mad," Jason said.

"I'm not." Annie quietly searched herself for resolve. She held her face still and worked very hard to let every word roll off her back.

"You seem like you are."

"Like I said, I just wish you could have been honest with me is all." It wasn't "all" but it was as much as she felt comfortable holding him accountable for. Everything with Jason had to be held in balance. A strategy had to be in place for every moment, always, but especially something like this. No, she couldn't just start screaming at him. No, she couldn't just feel whatever it was she was feeling.

She remembered one time as a teenager meeting a friend's boyfriend. They'd gone to a pumpkin patch to pick out pumpkins to carve. They'd both been looking forward to it, but when she got there, her friend's boyfriend was in a bad mood.

"Zach's pissed," her friend whispered.

"Why?" Annie asked.

And her friend just shrugged. Annie remembered looking over at Zach, who was standing an absurd distance away from them. His face looked brutish and sulky. The girls hurried along to get closer to him. They tried to engage with him, be happy, but he stayed like that the whole time. Annie could remember how she watched Zach toss a cigarette butt carelessly into the dry grass of the pumpkin field and then her friend dutifully lean down, pick it up, rub it against a rock to be sure it was put out, and hide it away in her coat pocket. At the time Annie had been in awe of that moment. But now here she was at thirty years old and she felt like much of her time was spent picking up cigarette butts that were seconds away from setting dry earth ablaze.

"It's fine," Annie said to Jason. "You can go."

Jason walked over to her, kissed her cheek, and moments later was out the door.

The next day, and the day after, she felt utterly sick about it. She thought about it constantly but mostly she just tried to convince herself that this pain she was feeling was irrational. *He just needs his space. What's so wrong about that?* she'd think. *Don't I like being alone?* But then as she'd think this, rather than feel soothed, she'd find herself shaking a leg or tapping a finger on her desk. A nervousness was manifesting in her body and that was harder to deny. *The person you're closest to has to get away from you,* she'd think and she'd feel herself falling, drifting, feeling like a fool. Today, though, she had a meeting with Arly, and she needed to put it out of her mind.

She wasn't sure what the meeting was about. It was rare that he'd ask to see her alone in his office. Usually it would be a group or if he wanted to talk to her one-on-one he'd stop at her desk and catch her for a few moments. The day before she'd gotten the email:

"Can you stop by my office tomorrow for a chat?—A"

She wrote back, "Sure! What time works? Best, Annie." She never felt comfortable just signing the way he signed his name. She thought he might take it the wrong way, like he would think she was trying too hard. She usually went with "Best" or sometimes she wouldn't sign her name at all.

"10?—A"

"Great! See you then!"

Arly's office door was open halfway, but she still knocked. She couldn't see Arly from that vantage point, but she could see Erin, his assistant, was there.

"Come on in, come on in," Arly called out.

Annie entered and stood just behind Erin. She didn't want to interrupt. She hated when people did that to assistants, like their work was somehow less urgent than their own. Work hierarchy in general was something she found to be unnecessarily cruel, and so when she had the chance she would do her best to rebel against it.

"Okay, great, I'll do that," Erin said to Arly. She turned and smiled to Annie. "Hey, Annie, how are you?"

"I'm good, how are you?"

"Great!" Erin always smiled a big smile, but it was rare that she didn't look exhausted. There was something about her that Annie couldn't quite understand. Even now standing beside her, something was there, heavy, full. She liked Erin though. She was smart, and she always dressed really well, which wasn't important but was easily enviable.

"I'll leave you guys to it," Erin said before turning to leave.

Arly was sitting, but he stood up as Annie approached.

"Take a seat," he said, gesturing to the chair in front of the desk. His office was messily chic. There were dozens of photos on the walls of him with important guests from over the years. On his desk was an array of knickknacks that looked hip in their disorder. And every empty space in the room seemed to be filled with a stack of books. Annie felt, whenever she was there, that this space was the place for her to be.

"So," Arly said. He walked to the front of the desk and leaned his body back against it so he was half sitting, half standing. He was a thin gangly type of guy. His hair was gray, but he looked younger than he was. Energy always seemed to radiate off of him. "I wanted to call you in here because I just wanted to let you know that you've been doing great work, and the team and I are discussing what kind of a role you should have next year because we want your role to reflect the work you've been doing, which is stellar. So in other words, I just want you to keep your nose clean and keep doing what you're doing, and I see big things for you on the horizon."

Annie could feel little flashes of lightening through herself. Those fibers that had been pulled apart by Jason and his Sundays were being thatched back together at breakneck speed.

"Wow, I don't know what to say, thank you so much, Arly. I—Wow."

"No, you don't have to say anything, your work speaks for itself." He walked himself back around the desk and sat down. "All right, you can go, just wanted to tell you in person. So, good work, my friend. You keep it up."

Annie stood up and thanked Arly a dozen more times before leaving his office. She felt elevated, alive, in a way she'd only ever felt a handful of times. There was a fourth-grade teacher who told her she was a good writer. Or that moment her mom said, "You know what, Annie, you're the smartest woman I've ever known." There was maybe even the first time Jason told her that he loved her. It was rare to feel this powerful. It was revelatory.

She thought to text Jason but decided to wait. She knew he'd be happy for her, but she just wanted to be alone with this a little longer.

She walked down the hall and decided to stop in at the bathroom on her way back to her desk. She'd been too busy to pee before the meeting, and she hadn't wanted to be late. As she got to the women's room and reached for the door, she noticed that the sign was badly broken. The stick figure woman's triangle dress had been half snapped off. The funny thing of it was not the sign itself. A broken bathroom sign, who cares, that isn't that strange. The funny thing of it was the feeling Annie felt seeing it. It was a quick jolt of a feeling. It wasn't logical and it wasn't tangible. It was elusive and almost ephemeral in its brevity. But she did feel it. She felt it in her gut, and attached to the feeling, a word came to her mind. It was as vivid as anything. She could almost see every letter in front of her spelled out. She could hear each sound in her mind, like her own voice was saying it. And then as quickly as it came that word was gone. That word was *violence*.

DANCED

Celine had recently come across an old video of herself as a child doing ballet. She'd taken dance from the age of three to the age of eleven, when she quit and started soccer to be with her friends. She didn't last long in soccer. Two years, and she hated every minute of it. Ballet she'd loved. She looked forward to it every week. Saturdays her mom would take her at 11:30 A.M. and she would dance and her mom would watch her and tell her how great she was, and then they would get Burger King afterwards. It was a very specific kind of wonderful. As she got older she started to doubt herself. She didn't think she was picking up the steps like she had when she was little. She didn't think her body was flexible enough. And, so, yes, when everyone was doing soccer, even though she didn't care about soccer, it was easy to tell her mom that was what she wanted, and, unceremoniously, she quit dancing just like that. But her mom had recently started digitizing all their old family videos, and she'd been sending them to Celine one by one. They were cute or funny or ridiculous. But there was this one of herself at nine years old in her dance recital, and she could not stop watching it. If you'd asked her what kind of a dancer she had been she would have said, "Average, I didn't stand out," but watching herself, her pointed toes, the straight lines of her body—she could see she was talented. She wasn't average. Not at all. And so she would watch the video over and over and think of what was or could have been, but she didn't feel particularly sad about it in relation to dance. Was she really going to be a ballerina? Of course not, but why had she given up on something she loved, that she was good at, without even a tear shed? What was it that made her doubt so much of who she was?

The same night her mom sent her the ballet video she'd gone over to Theo's. They'd decided to skip going out for dinner and just head to his apartment. The more time she spent there the more she liked it. Initially she'd really disliked the place. The first time he invited her over everything that was bad about it had felt so obvious. It was older, not updated. The tile in the bathroom was cracked so badly that it seemed almost absurd the landlord hadn't done anything about it. But as time went on she saw all the badness less and the goodness more. The place started to expand before her. It felt bigger and less shabby. It felt like some kind of semblance of home. *And really that's all I want,* she'd think vaguely as Theo sat on his bed and she sat beside him.

They had burritos delivered and ate them in his room. As she gingerly dipped chips in guac spread out on his comforter she questioned whether she'd regretted not going out to eat. After that they lay around and talked about nothing. Suddenly for reasons she wasn't quite sure of, she felt like she wanted to show Theo the dance video.

"Watch this," she'd said and pressed play. As they watched she could hear his roommate's TV in the background. It was always so loud that at one point she'd asked Theo if she was hard of hearing.

"What do you mean?" Theo had asked. He seemed completely surprised by the question.

"I just mean, she watches TV so loud. I just thought maybe she had issues with hearing."

"Oh, no. I don't know why she does that."

At first Celine found it irritating, but in time she kind of got used to it. The booming sound through the wall cut through the silence and helped her fall asleep when she slept over. Even hearing it in the background as she showed Theo the video made her feel, on some level, soothed.

As he watched she tried to study his face to read his reaction, but he just held the same half smile the whole time.

"Aww, cute," he said when it ended.

"I was good, right?" she asked him.

"Yeah, really good."

"I quit," she said.

"Why?"

"I don't know, to play soccer."

"I played soccer too."

And really that was their whole conversation about it. She felt disappointed, although she didn't know what it was that she'd expected from him.

The next morning she stood on one of the badly cracked bathroom tiles and tried to balance as she stepped into a fresh pair of underwear (she'd made sure to bring an extra pair since she knew she'd be sleeping over). Her body wavered a bit but she held it still thinking about pointe shoes and the feeling of leaping into the sky.

She took the train to work and around noon the only man who worked at Loom hit on her. He was a meaty guy with a big face and seemingly even bigger neck, not her type, but all the other women in the office crushed on him in a vague nonthreatening way, and so when he came over to her and asked her out for drinks, she felt not only flattered but also incredibly successful. She couldn't stop smiling, and the hours of the day spun by faster than they ever had. When she caught herself gleefully sending out an email about an upcoming meeting, she stopped dead. *This is the most accomplished and happiest I've ever felt in this office,* she thought. She racked her brain hoping to think of something else, any actual tangible accomplishment at work that would disprove the thought, but absolutely nothing came to mind. It wasn't entirely her fault—the job wasn't very rewarding—but even so, she couldn't feel anything but utterly pathetic over it.

She left work early, and when she got home she made herself a hot chocolate and sat on the beanbag chair she had by her little bay window. She rarely sat there. In theory the beanbag was for when guests came over, but in reality so few ever did. Her apartment was a studio, and it was really too small to entertain in. She hated the thought of someone mindlessly sitting on her bed, not understanding that just because there were no walls didn't mean there were no boundaries. Her lease was up soon and her landlord was talking about having her daughter move in.

"She's got a creative writing degree from Oberlin. She's got nowhere to go," her landlord had said.

Celine would have to move. Maybe to another studio, though she doubted she'd be able to afford it since the place she was in was rent controlled. She didn't want to move home. *Maybe I'll be moving in with Theo?* she thought and then, *But you don't even like Theo.*

Right as she had that thought she got another video from her mom.

"Finger painting in the bathtub!" her mom had captioned it.

Celine went to play it but stopped herself. She called her mom instead.

"Hi, honey," her mom said when she picked up.

"Hi."

"Did you watch the video I just sent?"

"Not yet." Celine felt disappointed. The conversation already felt like it wasn't what she wanted it to be, although by all accounts that seemed irrational. "I'm calling actually because I was wondering about why I quit dance."

"You wanted to play soccer."

"I know but I also . . . Nothing. What are you up to?"

"I didn't make you quit dance."

"That's not what I meant, Mom."

"Just checking." It was silent for a minute more, but Celine could hear her mom fumbling with something in the background, distracted.

"How are things with you and Theo?" she finally said.

"Good," Celine said. "We see each other a lot."

"Do you think it's serious?"

"Yes," Celine said without even thinking.

"That's good. Bring him around one of these days!"

"I will," Celine said. She felt like her answers were moving out of her face, if that was possible. *Is this what they mean when they say out-of-body experience?* she thought vaguely. "Can I ask you something?"

"Sure," her mom said.

"How would you have described me as a child?"

"Oh wow, you were bold."

"What?"

"Yes, and smart and beautiful, very sweet."

"Okay, but you said 'bold' as the first thing. You said 'bold.' "

"Yeah."

"Well, why did you say that? Why did you say 'bold' first?"

"Because, I don't know, you just were. You weren't afraid of a thing. I mean, you were a star."

Celine took in a breath but it didn't pull in deeply. She felt like everything was catching before it reached her.

"I don't think so."

"It's true. I remember one time when you were a kid and you walked down this aisle at the toy store and you put your arms up in the air and you just walked. It might have been funny or endearing if it were another child, but with you, I don't know, I just admired you instantly."

"Admired me?"

"Yes, admired."

"I just don't believe that."

"Celine, believe whatever you want, but it's the truth." Her mom sounded frustrated like when they used to fight all the time. "You don't even remember the eighties, shut the hell up," her mom had once said, and sometimes Celine felt like that tenor was the basis of virtually all their interactions.

"I don't want to think that."

"Why?" her mom said.

"Because I'm not like that at all now. I'm not."

Celine wished all her thoughts away. The conversation, the word *bold*. The vision of herself as a *star*. "It makes me sad," she said.

"What does?" Her mom wasn't acknowledging the jagged edge of what this was, so Celine changed the subject and they said their goodbyes and hung up.

She felt restless. She tried to think of herself walking around with her arms up. Now she never raised her arms, ever it seemed like. *Maybe just to lift something heavy,* she thought. She thought of

Theo briefly, one of their early dates when she waved to him from a café window to get his attention so he'd see where she was seated. He smiled but he didn't wave back because there was no need for him to do so. The thought made her even more restless and now she felt like she wanted to move her body. She got up and stood on the beanbag chair. In a big-postured move, she leapt off it like she was doing ballet. Her legs outstretched, her arms pantomiming a type of grace she was sure she remembered. When she landed, she felt silly in the little space of her apartment. Even so, she took a bow.

TINDERED

Joy hated first dates. She could not remember even a second of enjoying anything about them. Not once was getting ready for a date, or being on the date, or the hours after the date anything but torture for her. When she'd think of dating, a vision would pop into her mind of herself looking sloppy in a pair of gray jeans, something she could see with clarity thanks to an unfortunate mishap a few years ago. Her family was having its big Fourth of July party, and her uncle had set up a camera to film her young cousins lighting some sparklers for the first time. Everyone was gathered around and without realizing it, Joy had stood in front of the camera, which was on a tripod. When they went to watch it back a few minutes later, the view was one quarter kids with sparklers and three quarters sloppy ass.

"Who is that?" her uncle asked.

It took Joy a few seconds to recognize herself. Until that moment she would have never imagined that her butt could look that terrible. Surely she didn't have the best butt of all time, but this, this was a monstrosity. It looked more oblong and oddly folded than she would have expected. Her thighs seemed to be wider than her butt, which didn't make any sense given the properties of human anatomy that she could have sworn she was familiar with.

"It's me," she said.

"Oh, you stood in the way," her uncle said.

"I'm so sorry," she said.

And then everyone moved on and had potato salad because what more could they do? But something about the obliviousness of her sloppy self standing in the way aligned in her mind with dating, and whenever she did have a date, which really had been quite rare, she thought of her oblong ass blocking sparklers.

The Tinder date she had set up for tonight was with Rick. He seemed nice enough from his profile and from the few messages they'd sent back and forth. Her favorite thing about him was that she couldn't instantly find anything repulsive about him. *I'm sure he's nice,* she kept thinking to herself that day whenever she thought of canceling on the date, which was about twenty-eight times an hour, an impulse that she'd given in to with many other dates in the past. But this time she had extra motivation. Her plan wasn't to start dating to meet someone and to move on from Theo. No, her plan was to date Rick—or anyone she could stand really—with the hope of making Theo jealous.

She left work early to make it home in time to shower and get ready. She'd planned the date on a Wednesday because Wednesday was the least likely day for Celine to come over. At this point Celine was usually at the house Fridays, Saturdays, and most Tuesdays, with the occasional Thursday thrown in. Wednesdays she had to work late, a fact Joy had learned by meticulously paying attention to everything Theo said. Her plan was to get all dressed up and to have Theo say something like "Joy, you look gorgeous! Where are you off to?" And then she could say something casual like "I have a date with this great guy. His name is Rick." And then, best-case scenario, Theo would say, "Oh my god, don't you dare, I'm in love with you." And they'd kiss and that would be the beginning of everything beautiful and wonderful that she so believed could exist between them.

She hadn't given a ton of thought to what to wear, but she'd had a few things in mind: an empire-waisted dress with a subtle flower pattern; there was also the skirt that she thought hid her stomach pretty well. But when she went to try things on she realized that (1) Both articles of clothing were not nearly as nice as she'd remembered, and (2) She clearly had gained some weight all that time in the house fawning over Theo, and snacking with Theo, and stress eating because of Theo, and even if she'd been eating more salads lately, the damage had been done. *What the hell am I going to do?* she thought. A vague image of Celine crouched down by the fridge, her perfect lower back poking out over her pajama shorts, popped into her mind. *I never thought I could be so jealous of a lower back,* she thought. In the end the only thing she had that looked halfway decent was an oversized black sweater and a pair of jeans that were made almost entirely of spandex. She did her makeup as best she could and checked the time, 5:52. Theo should have been home by now. She'd have to leave in fifteen minutes or so. She started to get nervous. *Will I end up spending the whole night listening to Rick for nothing?* Mercifully she heard the lock click on the door. She listened closely to the footsteps coming down the hall. Once she could hear he was in the kitchen, she knew it was time. She slipped on the only pair of heels she owned and clip-clopped herself down the hall.

Theo was rinsing something at the sink. He didn't notice her come in. She'd had a plan of pretending she was looking for her keys.

"Hey, Theo," she said and kept on clip-clopping around the kitchen.

"Hey," he said, but he didn't look up from his rinsing.

She paused for a moment.

"Did you happen to see my keys?" she asked him.

"No, sorry," he said but kept rinsing.

"Well, I really need them because I'm going to be late." She was hoping he would say, "Late for what?" but he just kept on rinsing.

"For my date!" she said loudly even though he didn't ask anything.

He shut off the water and turned around.

"Date?" he asked smiling. "You have a date?"

"I do." Her heart was beating so hard she was worried he might somehow hear it.

"With who?"

"This guy I met on Tinder."

"I didn't know you joined Tinder."

"Well, you know, I'd been meaning to start dating again. I'd just been so busy with work that I'd been putting it off." All lies, but she thought it sounded good.

"This is kind of mind-blowing."

"Why?" She was asking it so earnestly that she didn't have time to hope for any type of answer from him.

"I don't know. I guess I just didn't think of you as someone who dates," Theo said.

They stood there staring at each other for a moment. Joy felt a lot of things, but more than anything she felt depressed. *Didn't think of you as someone who dates?*

"Do I look okay?" she asked him. At this point she was so discombobulated that she didn't even think before saying it. She just wanted, wanted, wanted something.

"You look good," he said, but it wasn't in any way that sexualized her in the least. It was as disappointing a "you look good" as anyone might expect to hear.

A few minutes later she was on her way to meet Rick. The sentence *I guess I just didn't think of you as someone who dates* ran through her mind over and over. She could not for the life of her parse that sentence in a way that made her feel encouraged.

Rick was older and fatter looking than his pictures, but there was relief in that for Joy. Whenever she created a dating profile she always worried that she'd post pictures of herself that would be too flattering and the guy would be disappointed by her in person. It was better to be as realistic as possible, a little worse than reality even; let them be pleasantly surprised. *Maybe I should just post that video of my oblong ass,* she'd thought on a few occasions.

"Hi, I'm Rick," he said shaking her hand.

"Joy," she said, shaking it back.

She'd suggested coffee or a drink—it was best to keep these kinds of things as short as possible in case the conversation was stilted—but he had raved on and on about a new Italian restaurant that he'd been wanting to try so she felt obliged to say yes even though she didn't want to. Now she was sitting there with fettuccini and doing everything in her power to keep the conversation going, a responsibility she took on as gravely as was humanly possible. She was on the front lines of defense against any awkwardness that could potentially make this man uncomfortable, a role she neither asked for nor wanted, but one that she dutifully performed.

"HR is cool. Was that what you went to school for?" Rick asked.

"No, I have a marketing degree, but I'm not sure what possessed me to go for that. I guess I just had this vision of myself being creative and coming up with fun ad ideas. I had no idea what I was getting myself into. I'm way too shy for something like that for starters."

"You don't seem shy," he said.

"Oh, I'm not super shy in this kind of situation per se, but I'm not great at asserting myself in a group. One-on-one I'm fine, but even in a group of three I find myself unable to, you know, just make my voice heard."

"I get it. I can be like that too," Rick said.

"What did you go to school for?"

"Drums. I wanted to be a musician."

"Oh wow, that's very cool."

"It would be, but I'm not that good at drumming, to be totally honest. I mean I'm good enough to get into a music program, but I'm not nearly good enough to make a dime at it."

"And you're in real estate now?"

"Yeah, I am."

"Are you liking it?"

"I like that it pays the bills."

"Yeah, no one talks about that when you're eighteen, do they? It's all just follow your dreams, do what you love. I think we all love not sleeping on the street."

"Very true."

It was quiet for a second. She could hear her fork clanking on the plate as she went to scoop up more noodles. *Think of a question, think of a question, think of a question,* she thought. "So are you from around here originally?"

Before he had a chance to answer, she felt her phone buzz. It was Theo. Her heart leapt at seeing his name.

"Sorry, I hope you don't mind me checking this. It's my roommate. Just want to be sure that nothing is wrong at home," she said. Ironically because he was her roommate, it sounded pretty legitimate. It sounded like she was worried about a burst pipe or a broken furnace.

The text was a GIF of a bride falling down a set of stairs in her wedding dress, something he'd sent many times and always made her laugh. From that second on, the date was nothing but white noise to her.

When she got back to the apartment, she was expecting Theo to be in the living room waiting for her. She'd already planned out a few things to say to him about the date: "He really didn't look like his pictures," "I had to make all the conversation," "He was an awful kisser." That last one she was the most excited for because she thought surely if anything would make Theo jealous, it would be the fact that she'd kissed Rick (something she didn't plan to do or even particularly like doing, but which felt pretty useful in this fantasy conversation she was sure she was about to have). She ran up the stairs as quickly as she could in her high heels. *Theo,* she thought. But when she got inside, the apartment was dark. He wasn't in the living room waiting for her like she'd hoped. He hadn't even left the kitchen lights on. The only light she could see was the light peeking out from her own bedroom door. She took in a breath and let out a sigh as she walked to her room, her heels clunking down, no longer rushing to be anywhere worthy. She tossed her purse on her bed and pulled off her coat and then she heard it clear as day:

"Fuck me, fuck me, fuck me." Celine was over. They were having sex. She felt instantly sick by it and she wasn't sure what to do. If she put on the TV or turned up music they'd know she could hear them and nothing seemed worse right then than that. She thought of running out of the house, racing down the street into the cold, away, away, away. But really the damage was done so Joy sat there and listened to the sounds of the person she loved more than she loved herself, having sex with the most beautiful woman that she knew existed. It was a span of ten minutes at most, but in that time she knew that something big had to be done. Some kind of major change had to happen, because this, this was unbearable, this was not right. So she pulled out her phone and typed out this message to Rick, "Great time tonight! Would love to see you again! Maybe drinks at my place?" She tried not to think too hard as she reread the message and pressed send.

LETTER

Annie could not stand talking to Joy about Celine anymore. For a while it was okay. She could understand why the whole thing was so devastating, and she tried to be as compassionate as possible, but now it was just sad. Joy's love for Theo had been present in their friendship for some time even without any confirmation from Joy. It was always there, in every interaction, every conversation. Before Celine was there it would be:

"Theo likes candy corn."

"Last week when Theo and I cleaned out behind the fridge we found three rolls of quarters."

"I'll ask Theo."

Usually it sounded like Joy was talking about a husband or a long-term lover. Someone who was there so permanently that it wasn't necessary to mention how they got there. But Annie could sense her friend was always dying to say more, to indulge in some small bit of intimacy. Sometimes Joy would stop herself midsentence: "You know Theo—"

Annie would feel most sorry for her then, but there was nothing that could be done to save her. She couldn't say, "No, tell me. I want to hear every little thing about Theo!" It was inappropriate. And so usually Joy would just end it with "Never mind. He just makes me laugh." As if somehow that made everything okay, like she was just hopelessly in love with him for chuckles. And so that was how it was, an unspoken truth that both of them were aware of, but that had to sit silent between them. But now that Celine was in the picture, all of that jerry-rigged decorum had gone out the window and what was quietly in the background had moved unforgivingly to the forefront.

"Do you know she calls him, like, all the time? Give him some space! He has his own life."

"You know what I hate is that she leaves her stuff in our place all the time. Not just in his room either. I found a hair tie in the bathroom that was definitely not mine."

"She finished up my almond milk! What a bitch."

For a while it was kind of fun. Who doesn't like ripping apart a woman with such perfect breasts? But as time went on, it was clear that the whole thing was unhealthy and obsessive. It was beyond the limit of what a crush could be, and now seeing it fully unearthed as it was, pulled up from the soil with all its twisted root systems, Annie came to feel that even before Celine was there, it wasn't right. *You should not be in love with a person who has never touched you,* she would think, and so even when she didn't mean for it to be, this was the sentiment that was simmering under the surface of every conversation she had with Joy, and Annie felt herself becoming more and more impatient and harsh with her friend.

"But she is his girlfriend so it makes sense."

"Yeah, I don't know. I think holding hands in the apartment is kind of sweet."

"I like shower sex too."

Poor Joy would often be left stuttering or stammering her way through, and then Annie would feel terrible, and she'd backtrack and the whole thing just felt unkind, and so she felt the best thing for both of them would be for her to distance herself even more than she had since moving out. She did offer this, though, in a conversation they had that morning.

"I'm like ninety-nine percent sure Celine is using my shampoo. Can you believe that?" Joy had said.

Annie took a breath in so that she wouldn't start screaming, "Why do you think that?"

"Because I'm, like, pretty sure I left it with the label facing out, and it was turned around the other way."

"Well, I mean, there's no way you could be sure about that."

"I'm pretty sure. I also think it's ridiculous that she showers here. She doesn't live here, go home and shower!"

"Yeah." Annie tried to remember what it felt like to shower in that apartment. She felt sorry that she couldn't think of it.

"Joy, can I ask you something? Does anything that Celine does, I mean actually more than just what she does—seeing them together—does it ever make you want to just move out?"

"What are you talking about? Why should I leave because of her?"

"I don't know. Sometimes I feel like if I were in your shoes, I would just get angry and be done with it."

Joy was quiet a moment. Annie didn't feel any need to fill the silence. For once she felt she wasn't being reactive or harsh. Briefly she thought of herself as a child walking along the thin edge of a sidewalk curb, something about the ease of it felt analogous to this moment now.

"I guess I just feel . . . not angry," Joy said. "I don't feel angry." And that was it. They talked about the shampoo a little longer and then Annie got off the phone and went to work.

When she got there Patrice was digging through a desk drawer.

"Erin quit," Patrice said without even looking up. "I'm trying to find a hairbrush she lent me."

"She quit? Why?"

"I don't know, but she's leaving today," Patrice said.

"Oh wow, why so suddenly?"

"I don't know, maybe family related? That was my guess."

Annie looked off to where Erin usually sat. She couldn't see her, but she could see the edge of her skirt sticking out from behind the cubicle wall. Then Erin moved her chair forward, and Annie couldn't see her at all.

"Well, I hope everything is okay," Annie said.

"I hope I can find that damn hairbrush. It looked expensive."

Around noon Arly stopped by her desk.

"Annie, would you mind interviewing a few gals for the soon-to-be, *very* soon-to-be I should say, vacant assistant role? I trust your judgment."

"Of course!" Annie said.

"Perfect." He drummed his hands on her desk before walking away.

After that she ate a quick lunch and then worked on the show for next week. At some point Reid walked by to ask her a question. She felt like he didn't really need the answer as much as he wanted the attention from her. It was something he did a lot.

"Oh I get it now," he said. "Cool, thanks." And he walked off.

After that she texted Jason and made herself a coffee. She

sent off a few emails, and around three Arly forwarded her the résumés of the women he wanted her to interview. She clicked through them without reading in much detail. All of them were fresh out of college. Their bullet points about experience were upbeat and scarce. Someone had written "Punctual" in bold font. *I guess that's as good as any quality to highlight,* Annie thought. In a way she felt sorry for all of them. They probably wanted to work in radio. She thought of herself wanting to be a writer. She'd once seen Toni Morrison read, and had cried because she felt so close to the dream. She too had been **Punctual**.

It was already well after six-thirty. Most people had left or were leaving. She was typing out a couple of notes to herself for tomorrow. She also had two more emails to answer.

"Here."

She looked up. It was Erin. She was holding out a white envelope.

"Erin, hi." She was surprised to see her. Earlier in the day she'd made sure to bump into her to say her goodbyes.

"I wanted to give you this," Erin said.

Annie took hold of the envelope. "Oh, thanks." She tried to imagine what it could be. Nothing in the context of Erin standing there with a stern expression on her face made sense. "What is it?"

"Someone left it for me when I got the job. I don't know what else to do with it," she said. And then without another word she turned and walked away. Annie got the sense that if she'd stayed, she may have started crying. Annie got the sense that maybe she already had been.

The envelope wasn't addressed to anyone. It looked old, like it had been around for a long time on the corner of a desk or in the back of a drawer. She flipped it over. It wasn't sealed. She opened it up and pulled out the letter.

To Arly's new assistant,

Please be careful. Arly was inappropriate with me many times. I consider it sexual assault. I reported it to HR and little was done so I quit. Please be careful.

My best,
A.

Annie could feel every word in her body. It was as if someone had scooped out her insides. She thought of many things: Arly, the soft-spoken brilliant man who believed in her and was championing her career. She thought of Erin on her first day of work getting this letter. Reading it to herself in silence. Maybe she was expected to make a coffee or write an email. Certainly she was expected not to look like someone had smacked her, and so what had she done all day? Smiled? Pretended there was no terror? She thought too of this woman, whoever she was. Annie couldn't see her face, but you don't need to see someone's face to feel like you can see *them*.

She looked around. She was alone as far as she could tell. Most of the lights were already shut off too. It was her desk lamp that was lighting her way. She didn't know whether to stand or sit. She took the letter and folded it back up but thought better of it. She unfolded it and took out her phone and carefully took a picture of it. She folded it back up and slipped it in her bag. It was time to go home. Home, sometimes it was just that. She shut off her desk lamp, but the hall was still bright so she could see. In the cold hard darkness, she moved her body towards the light.

STAR

It was the first time Celine had read *The Velveteen Rabbit* since she was a child. She and Theo had stopped into the bookstore after dinner and a movie. She came across the book as she meandered through the kids' section and sat down on a chair at the back of the store, reading it from start to finish. She was crying of course, but luckily Theo was preoccupied, so she didn't feel like she had to hide it. It felt too soon in the relationship to be crying over children's books in public in front of him. Her first-grade teacher had once said, "Whenever in life you see something clearly, you're like the Velveteen Rabbit. Once it's real, it's real." To this day Celine wasn't sure whether she fully understood what her teacher meant, but either way she felt so touched revisiting the story that she thought about buying the book. She even carried it under the Noam Chomsky book she was buying and a pair of novelty socks that had a picture of a girl talking to her pony saying, "I hate everyone too." They stood in line and Theo took notice of the little pile she was holding.

"You're buying that?" he said.

She felt silly for a moment, but then she realized he was also buying the Noam Chomsky. "Cause I'm happy to lend you this one," he said. For whatever reason that was enough to startle her, and at the last minute before she was about to pay, she tucked *The Velveteen Rabbit* on the New Fiction table and bought just the socks.

They went back to his place and had sex. After it was over they talked for a bit and then Theo fell asleep. Celine listened for some kind of sound but it was quiet. Joy had shut off her TV. The city streets must have been empty. Through the window beside the bed she could make out the Little Dipper so she counted each star to put herself to sleep. The next morning she woke up and felt disoriented briefly. She imagined herself at home, her apartment, or at home, her dorm room in college, or at home, her childhood bedroom. It was a letdown that it was none of those places. She dressed quickly and kissed Theo goodbye.

"What about brunch?" he offered. But she wanted to go back to her place. She made some kind of excuse about needing to get some work done—something vague—and minutes later she was on the train headed home.

The truth was Celine couldn't stop thinking about the conversation she'd had with her mom. She had been trying to contextualize herself as a child and herself now. A great chasm seemed to exist between the two and she couldn't figure out why. The dreams she'd been having about her ex were replaced with waking up in cold sweats remembering being six years old and eating peanut butter and banana sandwiches. *Bold,* she'd think as she remembered what it felt like to hold the cool plastic of a jump rope in her hands.

She tried to keep busy to avoid the whole thing, and she had been quite busy applying to grad school. She didn't have the money for it, but she was hoping something, anything, would put her in a position to earn more money. At this point her student loans were $798 a month. All her money went to her loans and her rent. Her mom still helped her out some, especially if she ever had an unexpected expense. She was living paycheck to paycheck, but she didn't feel as scared as she probably should have. Most of that was because every person she knew was living similarly, apart from the people whose parents supported them entirely.

Her friend from college posted a picture of herself and her fiancé in front of a house holding a SOLD! sign. She didn't talk to her friend regularly, but as far as she knew she was supposedly a documentary filmmaker. Her fiancé was also a documentary filmmaker. Where they'd materialized the tens of thousands of dollars necessary for a down payment seemed unfathomable. Celine messaged her, "New home?? Oh my god congrats!! I'm so jealous of you guys." Her friend wrote back, "My parents surprised us for our wedding present!!" And that just seemed to be how things were. For a long time she felt embarrassed that she was getting help here and there, but the more aware she was of every other struggling person around her, the more aware she was that few people were doing it on their own. Poor friends were getting help and rich friends were getting help. It was in a way the reason she wanted to go to grad school to begin with. *I want to buy a house without anyone giving it to me,* she thought, and even though the real goal was going three months in a row without asking for a few hundred bucks, she tried to think big. She paid her application fees on a credit card and hoped for the best.

She got home and tossed her purse on her bed. The apartment felt quiet and kind of morose in a way. A small palm tree she'd done everything on earth to save and didn't have the heart to toss out now felt accusatory in its deadened state. She decided to take a bath.

She filled the tub and let a blue star-shaped bath bomb loose in the water. She sank herself in and watched the color spread and fizzle around her. Her little bathroom immediately smelled entirely like black currant, a scent she'd been more enamored with before it fully consumed her as she sat in rapidly cooling bathwater. The bath bombs had been an attempt to get herself to enjoy bathing as much as she thought she should. Regularly throughout her adult life she'd tried to take a bath whenever she felt stressed out or overwhelmed, like she did now. But it never was what she wanted it to be and usually she found herself staring at the mildew buildup on her bathroom wall or watching a rogue hair float by. The steam would get to her too, and she never seemed to find a comfortable position in her small tub. *Maybe bathing is a thing for rich people,* she'd sometimes think. The bath bomb had been a last-ditch attempt to try to at least distract herself from the mildew and floating bits. In that respect it had worked, but the smell was so stifling that she wasn't any more relaxed than she had been from any other bath and here, mixed with black currant and the cold hard press of a rigid tub against the back of her neck, she thought relentlessly of every single relationship she'd ever been in.

She'd had her first "boyfriend" at the age of twelve. His name was Billy Savory, and every girl in their seventh-grade class was in love with him. He wasn't particularly bright, or even all that good at sports, but he looked cute with his big dark eyes and his well-thought-out T-shirt and shorts combos. He'd walked up to her at recess one day and said, "Hey, Celine, do you want to go out with me?" It wasn't a surprise that this was happening because for weeks the word had been "Billy likes you." And all that day it had been "Billy is going to ask you out at recess," and so she was very ready for this whole dramatic charade to play out, and when he walked up to her and said, "Hey, Celine, do you want to go out with me?" she knew exactly what she was going to say—she'd thought a lot about it since first period—"Yes," she said, and then there was lots of blushing and giggles and then that was it, and Billy walked away.

The whole seventh-grade class was abuzz about Celine and Billy going out. Girls she barely knew would come up to her and say, "I heard you and Billy are going out?" And she would say, "Yes, we are." And just like that there would be this feeling of power between herself and whichever girl it was. It was the most powerful Celine had felt her entire life. Instantly she was respected because beloved Billy had chosen *her.* That's right, of all the underdeveloped or overdeveloped twelve-to-thirteen-year-old children he could have chosen to hang his name with, he'd chosen *her.*

In reality she and Billy almost never saw each other. They ate at the same lunch table, but absolutely never next to each other, or even near each other for that matter. They had class together and he was nice enough to her there. Sometimes he'd see her in the hallway and goof around in front of her a little, but that was really it, until the single time they hung out. It was after school and he said, "Hey, Celine, can you hang out for a bit?" They walked around behind the school and Billy talked about lacrosse. She wasn't sure what to do besides smile a lot and laugh. Sometimes he'd ask her a question like "Do you have a dog?" And she'd say, "No." Then all of a sudden as they were walking he stopped in front of her and stood too close. She laughed uncomfortably, and then he leaned in hard to kiss her. This was no ordinary kiss. Aggressively and clumsily, he stuck his tongue in her mouth. She was so shocked by it that she didn't know what to do so she just stood there half laughing with his tongue in her face. After a few seconds he pulled back and said, "We just made out." When she got home after the whole ordeal she started crying. She wasn't sure why. It was embarrassment or loss of control. The power she'd been feeling over the last few weeks felt violently gone. More than anything, she just knew that she didn't want to kiss Billy or anybody else like that at all. She was panicked about what would happen the next time she saw him, but luckily it was school vacation so she wasn't going to see him for a while. When she got back to school a rumor was spreading that he "liked Ashley now" and that he "was going to break up with Celine." Considering the terror she felt at the idea of having to spend even one second of time near him, this should have come as a relief, but instead she was devastated by it. The thought that he who had chosen her was now unchoosing her, and was rechoosing Ashley? What did it all mean? Was she no longer the prettiest?? But Billy never formally broke up with her. The rumors were all it took in their childhood dating world, and soon after he was "going out" with Ashley, and Celine was "going out" with no one. A few other boys asked her out, but she said no to all of them. Billy Savory had her middle school heart.

In high school she dated Austin, who was similar to Billy in every respect, but his mom found out he was smoking, and so she moved him to private school three weeks into their relationship, which put an end to the whole thing. Then she dated Sean. He was also sporty, but smarter than Billy or Austin. She liked the way he called her "babe" and was always reaching to hold her hand walking down the school hall. She and Austin hadn't had the chance to kiss, so Sean was the first boy she'd kissed since the nightmare with Billy. She was happy to learn that kissing wasn't as traumatizing as it had once been, but even so, she didn't really feel a lot of joy in the whole thing. What she did like was seeing how happy and excited it made him. She loved the way he seemed almost entranced by her whenever they did anything physical. It was as if he was in another state of being. She found it so utterly compelling that when he begged her to take her top off, she did it even though she didn't want to. Just looking at him stare at her, she felt that same feeling of power she'd felt on the playground a few years before when she told girls that, yes, indeed, Billy was with her. Now it was in this room with just Sean and her. She felt exhilarated by it. For a long time it was lovely like that. But as time went on Sean became restless and expectant. He asked for a blow job every single time they were alone. He'd say things like "You know Cameron and Aaron are having sex already." Pretty soon Celine felt guilty that she wasn't as good to Sean as Cameron was to Aaron. She thought about blow jobs more than she thought about virtually anything else, and out of sheer fear that the relationship would fall apart, she found herself blowing him in his car. Soon after, they had sex, which was painful and miserable, and once again she felt like she was that same girl standing there with a tongue in her mouth that wasn't her own. She didn't cry about it though; that's what maturity brought, less terror, more acceptance.

At the time she really thought she was in love with Sean, but looking back with the fizz of a dissolved star pooling at her knees, she couldn't even begin to tell herself that she had loved him. She'd loved having him and she'd loved how obsessed with her body he was, but with him as a person? That wasn't love. If she honestly could strip away all the unhealthy parts of it, she probably wouldn't have wanted a boyfriend in high school at all.

Her first serious boyfriend really was her ex. After things ended with Sean she had been mostly single. She'd dated some in college, slept with a few strangers and felt pretty crappy about it each time.

"Our moms marched for a sexual revolution so I can have sex with some rando with a BO problem," her roommate had said to her once.

"I don't think that was the point," Celine had said.

"I don't know what the point is, but things are still shit," her roommate said.

It was soon after this conversation that she met Derk. Things with Derk were instant. It was magic. He played guitar and had an internship at an ad agency. His hair was nicely combed on most occasions, and he wore T-shirts of bands she'd never heard of. She met him at a party and she liked how much he knew about coconut oil. He asked for her number and texted her a few funny memes. She could not stop thinking about him. Whenever she'd see his name on her phone she felt more alive than she ever had. If he didn't text her back for a long time she reevaluated her existence in brutal existential bursts. *I'm so stupid,* she'd think. *I'm so useless,* she'd think. *Why won't he just answer me?* she'd think. Eventually they started hanging out regularly and soon they had sex. The sex was still not great, but for the first time she at least felt like she was a part of it. She loved the way he laughed, and she loved how he talked. She loved being by his side, and she even loved waiting for him. And that's what she did a lot. Six months in he had yet to say clearly in words what it was they were.

"This is Celine" was how he introduced her, and his relationship status on Facebook said, "Married to common sense." The whole thing was maddening and consuming, but rather than say anything to him or even say anything to herself, she worked tirelessly to make excuses and to patch the whole thing up. *Who needs titles? What difference does it make what you call it? Isn't the fact that we care for each other all that really matters?* And this was how she lived with it for over a year and a half. Finally, out of the blue one day as they were walking to the train station he said, "I'm glad my girlfriend gets it," referring to her. She felt her heart flip and flutter. A flash of herself as a child, a flash of herself as a water drop slipping into a puddle. But she didn't do anything.

She just kept walking alongside him cool and quiet as her insides floated in blood inside her. Soon after she used the word *boyfriend* liberally, and not too much later he told her he loved her. Derk left his internship at the ad agency and got an internship at a record label. Celine waited tables. His family had more money than hers did, and they could support him as he worked for free and lived with four roommates. It never really bothered her, but she didn't love how he rarely paid for dates. She found herself paying for both of them almost all the time, and if there was ever a concert he wanted to go to, he would drop little hints about it until she offered to buy them tickets. It increasingly frustrated her, but despite that she was still completely enamored of him. He always had strong opinions and just when she thought she had him figured out he would say something unexpected. It was exhilarating, if not hard to keep up with.

"I get being vegan and wearing fur," he'd once said, and she'd felt her head nodding.

"Seatbelt laws are absurd."

"If I had kids I'd let them pick their own names."

If she really didn't agree, she'd just be quiet about it. One time they were driving to an obscure beach seventy-five miles away, and he was going on and on about how recycling is just a way for people to feel that they have control of their carbon footprint and how in reality it doesn't matter. She didn't agree, but rather than say anything, she just sat there quietly. She counted seagulls as they got closer to the coast and as they walked in the surf, she felt sad and sorry, but she wouldn't let herself wonder why even for a second. Instead she kept on going and kept on paying and kept on agreeing. Her life was filled up with him. Her mind was filled up with him. Slowly, mercilessly she was bending and shaping herself to Derk. They did things he liked and spent time with his friends. She could hear his inflection in the way she spoke. The word *galvanize* (a favorite of his) slipped through her lips on a few occasions. She could fold and unfold who he was into every pocket of herself. It was madness, but it felt like fire. She was in love with him and every facet of herself newly cut through his prism was exalting. And then, unceremoniously, on a Saturday morning that was marked by an unexpected snowstorm, he broke up with her through text messages.

She begged him to reconsider, left quite a few sobbing voicemails, but he was certain that he "needed to be single" to "figure some stuff out" and so that was that. She was left extricating Derk from herself. And really she didn't do a great job of it. She was depressed. She found herself dating and mindlessly committing to meaningless relationships. She was bouncing, jingling, shaking around as she tried to find her footing. It was, in so many ways, the worst time of her life. But she had little clarity over it. Now, thinking of it and herself then, Celine could not get this one solid word out of her head: *erasure*. She wasn't sure why the instant her heart clicked along to his she had worked so tirelessly to erase everything of herself, and even now, sitting in the bath, could she say she was fully her own again? After they'd broken up she'd been terrified of being single. Each guy she hooked up with was a little bit more of something. A little flash of self-worth to get her through to the next moment of her life.

"You're so fucking hot," a guy she'd just allowed to see her naked said. "You have *the* perfect nipple."

And now that she was with Theo, it felt like more of the same. More quiet frenzy. More erasure and wishing for something she could barely explain. *Bold,* she thought. *Oh how I wish I was.*

And at that she decided to get out of the bath and shower off the fizz of the dissolved star. After the shower Celine brushed her teeth and as she caught sight of her reflection she felt the memory of it come back as fresh and as painful as ever. Just like she always did, she shook it from her mind and carried on with her day, but a few days later she'd pass the same bookstore she and Theo had gone to, and for whatever reason she'd think of it again. This time she couldn't shake it from her mind the way she had done over and over, year after year. She thought of her mother, she thought of herself. A star she was melting against her skin. She'd walk in the bookstore and find that copy of *The Velveteen Rabbit*. She'd hold it in her hands, and she'd think, *Once it's real, it's real.*

GLASS

Joy had never had good sex. She was at this point in her life pretty certain that good sex didn't actually exist. She found sex to be cumbersome and uncomfortable, painful sometimes. She had never once felt even a second close to orgasming. And the worst part of all of it was that she felt so unattractive during the whole thing. It was hard for her to imagine that a man, any man, would choose to look at her body to feel a sense of desire and so anytime she had been naked in front of a man she'd be sucking in and lying back and doing every physical thing possible to live up to a standard that she knew she couldn't live up to clothed let alone naked. It was depressing and draining. But recently she'd begun to feel better about things after a conversation with Annie. Historically, Annie had rarely talked about the sex she had with Jason. It was funny because she wasn't shy talking about sex in general. She talked about it frequently and crudely. Joy often found herself embarrassed by her.

"Really, Annie?" she'd say.

"What? It's true," Annie would say back. But that was it. It was always distant and impersonal. Then one day they were watching *Seinfeld* together on the couch and it was the episode where Elaine says that she faked orgasms with Jerry, and Joy said, "You know, I've never thought to fake an orgasm." And Annie said, "Really? I do it all the time." And Joy said, "You do?" But Annie didn't respond, and they just watched the rest of the episode in silence. It was a small moment really, nothing much at all, but it completely changed the way Joy thought about herself and sex. She wondered harder than ever if good sex existed. She wondered why women were lying to each other.

Joy wanted things to go well with Rick. She promised herself that no matter how self-conscious she was about her body, she was not going to question why he was sleeping with her. She was going to indulge in the whole thing as much as possible. She even bought a corset, an item that until now she'd been certain was meant only for women who had an easier time wearing trench coats without looking like Inspector Gadget. Now she was going to be like those women. She was ready to feel desired, sexy, wanted. And in the back of her mind, she was hoping that Theo would be jealous.

Joy spent an hour cleaning up her room. She didn't think of herself as a particularly messy person, but her room in its best natural state still seemed too cluttered with too much of herself. A faded robe with a duck embroidered on the pocket, a CD from 1998 that she still had out on her desk in a pile of other CDs from 1998. The knickknacks that lined her nightstand vaguely alluding to pieces of who she was: a turtle because she liked turtles, a dolphin because she liked dolphins, a matchbook from a cruise she'd taken because she'd taken a cruise. She shoved thing after thing into her closet or into a drawer, stripping her room down to a bareness that would be devoid of anything that might be othering herself from Rick. By the end of it, the only things she left out were a music box that didn't work and a candle she'd never lit. Oddly, when she went to clean the rest of the apartment nothing seemed to be hers. Everything was either a relic of the decisions Annie and she had made as they moved in together, childishly optimistic about what the home could be, or a reflection of her and Theo, but there was no optimism there, just her following Theo in every decision he made. He'd bought a set of magnetic refrigerator poetry with dirty words. "Cunt" it said every day when she wanted to make herself eggs. She didn't like it, but they'd actually picked it out online together. She'd laughed when he suggested it, and most of the time she wouldn't admit to herself how much she hated seeing it. There was also his craft beer, the empty bottles of which he had set out on a windowsill. She hated beer, but anytime they drank together she'd find herself drinking one and making tentative comments about hops. Later she'd stealthily dump out the majority of the bottle so he wouldn't take notice. There were his DVDs and blankets of his on the couch. His sneakers were always out even though she kept her shoes in her closet. It seemed so obvious now, but cleaning up for Rick was the first time she'd ever really looked around the space that was her home and seen that really everything that was hers—the turtles, the robe, a breathy song from 1998—was nowhere to be seen except in her little cave of a bedroom. It should have made her feel many things, but what it made her feel more than anything was childish. *It's like I still live in a dorm or my parents' house,* she thought, and she dusted behind one of the plants that Annie had left.

Theo was still out when Rick arrived, which was really a shame because Joy so wanted to introduce them.

"This is Rick," she would say. "This is Theo, my roommate." She really wanted the opportunity to address Theo as "my roommate" in front of him. She was hoping that he would feel at least some kind of pang at how vile and untrue that title was in the same way she always did.

Rick had brought flowers, which was something no man had ever done for her before. She was so surprised by it that she didn't even know what to say. "You didn't have to do that." She repeated it over and over so much so that she actually had to tell herself to knock it off, *Don't you dare say "You didn't have to do that" again, Joy. Stop being a fucking idiot.* She wasn't sure where to take him. The kitchen? The living room? She didn't want to take him straight to her bedroom, but anywhere else felt wrong: "And here is where I cook with the man I'm actually in love with." "Take a seat on the couch I sit on when I'm hanging out with the man I'm in love with." "He showers in that bathroom and so do I!" In the end she suggested they sit in the little dining room nook space that she and Theo hardly ever used.

"This is a really nice place," Rick said as he took a sip of craft beer.

"Thank you," Joy said. She was ready to jump into talking about Theo being her roommate, but she held back.

"My apartment is much smaller," he said.

"But you live alone," Joy offered.

"Yeah, I do," he said.

They talked for a while longer, but Joy hardly paid attention to the conversation because she was so busy trying to think of the least awkward way to ask the man to her bedroom. She hadn't given much thought to this before the date, but now sitting here, she couldn't for the life of her think of a transition that didn't make her sound like a whore bag. She could feel her stomach turning the longer they sat there.

"We went waterskiing last summer," she heard him say.

Waterskiing? she thought. *But how am I going to sleep with you?*

Finally she went with "Do you want to see my room?" which was the absolute best idea she could come up with. Rick's face turned red, and there was what felt like a long pause between them.

"Sure, I'd love to." And they got up, and she clumsily led the way down the hall.

When she opened the door, it almost didn't look like her space with everything put away. It was startling.

"Nice," Rick said. "I like your curtains."

The curtains had come with the apartment; they were beige and probably needed to be washed, but she didn't fault him on it. There was so little left to comment on at this point. "Thanks," she said.

Luckily she had nowhere to sit but the bed, so when she sat down he sat down beside her, one less transition to worry about. They talked a while longer and then it was silent for a second, and he leaned in to kiss her. The kiss was nicer than she'd expected. She felt happy briefly and almost present, but then he reached for her shirt and even though that was the plan, she felt herself stiffen up. He grabbed her breast over her bra, then leaned her back so that he was lying on top of her, kissing her still, holding her breast awkwardly. There was no time to consider the corset. Instead she was trying very hard to move along with it, to find a rhythm that made sense by following his clumsy lead. He had put his arm on the pillow to hold himself up and inadvertently was leaning on her hair. She tried to ignore it, hoping he'd move, but he just leaned harder and harder. It was getting uncomfortable and painful, but she just didn't feel right saying anything. She didn't want to ruin the mood. She didn't want to ruin any kind of illusion of herself as sexy or whatever it was that she was trying to be, and so she just stayed like that until mercifully, a minute later, he moved. He took off his shirt. He took off his pants. He got out a condom. She helped him where need be. She acted sexual at the moments where she felt another woman might. She did every motion right. But here is what she wanted:

She wanted a soul mate.

She wanted a husband.

She wanted a baby.

She wanted to be loved.

She wanted to love.

She wanted to feel beautiful.

She wanted to feel comfortable.

She wanted to have someone who was just her own.

She wanted to be happy.

What she didn't really want was to have sex with Rick, but that was exactly what she did.

When it was over they lay beside each other for a few minutes and talked. Rick said, "Do you want me to stay over?" And even though she did, she said, "Only if you want to." And Rick said, "I have work early. I think I should probably go." And so then they were getting dressed side by side. And then they were kissing goodbye at the door. Rick seemed sadder than she remembered him. His shoulders looked broader as he moved into the night.

She took a shower and lay in her room. She played a playlist of sad songs she listened to when she felt melancholy. She tried hard not to think of Theo in any way. She was sick of herself. Sick of her little life and everything that made her happy. Her phone buzzed. A text from Rick.

"I hope you had a nice time tonight. You're a lovely person." She felt her stomach jump in a nice way. *Maybe things will work out between us,* she thought vaguely. She texted him back something and the next day he'd respond, and she'd text again and then he again and then she once more, but then he wouldn't answer. That would be it. Their bodies pressed together in the most intimate depth, and then a few flat words on a screen, and she'd be there, just as lonely as before.

A few days later she was in the kitchen washing a glass at the sink. Her phone buzzed, a text from her mom. Lately things with her mom had felt uncomfortable and they'd started to talk on the phone less. It wasn't so much the secret itself that she was keeping from her mom, if you could even call it a secret. It was more just the feeling that she couldn't really open up about where she was in her life and what was going on.

"Are you crying?" her mom had asked once.

"No, I have a cold," Joy had said, but she had been crying.

She looked down at the text.

"More Trader Joe's coupons. Dropped them in the mail for your aunt but having second thoughts. Should have saved them for you."

Joy started to text back but stopped herself. Her mom complained about her aunt all the time. It was so much a part of their conversation and life that she hardly ever paid attention to it. But something about it struck her. How things were with Theo, sex with Rick, there was a palpable loneliness in her own life and it made her think of her aunt and the family trauma that had been relayed to her by her mom throughout her childhood.

Joy looked up to the crystallized branching of frozen condensation on the windowpane. Her hand moved over the glass she was washing, soap slipping through her fingertips. She pulled her phone back out and texted, "Can you text me her number? I think I'd like to visit her."

The ellipses popped up on her screen as her mom was typing a response. While Joy focused on her phone the glass slipped loose from her grasp and hit hard against the sink. It didn't shatter, but it had cracked all the way through. Any more stress and it would burst into shards. Joy hesitated for a moment, she held it in her hand and looked at the lines below the surface branching off, showing their inherent weakness; with little other option, she threw it away.

COW

Annie decided to go home and visit her parents that weekend. She hadn't told anyone about the letter yet. A few times she'd thought to tell Jason, but whenever she tried to, something felt wrong about it and she stopped herself. It wasn't as if she wasn't going to tell him, but she just wanted some time to think. She wanted a clear plan of what she was going to do before she said anything to him. That, and she and Jason had been fighting nonstop for the last two days. They'd been out at dinner and he'd said, "You know how people say that you know your wife right when you meet her? Like it's instant and you just know 'This woman is going to be my wife one day'? I bet that's how it is."

"What do you mean?" she said.

"I just mean that you hear that all the time and I bet that's usually how it is." He took a sip of his cappuccino. She wanted dessert but hadn't ordered it to save money.

Normally Annie would have given a lot of thought to what to say in response to something so diabolically insensitive. She treated so much of their relationship like a minefield, but this time she felt the words in her mouth and off her tongue before she had time to comb through them properly.

"Is that how you felt when you met me?" she asked.

Jason smiled nervously and nearly flinched. "What?" he said, but she couldn't bring herself to repeat what she'd just said. She already knew the answer just by his face, and really, she'd known it even before then, so they sat there in silence uncomfortably for a few minutes more before they got the check, split the bill, and took a long silent ride home. For the next two days she was miserable and found herself picking fights with him about everything. When she told him she was going to her parents' for the weekend, she wondered if he suspected that it was because of how rough things had been, but she didn't have the energy to confirm or deny any of his possible fears. Instead, she set out food for Simon with detailed directions on how to open a can and dump cat food into a dish.

Her parents had retired to their "mountain house." It wasn't really in the mountains but actually just a few hours north of the city, down the road from a big dairy farm. It had been their family vacation home, but it wasn't all that impressive a vacation home. Few people would choose to vacation two hours from home in a town with so little to offer, but her parents bought it for very cheap and had made it a cozy escape for long weekends and a few weeks in summer. There was a lake nearby for swimming and some decent hiking trails if you drove thirty minutes or so north towards the mountains.

Annie pulled up to the house and noticed the mailbox on its side on the ground. The last time she'd been there it had been hanging off the post and the time before it was leaning. Each time she visited it seemed like there was some other physical signifier of her parents' aging, and the subsequent panic she felt as a result was as present to her as her own heartbeat or the top of her lung as it pushed her breath out into the sky. She parked her car and walked slowly over to the mailbox. She reached down to pick it up, but instantly the feeling of metal in her hand gave her pause. It was cold. It was clumsy. It had its own weight and its own life. She certainly wasn't the answer to making it stand upright to become a mailbox again. She looked down the street. There were cows standing on the hill and grazing. She counted them briefly before turning to walk into the house.

Her mom opened the door. She looked older. She always did now. When they were still living in the suburbs, Annie would visit pretty often and would hardly notice any changes, but with these big breaks between visits now, what trauma it was each time she saw her. Her mom's hair was always grayer. Her skin looser. *Don't die, Mom,* was the thought, but it was less a thought than a foundational crack in her own humanity.

"Baby," her mom said and leaned in for a hug.

"The mailbox, Mom. It's on the ground."

"I know. I need to get another one."

"When are you going to do that?" Annie asked. Her mom had a whole list of things to get to that would likely never be done. The upstairs bath was broken. There was no heat in one of the bedrooms. The dining room table was buried under a monumental pile of clutter. Annie saw the house expanding and breaking around her parents but felt powerless to do anything.

"You know, I can call a plumber for you," she'd offered over and over about the bath, but her mom would always refuse. "Stop it," she'd say. "You don't need to do that," she'd say, and she'd continue doing whatever it was she was doing: cutting an onion, spreading peanut butter on toast, reading a book that she'd already read many times.

Annie felt paralyzed in her relationship with her. She felt like she was watching from the inside of a fishbowl, drowning, floating, scratching her nails against glass. But her parents seemed perfectly content to let things slowly go and to accept the tedious marching on of time, and so when she visited she didn't dare stay more than a night or two because she could not bear to watch them unthreading. No, mailboxes couldn't be easily picked up. Yes, the bath was dry.

"Hi, Dad," Annie said. Her dad was sitting by the fireplace doing a crossword puzzle.

"Seven letters for *tired,*" he said to her.

"*Exhausted.*"

"That's not seven letters."

"Well, I never claimed to be good at math," Annie said back.

"Don't say that," her mom said. "I hate when women say they aren't good at math like it's not something they should be embarrassed about. You would never say you aren't good at reading, would you? So why say you're not good at math? See how messed up that is?"

"It isn't that deep, Mom," Annie said, but she couldn't help but think that her mom was onto something.

"Do you want some cantaloupe?" her mom called from the kitchen. "I have some absolutely delicious cantaloupe right now."

"No." Annie was already exhausted by the trip and she'd only been there for twenty minutes (if you counted her time ruminating in the driveway).

She went upstairs to put her stuff in her childhood bedroom. Since this was their vacation cottage, the room had far fewer of her things than her actual old room had had, but even so, she'd managed to make the space cluttered with her younger self. There were posters on the walls of old WB shows she'd been obsessed with in middle school and a row of teddy bears that had valiantly collected dust. There was her old mirror with ticket stubs to concerts she'd gone to and a stack of DVDs. She lay down on her old bed, which increasingly sagged in the middle and seemed smaller and smaller every time she lay on it.

She took out her phone hoping for a text from Jason, but there was nothing except a text from Joy, which seemed short and distracted. The last few times they'd texted she'd gotten the feeling that Joy was sadder than usual. She wanted to ask about it, but she knew Joy wouldn't say what was going on. Knowing Joy, it was likely she didn't even know what was going on.

Annie flipped to her photos and looked at the picture of the letter. She felt sick to her stomach seeing it, and yet she kept looking at it over and over again. Her first thought had been to contact HR, let them handle it because that was protocol. But the letter already said nothing had been done and if this was true about Arly (and really why would this woman lie about this?), then she didn't feel right just letting this fall back into whatever status quo had gotten them there to begin with. Annie had never been harassed at work, but in college she'd had quite a few professors hit on her. One even invited her to his house, and at the time, she'd considered going. She admired him. Loved the way he spoke and the nice things he'd said about one of her papers. She didn't want to sleep with him, but she wanted to feel respected and liked and saying no to the invitation didn't seem like the way to get there. She'd told her friend Renee about it at the time.

"He wants you," Renee said and laughed, and even though Annie had been saying over and over to herself, *Maybe it's innocent, maybe he does just like me as a student and there is absolutely nothing wrong with this,* the second she heard her friend say it out loud, her fear was validated, and she felt able to say no to the offer. That was the power of other people in a situation like this. Words out loud that vibrated through the air and into your skull; they mattered, and so she knew that she wasn't going to just pass the buck with this. She was going to do everything in her power to do right by this person.

She'd gone over in her head every one of Arly's prior assistants that she knew of, but truth be told there had been quite a few of them, and was the letter even from an assistant? She couldn't say for certain. As far as she could recall, none of them had names that started with "A" and so she'd started to believe that the *A* was for *anonymous*.

Annie turned to her side and looked at the view from her old bedroom window. It hadn't changed, but it felt different, the whole room did really. Everything was aging and dirtying even with no one there. *You're old, Annie,* she thought. Her mortality seemed inescapably intertwined with that of her parents. But her parents, on the other hand, didn't seem aware or worried at all. Her mom had recently joined a choir. She was singing on her weekends. A far cry from the dust-encrusted bear that sat on Annie's old dresser.

"Annie," her mom called up the stairs. "Do you want something to eat? I'm making lasagna."

Annie got up to go back downstairs and felt her phone buzz in her hand. "Jason," it said.

"I think we should talk about this whole marriage thing," the text read.

Annie felt her heart leap in place. She felt equal parts joy and terror. Her first instinct was to text back immediately.

"What do you mean? Do you want me to call you?" which would have more accurately been written as "You mean you want to marry me????????????? Please let's talk on the phone and you tell me it's exactly that so I can enjoy my weekend and feel real happiness!!!!!!!!!!!!!"

But she knew better than to text Jason right away. Jason needed complicated finesse. She had to wait and answer after just the right amount of time. Too soon and he'd be scared off, too late and he'd assume it wasn't pressing enough and he'd not respond until probably the next day. She had developed so much culture around him that she knew exactly how to time any important text as well as she knew the way her own body moved when she tossed and turned in the night.

She came downstairs to find her mom still in the kitchen and her dad sitting in the exact same place he was when she'd arrived.

"Do you eat gluten or are you against gluten?" her mom asked.

"Why would I be against gluten?"

"I heard that's what the kids are into now," her mom said as she rummaged in the back of a cabinet.

Annie had gone carb-free her sophomore year of college in anticipation of a spring break trip she and her friends had planned to Cabo. She had never in her life gone on a trip with a group of girlfriends, and the thought that she and her saddlebags were going to be measured up against the saddlebags of lesser saddlebagged girls was enough to put her into an anxious tailspin. For months she ripped all bread from her life. Her mom had been appalled by it and still wouldn't let her forget how stupid the whole thing was. "She wouldn't even have pizza. I had to talk her into having a slice of cake on her own birthday," she'd said. Annie couldn't disagree that the diet was extreme and stupid. She lost ten pounds, but her saddlebags looked the same, and when she went on the trip, the majority of the time was spent not on the beach but in the hotel room comforting a girl who'd found out her boyfriend had sex with her best friend. Annie would never forget the way that girl cried. Her eyes were so soaked with tears that they looked like glass.

"I'm not dieting, Mom," Annie said.

"Thank god. Just eat healthy, don't be vain," her mom said.

Annie wanted to say something back, but she stopped herself. She remembered her mom eating salad after salad when she was a child. She knew better than to believe that was all health related.

She sat on the small sofa next to her dad on his recliner.

"Four-letter word for *ostentatious,*" he said.

Annie shrugged. "Crosswords are stupid."

"Sounds like you don't have a four-letter word for *ostentatious,*" her dad said.

"How's Jason?" her mom called from the kitchen.

"He's fine," Annie said.

When she and Jason had first started going out, she'd told her mom everything about their relationship; mostly she was just complaining about what an asshole Jason was being. After a while her mom started saying things like "You deserve better" or "Don't waste the pretty," which for a long time Annie thought was something her mom had come up with only to find out it was a saying of Oprah's. There was apparently a whole show where Oprah told women that they shouldn't "waste the pretty" on terrible men.

"So now you're just feeding me lines from the Oprah show?" Annie had asked her mom when she found out.

"Do you not agree that wasting your time, your very precious time, as a woman who has only a short fertility window is foolish?"

Annie wanted to argue, but she couldn't help but feel her mom and Oprah were probably right, so instead of fighting it, she just stopped telling her mom her frustrations, and when she was asked how things with Jason were, she'd say, "Fine," and hope her mom would leave it at that.

"You should bring him next time," her mom said. "I feel like we haven't seen him in ages."

"Yeah," Annie said.

"Do you want zucchini with yours?" her mom asked her dad.

"What do we have?"

"I'm making zucchini, but we have leftover broccoli if you'd rather have that instead."

Her dad thought for a moment. Annie could not believe her mom was still serving him like this. She was hoping now that he was retired they'd be sharing more of the household duties but nothing had changed. If anything things were worse than ever. Annie remembered her mom working a full day and coming home and helping with homework and cooking dinner and cleaning up in between all of that. Her dad did a few things too. He'd shovel the driveway when it snowed. He took out the trash. But by far and away, it was her mother who kept their household together. Without her they may not have starved, but they would have at the very least been deeply malnourished from eating microwave chicken nuggets for every meal for eighteen years straight. For a long time Annie blamed her mom for it.

"Don't pick up after him," she'd say or "Why doesn't Dad make his own eggs?" But now she just looked at her father, watched the way he sat there and let a woman carry him like that, and she couldn't help but feel that it was all his fault. She couldn't help but feel that it was shameful.

"Zucchini is good," her dad said.

After dinner Annie sat around with her mom awhile and talked. Her dad went to bed early. She had texted Jason back about halfway through dinner, so she was obsessively checking her phone as she sat there.

"Do you watch *Mad Men*?" her mom asked.

"No, I haven't."

"I think it's quite good," her mom said. "What about *Breaking Bad*?"

"Yeah, I've seen *Breaking Bad*."

"I like Jesse."

Annie checked her phone, nothing.

A while later she took a shower and was back in her room. Her mom was downstairs watching *Mad Men,* but Annie didn't join her. She wanted to email Patrice about the whole Arly thing, and truthfully, she also wanted to be sure she wouldn't miss Jason if he happened to call like she was so hoping he would.

She got out her laptop and started writing to Patrice.

> "I didn't want to talk to you at work about this, but I'm very concerned. Erin gave me this letter. I find it—"

She stopped and checked her phone. It had been almost two hours since she answered Jason and it was getting late. She'd texted, "Yeah, we should definitely talk about it," which she thought was very clever because it didn't put pressure on him to call, but it left it open enough that it was possible he would think to call.

She went back to her email,

> ". . . incredibly troubling. I'll attach a picture of the letter below so you can read it for yourself. I'm trying to think of what the proper channels for this might be while still recognizing that this person clearly already looked for help and did not receive it."

She stopped and reread what she'd written, but for some reason none of it felt right. She deleted the draft. She felt her phone buzz beside her. She swiped open the text as quickly as she could to recognize his name, which she no longer read so much as felt like electricity at the way the letters sat stacked beside each other: *J* into *A, S* into *O,* and then that *N.*

"Did you get my text?" the text read.

She quickly typed back, "Yeah, I responded. Did you get mine?" But she could see her text wasn't going through.

She got up and went downstairs. Her mom was lying on the sofa in front of the TV.

"My texts aren't going through," she said.

"Oh yeah, they took down that cell tower. I get almost no service now, which is why I call on the house phone. If you go outside though it usually works fine."

Annie raced out without even letting her mom finish her breath. It was pitch dark out now. There weren't many streetlights and the nearest house was far back from the road. The brightest lights were on the barn of the dairy farm, but they would light nothing that fell in front of Annie's way as she stumbled around looking for service.

Suddenly her phone lit up. Jason was calling.

"Hello," she said.

"Hey, I've been texting, is everything—" But his voice started breaking up.

"Hold on, I can't hear you. I don't have any service out here, hold on."

She walked farther into the field behind her parents' house.

"Jason, Jason, hello," she said.

Her feet moved over slick ground. It was cold, and dampness pressed the grass into the earth.

"Jason, can you hear me?"

"Yeah, I can hear you did—"

"No, sorry, you're cutting out again, hold on."

Now her house was farther away. Now she couldn't even see the streetlights.

"Hello, hello," she heard him say; his voice was distant and present. Her mind was alongside it and nowhere else. Just then she stopped dead. A cow was standing right in front of her. Her body was massive. Her face looked like it was carved from the night sky. She was staring at Annie. Around them was just darkness and the earth that Annie had walked across to find herself here. She wasn't scared, but bravery was not it either. She let the phone fall to her side.

"Hello, hello," she could hear Jason say. Then it was silent and it was just her staring into the deep dark eyes of the animal before her.

PART FOUR

ANONYMOUS

It was a dream job. I've always wanted to work in radio, and with Arly? Everyone wanted to work with Arly. He's a legend. He's why you believe that big things can happen to you when you're dreaming big things for yourself and your life. At first I really liked him. He was always respectful and kind. He'd even ask my advice on things that I had no business having an opinion on. If anything I think he really likes women as people. I know that sounds like a little thing, but so many men I've worked with, even if they aren't doing something misogynistic or dickish, they still don't take you seriously. They just look at you with this certain look on their face. I can't describe it really, it's vacant and yet there's thinking behind it, there's judgment. The glass ceiling I think is just that gloss in men's eyes. Probably all men had it a long time ago, now it's only most of them.

When Arly asked me to come help him do some organization at his summerhouse I didn't for a second hesitate. He told me he had all these old files in his office that he wanted to get straightened up, but that there were too many to bring to the city. He told me I would sleep in the guest cabin and that I was more than welcome to bring a friend or "a partner," as he said it. He also said he'd pay me $3K for the weekend, which I cannot even tell you how much money that was to me at the time. I was just coming off of two unpaid internships and I'd been deferring my student loans to the point that I'd already accrued $10K more in interest. Nobody in my position would have done anything but jump at the opportunity to dig through some old files for two days at a ritzy cabin in a resort town for that kind of money. I actually did ask a friend to go with me, but she had to work that weekend too so I went alone. I beat myself up about that a lot. I know I shouldn't, but I do. I'm not positive things would have been different, but I still wish I'd had someone there with me to make me feel less alone through all of it. I don't know though. It's hard to know what could have made it better.

His house was about a five-hour drive from the city, but it was gorgeous, and I remember getting there, and I just could not believe how stunning it was. The house was picture perfect and right on a lake. When I pulled up he came walking out and he was waving this big wave with both arms. That memory is burned in my brain for some reason, him on his porch with his arms up and waving. I was driving, but I still waved back because anything he did elicited that kind of response: you wanted to be the answer to his question.

My little guest cabin was lovely, and Arly was supernice as always. I unpacked and spent the afternoon in his house going through files and organizing them. He was up and about. He checked on me a few times. Offered me a lemonade, which I agreed to, but rather than get it himself, he called in a housekeeper to get it for me. For some reason that was the first shock of that weekend. I don't know why, but I would not have expected him to have hired help. He always just seemed so salt of the earth to me before that. Not a person that has an old lady walking around to fetch things for him. And she was older. She reminded me of my mom or one of my aunts. I didn't like seeing her pouring a drink for me that I could easily have gotten for myself. The whole thing was very uncomfortable. I felt helpless watching her, with her shaky short step, walk that lemonade over to me.

After that I just kept working, but I didn't feel the ease I had before. I was alone most of the rest of the afternoon. At a certain point I could see Arly was outside playing tennis. He was swinging a tennis racket wildly and smacking hard at a ball. From my vantage point I couldn't see the other player though. It looked like he was playing with no one.

A few hours passed and it was getting dark out. I was finishing up what I was working on and I was planning on heading to the cabin but then Arly came in. He was all sweaty.

"I'm all set here" is what I said to him.

"And I'm all sweaty here" is what he said back. And I laughed, but I did think it was odd that he brought himself up like that. Even that felt vaguely too intimate. I certainly wouldn't have said that to my boss, or a co-worker even, but I figured maybe he was embarrassed by how he was looking, and so I brushed it off. That's what a person does. We make excuses for other people. We invent reasons why something is off or odd or wrong. We give people a latitude of empathy that sometimes is warranted and sometimes isn't. That's what a person does. Or at least that's what a woman does.

"Do you have plans for dinner tonight? I'm eating in and would love the company if you're free," he said.

If you'd told me a week before that Arly would be offering to have dinner with him I would not have believed you. Keep in mind this man is a pillar in the industry. He doesn't waste time with people like me ever, so this, for someone trying to make their way in the industry, this felt like *the* breakthrough moment. I was over the moon, honestly. I didn't give any thought beyond that. The sweat comment, the unease of the lemonade, it was gone, just like that.

I went back to the guesthouse and showered and changed. The other big part of that weekend, and I often forget about this when I think back, but my friend kept texting me because she broke up with her boyfriend. She wanted to call, but every time she did the service was bad and she couldn't get through. To be honest I was thrilled their relationship was over. I mean I was sad for my friend because obviously I didn't want her to be sad, but I was thrilled for her as well because the whole thing was really unhealthy. It wasn't so much that I didn't like him—to be honest I didn't know him enough not to like him—but what I hated was *her* around him. Suddenly she was into every stupid thing he liked. She was going to baseball games and football games, NASCAR even. She once told me they played videogames together. None of these were interests she had before she met him, but now his world was her world. Last winter she invited me along to this cabin they'd rented in the woods. When I got there he wanted to go hunting, and she just went along with it like we were in some kind of nightmare. We took his truck out and we were riding through the snow and I could hear my heart beating in my ears. I love animals. I didn't want to see anything die. I was horrified. Finally I said, "I'm scared. I don't like this." I looked over at her and she had tears in her eyes. She was like me. We went back to the cabin after that, but on the way, there was blood in the snow. Something had died and had been ripped apart. I'll never be able to feel like we weren't a part of that death. Later my friend made cocoa for us and looked happy. Now that's all that's left, blood in the snow and the bubbly look on her face as she melted chocolate into a mug. I hope she never speaks to him again. I hope whatever it was that let her cry but not speak is never in her again. But yes, that weekend I was consoling her and that, those feelings, were mixed up with everything with Arly. I think that's important to remember because—honestly, I don't know why.

I didn't have anything to wear to dinner. I only had clothes to work in because I hadn't expected to do anything but work and sleep. It was too warm to wear my jean jacket that I'd brought along, but I did because it was the most professional and appropriate thing I owned. That's how misguided I was about what this would be. I was willing to boil myself alive over it because I thought it would make me seem smart, as if he gave a damn.

When I came to the house Arly let me in. We embraced in a professional way and he was already chewing something he'd taken a bite of.

"Come in, come in, come in, come in," he said.

We ate at the big dining table. That same housekeeper served us food that looked very expensive. I was incredibly nervous.

Most of the night we talked about all kinds of different things that you would with any person you didn't know well. He asked me about my family and where I grew up. He asked me about what I'd studied in school and my future plans. After a while he said something like "And what about a love life? Seeing anyone?" I thought his use of the phrase *love life* was very odd. He always seemed so eloquent with words and this just seemed, I don't know, so outdated and out of touch with language, or maybe it was more just that it was out of touch with me, another human being sitting before him who wouldn't want to talk about my "love life" with my boss.

"Oh, I'm single," I said.

"Single and happy?" he said.

"I guess so, yeah."

"I sense some hesitation," he said. At this point it felt uncomfortable that he was pressing, but I ignored that feeling and soldiered on through the conversation.

"Well, I mean, I guess I'm looking for someone, just like anybody would, but I'm not, you know, unhappy," I said.

"That's good." He took a sip of wine, and then he leaned back in his chair, a way he always sat. That's something I've taken note of, how I was leaned forward the whole night. Eager, pathetic really, while he was just leaned back, relaxed, searching himself for what inappropriate thing he'd say next.

"I never liked being single. I'm divorced, you know."

I nodded. I did know, but I wasn't sure what to say.

"What I miss more than anything is sleeping with someone." Here he took a pause waiting for me to respond, but I just tried to keep my face as still as possible.

"Not sexually, that's not what I meant, although, well, you know . . ." And he laughed. "No, I just mean I miss having someone warm in bed with me each night."

I started to feel a churning inside. My brain was already there. *This is fucked up,* it was already saying.

He changed the subject after that and we finished the meal. He offered me an after-dinner cocktail, but I declined.

I'd had wine with dinner, but I certainly wasn't interested in getting drunk or even buzzed around him right then, but I did have a coffee out of trying to be polite. At this point I was doing everything under the sun to tell myself that any feeling I'd had so far of anything being off was wrong. I felt nervous and on guard still, but I was doubling down on trying to talk myself out of it all, and it wasn't that hard to do at that point because he was being normal again. He asked me what my plans were that summer and if I liked living in the city. He asked me about a trip I'd taken to Paris that I'd mentioned a few weeks before. Slowly my trust was rebuilding, and I felt calmer and hopeful.

The night was winding down and Arly walked me to the door.

"You know what, on your walk back be sure to take a moment by the lake. If you walk down the dock you can see all the stars reflect on the water. It's gorgeous. I highly recommend."

"I'll do that," I said, and we once again gave each other a professional hug, and I headed back to the guesthouse.

On the walk back, I can't even remember what I was thinking. I know I was, once again, trying to talk myself out of the queasiness I had felt. I know I was reliving that queasiness. And then I got to where the dock was. I wasn't planning on walking down it because it was late and the thought didn't appeal to me, even as nicely as Arly had laid it out, but I felt like I had to do it. I felt like if I didn't, he'd bring it up and ask me and I'd sound rude or like I didn't care. Really it's like this, I felt in that moment like my entire future might depend on walking down the dock of a rich man's lake and looking at his stars reflecting back at me. And so I went down the dock, and I stood there for a minute and it was peaceful and I could see the stars above me and all around me and for a second it felt okay. Then I looked up or out or back, whatever direction you might call it, and Arly was walking down the dock towards me. And just like that, it snapped. The sirens that I'd fought against were full force. My heart, which was alone in my chest, let all the blood out through my body hard and fast and relentless. I thought, and I'll never forget it, I thought, *I'm dying.*

He came up and stood beside me.

"It's gorgeous out here," I said, loud and chipper, trying desperately to desexualize anything that might happen by acting like it was perfectly normal to be standing here in total darkness with my boss at my side. He didn't answer me. He just stood beside me, very close, and put his arm around my shoulder and we stood like that looking up at the stars. You might wonder why I didn't move away, and fuck you for wondering. After that it was silent for a minute more and then he turned and walked back down the dock.

"Have a good night," he said. Once he was out of sight, I went back to the guesthouse as fast as I could.

I remember locking the doors twice. I felt so scared and overwhelmed and—and this is really the important part—I felt lonely. I didn't know who to call or what to do. If I'd told my mom she would have been so worried about me, and I didn't want to deal with her fear or her expectations. If I'd told my friends they would have told me to quit, and was I going to quit? This was a dream job. This was what I worked so hard for, and where I wanted to go in my life. Was I going to give that up because the guy put his arm around me on a dock? I started doubting myself again, but at this point I knew he was at the very least being flirtatious, but was this crossing a line to the point where I should drive home right now or quit? I felt dizzy from all of it. I felt like that feeling you feel when you catch yourself before a fall.

"He's not answering any of my texts. I want to tell him about me finding Bumble on his phone, but I want him to answer me first before I confront him," my friend texted me. I was almost tempted to text back about what was going on, to say something like "I'm double-locking my doors so my boss doesn't come and rape me tonight," but I stopped myself and just texted something supportive back to her.

I can't remember everything I thought about that night, but I know I thought a lot about every sexual assault of my life. When I was in seventh grade a boy ran up to me in gym class and grabbed my breast and made a honking sound. I was so embarrassed by that that I didn't tell anyone for years. The first person I ever told was actually my college boyfriend, who said, "What a little prick."

"He was just a kid," I said. "He was just joking around."

"No," my boyfriend said. "He was a little prick."

His anger, believe it or not, was the first time I allowed myself to feel anything but bad about myself over it. I had taken on the incident as a little piece of shame that I tucked away and carried around, and that was it; never did I let the burden fall on anyone else's shoulders but my own. In college a guy at a party grabbed my butt as I walked past him. He said something to me like "Hey, gorgeous." I just kept walking and didn't acknowledge it. I wanted to turn around and say, "Fuck you," but my instinct was to just leave the party as soon as possible, so I did. I cried about it later that night. I was alone then too. The funny thing of it is, you feel two ways when someone touches you when you don't want them to: you feel devastated, and you feel stupid for feeling devastated. The last time someone grabbed me was on the subway. It was during rush hour and the car was packed. As I was getting off at my stop, someone touched my butt as I shuffled out the door, but I couldn't see who did it. I know it happened, and I looked back to see, but I couldn't figure out who had done it. Do you know how many people have touched my butt in my life? Five. And two of them were people I didn't want to touch it. I'll never even know who one of them was.

In the end, I made the decision to stay for the rest of the weekend. I figured that even if he was flirting with me, I could handle it and it would be totally fine. No real lines had been crossed. I wasn't in actual danger of an *actual* assault. I would do my job and be back at the office on Monday where I would be safe. But I wasn't about to go to bed anytime soon. Instead I turned on all the lights in the cottage and sat on the sofa fully clothed. I fell asleep texting things back to my friend like

"You deserve better."

"You have everything to offer."

"This isn't love."

The next morning I had a plan: avoid Arly as much as possible and try to stay in the kitchen, where his housekeeper was most of the time. When I walked back to the house I felt a frenzied sense of terror. I looked down the dock as if he would be standing there waiting for me. I felt like at any minute he'd jump out and I'd have to deal with it all again.

But I didn't see Arly all that morning actually. His housekeeper let me in, and after eating some eggs she had made for me at Arly's request, I shuffled back into his office and grabbed some files to bring into the kitchen to sort. By noon it was still just me and the housekeeper, and I started to feel a sense of relief. I ate lunch by myself and got most of the files done. I brought out more files and kept working.

I think it was around four that I decided to get the bookshelves done. They were in the living room lining the walls, and he'd asked me to organize them a bit. His housekeeper was up and about, so I didn't worry too much about being there versus in the kitchen or anything. I could hear her vacuuming in another room. I was there awhile, stacking books, throwing out anything that was too shabby, and then I remember holding a book in my hand and thinking about the way the edges had frayed. It looked like they'd been gnawed on by something or someone. It was an old book and I remember thinking, *It still looks good though*. And then I heard someone walking behind me and I knew it was him. I knew it the second I heard it. And so I turned around, and there he was, and he was naked, completely naked. I turned away from him immediately and said, "Oh my god, I'm so sorry," like it was my fault. I was so shocked; I didn't know what else to say.

"No worries," he said. "I just got out of the shower."

And then I stood there for a second, but he wasn't leaving the room. I heard him continue on as if somehow this was all normal. I started to feel dizzy. My ears felt very hot. And yet I was compelled to make the situation okay. To make everything normal. I didn't want to do anything, I didn't want to have any kind of reaction to make anything uncomfortable. Can you imagine that I was worried about that? I was worried that I would make something uncomfortable? I was so terrified and the whole thing was so bizarre and confusing. Are there words really for what kinds of emotions I was feeling? I'm not sure language has invented them. Men have probably kept us from coming up with a word that would describe that feeling you feel when a man does something like that to you.

And so I felt like all I could do was stay there, and that's what I did. I sat back down and continued going through the books. I remember my hands were shaking. My mind was fully focused on him. I didn't turn back around, but I think he was sitting on the sofa and reading a newspaper. It was silent between us, and I just stayed there in that feeling that there are no words for. Finally after some time he left the room, and I finished the books as fast as I could and the next thing I did was go back to his office and grab the last stacks of files, and I went to the kitchen, and I went through them as fast as possible. I just wanted it all to be done. I just wanted to be able to leave and not to have to confront him about why and how and what this all was. I wanted my job. I wanted my life. I honestly didn't know what the hell to do because—and let me be clear—no one knows what to do when something like that happens. You might think you do, but you don't. I was trying to make sense of myself and my heart and the way it was pounding in my chest. I was trying to make sense of humanity and the way it could slip away from you while you held a book with frayed edges in your hand.

It was nearly seven and I was just about done. Arly came down to the kitchen. Clothed this time. He went to the fridge and poured two glasses of wine.

"That's good enough," he said. "You've done plenty."

I looked at the task in my hands. The papers that even in my terrified state I had spent so much time on. Clearly none of it mattered to him. It was all a ruse for whatever hellscape this was. How many women were busied with work throughout history as men made plans for their bodies? How many of them thought they were factors in their own destiny? *What a fucking idiot I am,* I thought.

He walked over with the glass of wine and put it in front of me.

"Let's enjoy the evening," he said. "Congrats on a job well done."

By this point I was going to get the hell out of there. It was over. I was not about to see this man's penis again, so help me god.

"Thanks. Actually I feel kind of under the weather. I was sick to my stomach all last night."

I was hoping he wouldn't realize it was an excuse, but I was so certain that I had to get out of there that I was willing to risk it. That's the thing, I was still, even then, worried about how he would perceive me. I was still shadowed by who this man had been to me days before: Arly, a demigod of radio.

Luckily, he took the excuse and walked me to the door. I know he said something about me coming out again and this time getting to enjoy the property and not be cooped up. I agreed in as pleasant a way as possible, though I knew that was not going to happen. At the door he reached for a hug and I obliged, quickly and distantly.

As I was leaving I could see his housekeeper getting into her car. She looked like a different person outside of the house. I wanted to run up to her and to tell her everything. To beg her to hold me for a second. Of course I didn't. I waved to her though, but she didn't wave back. Sometimes people don't see you in moments when you really need them to.

I ran back to the cottage. I didn't walk. When I got there I started packing my stuff as quickly as possible, and I got in my car and I drove back to the city, and when I got to my apartment, my apartment, my space, my things everywhere, I burst into tears. I felt so scared and so out of control. I felt like a joke in my own life. I felt totally and utterly alone. My roommate was asleep, and even though we weren't close, I woke her up and told her everything. And she listened to me and was quiet when it was right to be quiet and said the right thing when it was right to say the right thing. I could not be more grateful to her for that night. If I hadn't had her there I don't know what my night would have been.

"I love you," she said to me before I went to bed. I don't think my roommate loved me or loves me. I think she was talking about love and loneliness. I think like there are no words for how it felt when Arly did that to me. I don't think there are ways to express to another woman this: I know the hurt you hurt. And so it was the best she could offer.

The next day I had to be back at work. I thought about calling in sick, but I decided not to. Mostly I was afraid that if I did, I would just be prolonging the torturous anticipation of what this would all be. But when I saw Arly things were back to normal. He acted like he had before the weekend. Professional and distant and cool in all the ways anyone would admire about him. I didn't expect that he'd continue to be naked or inappropriate, but I thought something would be there that would give me insight into what this would be—my life, my future. In so many ways I was waiting for Arly to tell me what was what. The next day was the same and the day after that. I was just waiting for something to happen.

And then one day, a few weeks later, I was in a meeting with him and a bunch of other people, and I looked around the room, and I was the only woman there. And I looked at Arly, and he was smiling about something, and I just knew I couldn't do this anymore. I couldn't wait around to see what these men had decided for me. So I quit. And I don't work in radio anymore. It's not easy to get those jobs. Right now I'm just living and working. Am I happy? How could anyone be.

PART FIVE

JOY

The whole drive to my aunt's I kept thinking about Theo. At this point I wanted to stop thinking about him. I didn't want every single thought of mine to be about him because he was with Celine and that was that. Last night he and I ordered in a pizza and we ate together, and I noticed that I've started to chew like him. When he eats pizza he rips off big pieces with his teeth rather than take normal bites. It's like he tears the pizza in chunks. I once made fun of him for it. I said, "Wow, what did the pizza ever do to you?" And we laughed. I noticed last night that somewhere along the line, I've started eating my pizza just like that. I didn't even think of it, and it just happened to me. Now I'm tearing instead of chewing. It made me sad, but I still ate with him and then we hung out and watched TV together. He does this thing where when we hang out he puts his phone down and doesn't text. Before Celine he used to text or use his phone when we hung out just like anyone would, but now he puts his phone aside. It's like he wants me to know that the time we have together is our own. Sometimes I'll hear his phone buzz and I'll even say, "You're getting a text," and he'll just say back, "It's okay. I'll answer it later." It shouldn't make me feel special, but it does. I'm exhausted by it. I'm exhausted by myself. I'm exhausted by how good it felt when he said, "What color are your eyes exactly because they almost look like two colors mixed together?"

I actually wrote that down so I could remember it. I reread it too sometimes. I wonder if there's a man in the world out there who has ever written down something a woman has said about his eyes. I wonder if he's read it to himself to make him feel more like who he is.

Joy had grown up with family lore about her aunt. It would be impossible to pinpoint when exactly she'd first heard it because she'd heard it so often and so consistently that there was no distinct memory of when her mom first told her about it. The best she could come up with was a memory of herself in the back seat of the car at around age nine, and her mom was angry at her aunt for something, although Joy could not for the life of her remember what that was, and then her mom said, "She's never been the same since the baby accident. She'll never be normal."

And even though Joy had heard about "the baby accident" as her mom often called it, she'd never heard her mom say explicitly "She'll never be normal" before. Certainly her mom had implied it a million times over. Anytime her aunt said something off-color or was late to a family gathering her mom would roll her eyes, and right before she would get mad she'd say, as if stopping herself from losing her temper, "I should be patient with her. I should. She hasn't had it easy." And Joy would know instantly what she was referring to.

As Joy got older, the conversations changed. "Your aunt never met anyone, and I really think it had to do with that baby accident. She wanted a family," her mom would say. "believe me she wanted one. But she just could not get herself together enough. Now she'll probably die alone."

Joy had heard the story of the accident told like this:

Her aunt had been driving when all of a sudden, out of the blue, a newborn baby landed on the hood of her car. A woman had just given birth and had thrown her baby off a balcony, and it was her aunt who was driving by right then. The baby landed on her aunt's hood, and she pulled the car over and ran out but the baby was dead. Its body hardly looked like a baby at all. She started screaming, "Help, we need help!" and soon there was an ambulance and the police. The woman on the balcony was taken away in handcuffs. After that, her aunt was never the same. She became depressed, had nightmares, constant anxiety. She dropped out of the graduate program she had been in and quit her job. Not too much later she moved off into a small house in the middle of nowhere. Now she just did odd jobs to pay the bills. She didn't have a career or a family. She should have gotten more help than she did but those were the times then. People were expected to cope quietly by themselves and that's exactly what her aunt had done. She'd found a space, a path, a way to keep living despite the mangled baby in her mind.

Joy didn't plan what she was going to say to her aunt. She just suddenly felt relentlessly compelled to understand it all. She no longer wanted it to be lore. She no longer wanted her mom's words to define the story. She felt the need to be close to her aunt, in a real way. She hadn't put it all together, but she was driving over there and she was telling herself she was ready.

Her aunt lived about three hours from the city in a very wooded rural area. Joy had been there only once or twice when she was very little, until her mom had put a stop to the whole thing.

"We're not driving all this goddamn way when she doesn't even have a drink to offer us besides tap water," her mom had said as they were pulling away.

Joy remembered her aunt's home as being a fun place, where she ran around happy and oblivious, but so many places from her childhood elicited that same response that she wasn't sure if she should trust that memory.

When she pulled up the house looked different than she remembered. It was little more than a glorified mobile home, and the yard was in bad shape. Her aunt didn't seem to have a driveway, so Joy parked in the street. For a second she didn't feel like getting up and going inside. *I'll just let myself* . . . she thought vaguely and sat still for a moment. She pulled out her phone and scrolled through Instagram. Annie had posted a picture of a book she was reading and tea she was drinking. It made Joy feel sad, and in that sadness she thought maybe she wasn't sad as much as she sensed that her friend was sad, *and maybe it's all that sadness between us that keeps us all together.* She double-tapped the picture.

Suddenly from her periphery she could see the mobile home door opening, and her aunt coming out to greet her. Instantly she got out of the car and pretended that she had not been just sitting there doing nothing.

Her aunt waved a big wave at her as Joy walked through the overgrown yard and up to the door.

"Joy! You look amazing," her aunt said.

So rarely had anyone used the word *amazing* to describe how she looked that Joy was almost stunned. She hesitated for a moment.

"Thank you, you look great also," she finally said back. She handed her aunt the cake she'd brought as a gesture, and her aunt seemed genuinely touched.

"You didn't have to do this!"

"It's a ginger cake," Joy said.

"I don't think I've ever had a ginger cake before. This is so thoughtful." Her aunt pulled the cake in close to herself as if, had it made sense, she would have embraced it.

They stepped inside and Joy took a moment to look around the living room she was now standing in. It looked nothing like she remembered really. For starters it was much smaller and there was nothing very remarkable about any of it. If you took the things of her aunt's out of it, it would have been nothing but a white box with windows that seemed disproportionately small. None of the things in the home seemed like the things that might have been there twenty-plus years ago, and so instantly, and without meaning to, Joy felt the enormous loss of time passing.

"Take a seat," her aunt said, pointing to a leather sofa that looked freshly sat on.

Joy sat down, and her aunt went towards the kitchen with the cake.

"Would you like tea?" she called back after herself.

"That would be great, thank you," Joy said.

Her aunt popped her head back into the living room. "Oh no, you know what? I only have ginger tea. Would that go with ginger cake? Wouldn't that be too much?"

"I'm fine with that," Joy said. She felt her aunt was more invested in this meeting than was appropriate. All the complaints her mom had made over the years were flooding back to her.

"People would call it 'being scatterbrained,'" she remembered her mom saying once, "but I think there's more to it than that."

"Okay, great," her aunt called from the kitchen. "Ginger it is."

Moments later they were sitting together sipping tea and exchanging the pleasantries you would expect in a conversation between family members who had not seen each other for a while.

Joy kept thinking about how to say what she wanted to say, how to ask all those horrifying questions about the baby, but she felt herself completely arrested by fear.

"I've been thinking about getting bees," her aunt said. She took a bite of cake and was looking off a bit towards the window behind Joy. "So many flowers around here it seems like there should be more bees."

"Bees sound like fun," Joy said.

"Have you heard the bees are dying?" her aunt said.

"I have. It's terrible." Joy didn't want to talk about bees anymore. "So are you working much these days?" The last Joy knew her aunt had been trying to get her realtor's license.

"Not a whole ton," her aunt said. She took another bite of cake. She looked sadder and less fretful than she had earlier. "I still do the antique furniture stuff on eBay. You'd be surprised how many people are desperate to get rid of old furniture. All you have to do is come get it, and they'll give away stuff that's worth, you know, usually not thousands, but sometimes hundreds of dollars."

"Do you have a truck?" Joy asked.

"No, I don't drive," her aunt said.

Joy could feel her heart in her throat. This was the moment she'd been looking for.

"There's a guy I know who has one though. He helps me pick up the furniture. I offer to pay him, but he always refuses.

He's very nice. His wife is very nice also. They live up north with their son, who is probably your age. He lives at home."

"Why don't you drive?" Joy felt almost sick as she asked it.

"I just hate all the windy roads out here. And honestly, it really doesn't make sense for me to have a car. I have my bike, which gets me into town and back, which is all I really need. I can always rent a car if I need one."

Joy was quiet for a moment. She looked down at her cake. The frosting was smeared to the side. The piece, which she'd eaten most of, looked molested sitting there with all the bites taken out of it. The whole thing made her feel stupid. *What did I think? I was going to come here like fucking Sherlock Holmes and suddenly my life would make sense?* She felt more childish than she had in a long time, and really that was saying a lot because most of the time in her life, at work and at home, she did feel like a child.

"Did you think I was going to say 'the accident'?" her aunt asked with a smile.

Joy just stared at her, unable to move.

"No, your mom thinks everything that goes wrong in my life is because of that day. I'm not afraid to drive."

Joy still didn't know what to say, but she felt herself stammering words out into the air. "Yeah, I've always, you know, wondered about what happened. My mom told me. I mean, the details and all. I just, I mean, I always felt I should ask you about it."

"Yeah, it was awful," her aunt said. She put her plate down and picked up the teacup. "The baby died. I was twenty-three when it happened. It was really traumatic."

"I can imagine—I mean I can't imagine. I don't know how I would handle something like that."

"Well, I think I handled it as well as anyone could. I did go to a counselor. Your mom always tells people I didn't, but I did. I think for me the big thing I would always think of was that mother and why she would do something so violent like that to her child. Killing your child in any circumstance is unfathomable, of course, but why would you choose something like that where you know that it's just so violent? I always figured she must have just snapped. She must have just picked the baby up and just tossed it, just like that."

Joy could see all of it in her mind. A young mother, a crying infant, a sweeping motion, and then death far below. She could feel it in her bones the way any evil is there, most of it known but so little of it felt in one's own life. Mothers snapping, babies dying, bees going extinct, and the end of mankind.

"Anyway, like I said, I did counseling and that really helped. I stopped thinking about it so much, and I think now I handle it as healthily as anyone would."

"Can a person handle that healthily?" Joy asked.

"Well, I mean there are doctors treating babies with brain cancer. There are firefighters seeing whole families burned alive. Think of Holocaust survivors. You have to deal with it and people do."

Joy was taken aback by how together her aunt seemed to be. It wasn't the vision she'd been sold for so many years.

"Do you think it's affected your life?" Joy asked. "I mean do you think you'd be living differently if it hadn't happened?"

"I don't think so really. I think your mom worries about me because I never met someone, but the truth is, I just never did. I would have loved to have met the right guy and have gotten married. God knows it would have helped with the bills to not have to do it all alone all these years! And yes, I wanted a baby like anyone does—I mean I guess not everyone does, but I did.

So yeah, I just didn't meet the guy." Her aunt shrugged. "Is it cold in here? I feel like I might put the wood-burning stove on."

Joy just stared at her aunt as she watched her get up and move about the room trying to start a fire. She remembered the thoughts she'd had about luck in college. Life seemed suddenly so much more dangerous. So much more reckless. She had thought of her aunt being the victim of a baby being tossed on her, but really her aunt was the victim of just being tossed. She hadn't found her footing. She hadn't built a career or fallen in love. There was no baby. Joy could feel within herself a level of frenzy that felt newly unearthed.

She remembered the cavalier way her mom would say *die alone* about her sister, like it was nothing to just other her like that: *We* who *don't* die alone. *She* who *does* die alone. Her mother had pinpointed a hideous mishandling of trauma as the root of her sister's failure. She herself had met someone to love, and her daughter, who wouldn't balk at pain, would meet someone and would not *die alone* either. Her mom held such blind faith in her daughter and in her daughter's future that she effortlessly let the downfall of her sister's life slip off her tongue any chance she got. How fierce could love be. How vicious deception.

"And what about you?" her aunt asked as the flames rose in their own little oven. "Are you seeing anyone special?"

"Yes," Joy said. "I'm dating my roommate."

ANNIE

Jason and I watched a movie on Sunday. It was really nice because, you know, he usually goes off on his own Sundays and sees his friends, so when he asked if I wanted to stay home and just watch movies with him, I felt, I'm not going to lie, I felt so incredibly excited, which put me in a bad mood because I've been telling myself for a while now that I don't mind that he leaves me alone every weekend like that, but clearly I do because I was so excited when he said he'd stay. One time Patrice had said something to me like this, she said, "Bad boyfriends: the highs are so high because the lows are so low." She was talking about someone else we knew, a woman who used to work in the office with us. She dated this guy who cheated on her a lot. I used to think of that relationship whenever I wanted to feel better about my own, but here I am feeling like the highs are high only because the lows are low. The movie we watched was *Free Solo,* which is a documentary about this insane man who climbs mountains without any ropes to catch him if he falls. I thought it would be a good movie to watch because with documentaries I feel like they're the least likely to remind you of your own life. But it turned out to be a terrible idea because in the movie the guy has this girlfriend who follows him around and supports him, and says "I love you," but he doesn't say "I love you" back until after he climbs some big-ass mountain. She was so happy he finally said I love you that rather than be mad that he hadn't said it the second he felt it, she was just thrilled he'd said it at all. Why would someone do that to someone they love? Why would anyone withhold saying "I love you" for any reason other than control? I could see myself the same as this girl standing on a mountainside looking up at a man risking his life without the strength to risk his heart. *Men are cowards,* I thought, but I didn't let myself think much more than that. I too was afraid, and seeing myself like that, afraid and looking up, I felt sad and angry. I went to bed and forced myself to sleep, and in the middle of the night I felt Jason's foot pressed against my ankle, and I felt happy he was there. That's it.

When Annie got home from her parents' she opened the door to the apartment and the lights were off. Candles were set up all around. On the mantel, the windowsills. Every tabletop. *Oh my god,* she thought. But she felt too shocked to think much else. She stepped in the doorway.

"Jason," she called out, and as she did, she noticed music was playing.

She walked down the hall and Simon made his way up to her. She patted him distractedly and kept walking. *Is this* . . . But she felt such a level of thrill she would not dare let herself finish that thought.

"Jason," she called again.

"I'm out here," he said, and by the muffled sound of his voice she could tell he was on their balcony.

She made her way over to him and he pushed the sliding glass door open for her.

"Hey, Annie," he said. He smiled warmly.

"What is this?" She stepped out. It was freezing. Far too cold to be outside. Her teeth started chattering.

"Here." He handed her a blanket.

"A blanket?" she said. She wrapped it around herself. He pulled her body in close to him. She loved the feeling of his arms, his angled physicality. Every bit of it felt like something she knew so well.

"Look up," he said.

Annie looked up at the sky. It was a pretty clear night. The moon was a slice of a crescent. Despite the lights from the city, she could see some stars.

"Annie, listen, I might not be ready to get married yet, but I know that one day I will be. And I just wanted you to know that I love you."

Her first thought was *So this isn't a proposal?* And then her second thought was *I'm absolutely freezing out here.* She felt too tired to have much more of a reaction than that. It felt like a few months ago she would have been more excited by the gesture.

"I love you too," she said.

"Good things are coming for us, Annie," he said and pulled her in tighter.

"Where'd you get all the candles?" she asked him.

"I ordered a big pack from Amazon."

"Oh, that's good," she said. "We should go blow them out before the apartment catches fire."

"Do you like them?"

"I do." Annie did like the candles. The candles and the feeling she got from seeing them was the best part of what that night was for her.

They blew out the candles one by one and the house smelled like every birthday Annie could ever remember. That night they lay in bed and Annie told Jason about Erin and the letter.

"Jesus," he said. "Men suck."

"I know," she said.

"So what are you going to do? Want me to beat the shit out of him?"

Annie smiled. There were few things in life she loved more than a man expressing his antiquated desire to protect women from violent men.

"No, I can handle it."

"You can handle anything," Jason said.

And just like that, she stopped feeling bad about the nonengagement.

Annie didn't hesitate when she got to work on Monday, even though she could feel her heart pound in her chest all morning and all day. She thought too of things from childhood that gave her a similar sense of unease: the man next door who yelled at her for running on his lawn, her mom crying over something Annie was too young to understand, a beloved teddy bear lost forever. It was fear, unmistakably so, but that was not about to stop her.

Despite what the letter said, she felt she should go to HR first. It was what policy dictated, and she wanted to be on record having done everything right. She emailed Meredith. Meredith was an older lady who'd been with the station longer than anyone besides Arly. She'd been there even before the show was Kathy's and was instead hosted by a very boring man named Roger. Annie had vague memories of what the show had been before Kathy took over. She remembered her dad used to listen to it on occasion as he drove her to school. The show was mostly about history with some politics woven in. She had a distinct memory of her dad saying "Windbag" and shutting it off once. When Kathy took over, it was a revelation. She was warm and smart. The show was still very academic, but Kathy understood what made things interesting. One time Annie had overheard her say, "People don't care about war they care about death," and that kind of brilliance was what made Annie so proud to work on the show.

Meredith was never quick to respond. A week was usually the bare minimum for a response from HR in general, but especially from Meredith, who typed using only one index finger. So when Annie scrolled to her inbox minutes after pressing send, and saw the "RE: Important Matter Regarding Sexual Assault Allegation," she couldn't believe it. *This is real,* she felt herself think, her hand wavering over the email before tapping it open. It read:

> Dear Annie,
>
> Obviously, we don't take these kinds of matters lightly. I would like to see a copy of the letter as soon as possible. Would you mind meeting me before end of day? I'm free anytime.
>
> Best,
> Meredith

At first Annie felt hopeful. This was exactly the kind of response a person would expect from HR given the circumstance, but when she got to Meredith's office later that day, the energy, the competent haste she'd been assuming, was really more frantic and fretful than anything else.

"Could you please shut the door behind you?" was the first thing Meredith said. She wasn't wasting any time. "Could I see the letter please?"

She grabbed it and held it in both hands as she read.

"It's not signed," she finally said.

"Yes, I know," Annie responded. "I don't think the person wanted their identity revealed."

"Well, I can't do anything without a signature," Meredith said.

Annie felt instantly angry as hell. "She said she already went to HR and not much was done. Do you remember anyone coming forward with something like this?"

"No, and if they had this matter would have been resolved immediately. If someone accuses someone of—how did she put it?" She looked back down at the letter—" 'sexual assault,' then we take that very seriously. No one here would have ignored that."

Then why the hell would she write that? was Annie's first thought, but she stopped herself from saying it. "I know you would have, but I also have to take this seriously since it was presented to me by a co-worker, and I feel it needs to be properly looked into."

"Well, who brought it to you?"

Annie hesitated. "I don't feel comfortable giving that information out without her consent."

"Well, I don't know what you expect me to do," Meredith said. Her tone was becoming increasingly belligerent. "I can't go accusing people of sexual assault based on anonymous tips. As far as I can tell, if this letter is correct, it was already brought up to HR and the matter was dealt with."

"And how was it dealt with exactly? Could you at least look into whether this kind of issue was brought up to HR against Arly?" His name burned off her tongue and past her lips. "I'd like to know what was done and how it was resolved."

"I can't give you that information, I'm sorry. If an accusation like this is made, the accuser and the accused are the only people who would be privy to it."

"So basically you're telling me that you don't know if anything was ever done, and even if you did know you couldn't tell me what it was, and there's absolutely nothing that can be done now?"

Meredith stared at her for a moment. As far as Annie could tell she was not used to young women talking back to her. Most young women were afraid to make waves, be loud, seem mean, but Annie had worked with a lot of men for the last decade and she was not about to balk just because this woman had let dregs of patriarchy into the deepest recesses of her heart. *And what about you? Who has mistreated you and your body? Who has stolen from your goodness?* Annie thought. *Be a sister, Sister.*

"Unless one of these women comes forward nothing can be done," Meredith said.

"Thank you for your time," Annie said, and she turned to leave.

"Annie," Meredith called after her. Annie paused at the door and turned back around. "I've known Arly for more than thirty years. He's a good man."

Annie didn't respond. She stood and stared, and seconds later she left the room.

Back at her desk, she tried to organize her thoughts. She took a breath in and let a breath out. Her hands, her legs, everything felt like motion and she wanted to move. Move up, move forward, move out. She wasn't going to let Meredith and her unfathomable disinterest be slowing or halting or ending anything. She didn't have her email or a way to contact her, but Annie was going to find Erin.

CELINE

I was not so poor in college that I needed to do it. The truth is that my friends were going to Paris, and I didn't have the money to go with them. I didn't get to travel like a lot of my classmates. I'd never left the country before. Paris sounded amazing, and I just really wanted to go. My friend Myriel suggested it. She said she'd done it a bunch, and it was no big deal. It didn't sound like a big deal, and it paid well. But afterwards I instantly felt bad about it. It was like the feeling of drinking something cold and feeling the coolness go down through your chest and into your body. Some people might say that feeling is refreshing, but I always find it disturbing. I tried not to think about it. I went to Paris, I took pictures and laughed with my friends. Everything around me was beautiful, idyllic, but I could still feel it there in my chest. And then when I got home it was still there and still there and still there. You can't always take everything back. Apologize to yourself and it doesn't mean much. Yourself knows yourself. Even now, here I am, and I can feel that coolness draining down into me. I took the sip, but the water is the one that seeps, spills, rolls over the warm thin layer of my insides. This is all to say, I regret it.

⁂

Celine made the video herself in her dorm room bathroom. She had been told she did not have to do anything sexual, just to brush normally as she would on any other day of the week. She'd be paid five hundred dollars for the video, and it would go to only one person and would not be posted anywhere online. She didn't think much of it ahead of time. She felt a sense of resolve once she'd decided to do it, but she made sure to wait until her roommate, Olivia, was out. Not that Olivia was in a position to judge. She was the most sexually reckless person that Celine had ever known.

"I had sex with two guys last night," she'd said once. She was flipping through a stack of mail as she said it and Celine could see both her arms were bruised badly.

"Oh my god, what?"

"Yeah, I met them both last night. Had sex with one at the club in a bathroom and the other at his place."

She acted happy about it, but Celine didn't think Olivia was happy. Olivia, of any woman she knew, seemed defeated and brittle. Sometimes she'd hear her crying softly to herself at night. Celine thought to say something, she thought to say, "Olivia, are you okay?" or "Olivia, please be kinder to yourself." Instead she left her roommate her privacy. Who knew what was right? Whatever the case, she was not about to make this video in front of her.

Celine set the camera up on the bathroom vanity. She felt particular about what she was wearing even though her body wouldn't be showing. She wanted to be covered, to feel like this was not about sex at all, like this was any other day just brushing her teeth. She put on a USC sweatshirt that her cousin who went to USC had given her. It was old and stained and no one could possibly think it was sexual in any context. She did exactly what Myriel had told her to do.

"Make sure you put the toothpaste on the brush in front of the camera. They want to see the whole process."

Celine first met Myriel their junior year. They'd had a film class together where Myriel was often late or complaining about intricacies of film theory no one else had the energy to care about. Celine didn't like her, but she also didn't pay much attention to her, and not too much later they ended up at a mutual friend's house for a party where they unexpectedly hit it off.

"I hate people who think doing drugs makes them interesting," Myriel said. Celine laughed and soon after they were hanging out all the time. Celine loved how chic Myriel always seemed. She wore clothes from H&M like they were couture. Her style was effortlessly together and cool. She was everything every girl wanted to be. She dated all kinds of rich and powerful men, and very often Celine felt herself jealous of all the fabulous places Myriel seemed to go and all the fabulous people she always was surrounded by. It was Myriel who came up with the idea for the trip to Paris. It would be her, Celine, and a group of Myriel's girlfriends.

"I'm broke," Celine said.

"What? Come on. The tickets are not that much. I'll pay for the hotel and you can room with me."

"I honestly can't. I just bought my books for the semester and it was a fortune."

"You know what you should do? You should do one of those toothbrushing videos."

"The what?"

"You brush your teeth in a video and guys buy it."

"Buy it for what?"

"To jerk off to."

"They jerk off to toothbrushing?"

"Yes, it's a fetish. You don't even show your face or do anything sexual. It's literally just a close-up of your mouth. I do it all the time. I've made like three grand doing it."

"Three grand?"

"Yeah, it's through this guy I know who has this hookup to rich people."

"They pay that much for it?"

"They do if you're pretty, and you're really pretty. You could probably make more money than I do. You have great lips."

"And it doesn't make you feel weird?"

"Not at all. It's not even my whole face. I honestly would feel stupid not doing it."

Celine didn't have any doubts at first. There was something about the ease with which Myriel talked about it; it all sounded as effortless as the big summer hats she wore or the brightly colored leggings that thinned her legs in a way improbable on anyone else. Celine told herself all kinds of vaguely empowering things about it too. *Independent woman,* she'd think or *The man is the one being exploited here*. She went into the whole thing almost energized by it.

Myriel lent her the camera and told her she'd email the video to the guy she knew, who would send it to the actual guy who was buying it.

"It's all very professional. You don't ever find out who the guy is who has it, and he has no idea who you are."

Celine nodded.

"It's easy. You got this." Myriel tapped Celine on the shoulder in a reassuring way, and then as she was about to leave, she swung back around. "Oh, and make sure you put the toothpaste on the brush in front of the camera. They want to see the whole process, especially when you spit it out."

The words hit Celine, singular and suffocating, *spit it out*. She thought of herself as a child briefly. Herself walking in the black of a dark basement and a mouse running by her foot. That same feeling was there, terror at what sees you as you move in darkness. "Got it, thanks, Myriel. I'll text you when I'm done." Her body, her voice, all of it was just moving forward as she was still in her own little darkness with spit and a mouse who ran past her a decade before.

She was careful to be sure the shot was in tight to just her mouth and showed nothing else, but even seeing just her mouth in the viewer was strange. It was like seeing someone else's face, someone else's life. It was like watching someone else do something sexual—and it did feel sexual even though she'd tried so hard to believe that it wouldn't. Getting the paste on the brush was hard because her hand was shaking so she started over a few times until it looked okay. She brushed back and forth and back and forth in what she felt was normal brushing, but the whole process didn't feel normal, and every second she questioned if what her hand was doing was what it would have been doing if this wasn't for porn. After a few minutes she was ready to spit. But now she wasn't sure what to do. If she leaned forward she'd move out of the shot and trying to pick up the camera now seemed risky in terms of keeping her identity concealed. She hesitated for a moment and then just spit right where she was even though it had no chance of going into the sink. The toothpaste and spit ended up all over the floor and down the front of her USC sweatshirt. She felt embarrassed and quickly shut off the camera. Now, as she stood in the mess, everything that was bad about this seemed so much worse. She caught a glimpse of herself in the mirror. She looked no different than she had at birth, or three years old, or seven, or ten, or in high school. She was Celine, still a person, and to someone else she would be an image of foaming toothpaste and suds flying out of a mouth and down a chin.

She wiped her face and cleaned up the floor. Her sweatshirt was thrown in the hamper. A few minutes later she'd play back the footage and edit out herself turning on the camera, and her few shaky first attempts, and herself at the end frantically shutting off the camera. Overall it looked as good as she could have hoped. It was just a mouth on-screen, hardly her own, or anyone's, and so she could convince herself that here and now was where she'd leave any misery she'd felt. The chalky streaks were gone from the floor and from her face. It was possible to feel like she'd easily move on.

She sent the video to Myriel, who wrote back. "Perfect! I'll give you the check next time I see you!" Not too much later they'd be on a plane to Paris. She'd stand like so many others waiting to snap a picture of the *Mona Lisa,* waiting to stand on top of a tower from which the whole city would be in her sight.

"Wow, is this America?" a French man catcalled to her in broken English by Notre Dame. "If this is America take me with you!"

"Every man is in love with you," Myriel said, laughing.

"He's talking to all of us," Celine said back.

"No, he most certainly is not," Myriel said. "He's talking to you."

Celine could not stop thinking about the video the entire trip. Every time she did, she felt a flutter rising up inside. It felt almost like that moment had been a rebirth for her, but not a rebirth in a beautiful, stirring, motivational way, a rebirth that felt like she had decided wholeheartedly what she was as a person. A mouth, a moment, five hundred dollars. These limitations were limitations she had set for herself. All her life it felt like she'd been fighting for the right definition of herself.

"Don't ever let a man treat you like that," her mom had said.

But here she was letting a man treat her like that. Here she was letting herself be treated like that by herself. She set the price. She set up the camera. She spit on the floor.

On the last night of the trip she couldn't sleep. The day had been long and exhausting, and her thoughts had been vicious from the minute she'd woken up till now. She couldn't take it.

"Are you awake?" Celine asked Myriel.

"Yes," Myriel said, her voice cracked and shaking like she was already asleep.

"I'm worried about the video," Celine said.

"What video?"

"The one I made."

"Stop, you're crazy," Myriel said, and then she turned over and that was it.

They flew home and life went back to normal, but Celine was still bothered. She'd try not to think about it in terms of herself. Anytime the image of her lips or her face with toothpaste on it would pop up in her mind, she would start counting in her head or she'd do this thing she'd heard this girl with anxiety once describe to her.

"Every time I feel myself start to have an anxiety attack I just describe a stop sign to myself in my head: 'It's red, it's an octagon, it says S-T-O-P.' "

Pretty soon all day long Celine would be repeating to herself over and over, "It's red, it's an octagon, it says S-T-O-P."

She had planned on taking summer classes and working at a café near school, but at the last minute she changed her mind and decided to spend the summer at home.

Her mom took her shopping and they spent time by the lake. She didn't see many friends. It was a respite from her life and all the reminders of the video. She felt less panicked. She felt less unsure.

But once she got back to school and the dorm, everything came piling back. She felt no different than the day she'd left. It was still "It's red, it's an octagon, it says S-T-O-P."

She started staring at men in public, wondering if any one of them could be the man who'd watched her video. It didn't seem impossible that one of them would recognize her from her mouth. She had nightmares of them coming up to her and saying something like "Oh wow, you're the whore from the video I bought."

She'd search on subways, in class, at work. She'd pass men on the street and think, *Is that him?* Whenever she'd have to interact with some new man she'd wonder if he was the one who had had an orgasm at her face. It made her quieter, more reserved.

"You're so coquettish," a guy would say to her once on a date when he thought she was being coy.

If you only knew, she would think. And no one knew. She wouldn't even tell Derk about it when they started dating not too much later. It was herself and Myriel and two other strange men and no one else. She was alone with it, and that's where it was, a little hole in her heart that she carried around. And she just lived like that and over time she didn't think of it less; rather she had found ways to set it aside, put it away, fill other voids in her heart adjacent to this one.

But now she wanted to do something, to feel something, to change the pain if she couldn't cure it. The first thing she thought to do was to call Myriel.

LAUNDRY

When Joy got home from visiting her aunt she took two sick days and spent them cleaning the apartment. She had made a decision about her life. It was not a decision she decided on, though. It was a finality born of an impulse. Really what it was was fear. And so she decided that from now on things were going to be different. She would not die alone.

She organized the hall closet and cleaned the bathtub. As long as she'd lived there, the cabinets had never been washed, so she washed those too. After that she prepped for dinner. She had plans to make something elaborate and French. Theo was out with Celine, but she tried not to dwell on that. Instead she put her body and soul up against their home. She folded herself inside the space deeper and deeper until it was becoming its best version of itself and into it she spun out feelings about herself that felt markedly superior to the feelings she'd had before. There was a level of triumph in all of it.

In college she'd had a lit professor who said, "Cleaning was women's work because women's work becomes undone." That statement was something she'd held on to and thought of anytime she cleaned or cooked or streaked makeup across her face.

The thought of women having this endless undoing to uphold, it felt very true and it felt very powerful. Maybe it was meant to be the opposite, an examination of how women were tasked with labor that was, in many ways, thankless, but to Joy the recognition of that thanklessness was what felt powerful. *Yes, we're strong enough to do work that goes on forever,* she'd think. Now though, as she pushed the couch away from the wall to pick up one of Theo's socks, she didn't think of what her professor said so much as who her professor was. She was the bitchiest teacher she'd ever had. She made students cry. There was one student in particular whom she actively made a fool out of almost every class. And—and this is something that stuck out more now than it had at the time—she favored the male students. If they had something to say or to add she always seemed to instantly respect it more than anything a female student would say. Joy herself was too terrified to ever participate, but she did get a few graded essays back with notes like "What does that even mean?" and "Lazy." Joy had learned a lot from that professor though. She'd learned about not only women's work but also all kinds of literary theory. It was in that class that she first read Virginia Woolf. But now, so far away from it all, as she vacuumed up old cereal, and worked at a job where she spent the majority of her time writing emails that were so banal they could nearly be produced by a machine (and likely one day would be), it seemed that any of the goodness the professor had brought her was more or less useless. *Kindness is all that matters,* Joy thought, and she pushed the couch back against the wall and went to make dinner.

When Theo got home he was stunned.

"Wow, Joy, the house looks amazing. You stayed home cleaning all day?"

"Well, I just wanted it to look, you know, more organized."

"It looks perfect."

They had dinner and watched TV side by side on the couch. They made brownies much later than was reasonable, and it felt like old times.

Theo smiled as he dipped his brownie in peanut butter, a habit of his that she still found endearing, even now as so many things that she'd once considered endearing about him had kind of dissolved.

"You know what, Joyous?" Theo asked, brownie in hand as he chewed thoughtfully.

"What?" Joy said.

"You should never go away again. The house is too empty without you."

Joy could feel her heart simmer. She smiled a big smile and turned because she could not take another moment of eye contact with him. "You're just saying that because I cleaned the whole damn place."

"No, I'm not," Theo said. "I just think, you know, us, this whole thing, it works. I'm happy here is what I mean. I always feel like, you know, this is my home."

"Me too," Joy said. *I love you* would have felt like the next natural thing to say.

And then Joy took the words *this is my home* and based everything in her mind on them and that feeling of sitting there with Theo. She wanted to be that for him and for them. So she kept cleaning and she kept cooking. She started packing him elaborate lunches for work. He was so impressed and surprised by the gesture that he started taking pictures of each lunch and posting them on his Instagram with the hashtag #joyfull. She would see them and feel that same simmer in her heart. The dead baby of her aunt's, the bad dates of her youth, the feeling of not being good enough or thin enough, all of it was being buried. Her fervor, which had been directed at making some kind of relationship manifest, was now more about keeping that feeling between them, that *home,* alive and real. It felt good to have a man sit beside her at the end of the day, and whatever future there was or wasn't, she was not going to let herself move away from this goodness. In a way it was the first time Joy had ever felt successful as an adult. At times she'd tell herself she was even happy.

But then there were other times, like that early morning when she got up in a sleepy haze to go to the bathroom and she heard the stirring of not Theo but Celine in the hallway. She cracked open her door and could see Celine standing there with a crop top and short shorts and her body was sleek and perfect and so skinny. There were, in the space between herself and that perfect thinness, miles and decades and every splitting cell of the universe. Joy felt like she was a stomach. Defined by it and living in it. *You dumb bitch,* she thought, but who the thought was for was unclear.

Two days later Joy would be in Theo's room. She was doing laundry, something she did for both of them now. At first he'd leave his hamper out, but at this point she just went around the room and picked up whatever looked dirty. She knew his clothes and his routine so it wasn't all that hard. As she leaned down to grab a gray T-shirt she saw beside it, right there, as stark and skinny as the image of Celine in the hallway, a pair of her underwear. They were dirty it was clear. Women's underwear, unlike so many parts of women's lives, would not and could not lie about the humanity of the person who wore it. Joy stood there. She let different thoughts in and out of her mind, but then there was also not so much thought. There was a feeling like the feeling you feel when you hear your aunt is an old maid because of trauma. There was a feeling you feel when you have sex to prove that you have worth. There was a feeling when you squeeze your own flesh in your hand and wish you could rip it off your body to spare yourself a pain so chasmic that it almost seems intrinsic to the deepest parts of yourself, that same part that lives inside your simmering heart or expresses itself in clear sticky streaks on your underwear. She took a breath, leaned down, picked them up using Theo's T-shirt, and tossed them into the hamper.

WEDDED

Annie hadn't seen Joy in months. All their communication had been via text or the occasional comment on Instagram, but she wanted to ask Joy what she thought about reaching out to Erin. She thought Joy might have some insight from an HR perspective, and to tell the truth, she just wanted to call her.

"Hello?" Joy said as she picked up.

Her voice—hearing it—was jarring at first. It sounded like an old lady voice almost. For a brief second Annie felt like crying. She wished she could hug Joy close and say, "I miss you. It hurts." She didn't, though. Instead she did what she often did and responded with rage.

"You haven't called me in months."

"I know, I'm sorry. I've just been busy with work."

"And with Theo?" Annie said.

Joy was quiet a second. Annie could hear her breathing, and she felt once again like she might cry. "Look, I'm not calling to be a bitch. I just need some idea of what to do."

"About what?"

"I got this letter. My boss, well, his assistant—former assistant—when she was leaving—she gave me this anonymous letter she'd received from another one of Arly's assistants. It accused him of sexual misconduct."

"Oh my god."

"Yeah, I'm really shaken up about it."

"Well, are you going to go to HR?"

"I already did. They're not doing anything. They're useless."

"You should have come to me first. I could have given you at least some pointers on the best way to approach them with this."

"I probably should have."

"No, really, I could have helped. Really, I'm sorry you didn't."

Annie was taken aback by Joy's vigor. It felt nice to feel that directed her way, directed at their friendship.

"So they wouldn't help?" Joy said.

"No, they said because it's anonymous they couldn't do anything. I feel like the only thing I can really do at this point is try to get Erin—that's the assistant who gave me the letter—to come forward. I think something similar happened to her. I think that's why she left, but I'm worried about it. I don't know if it's a good idea to reach out to her when obviously she didn't want to come forward herself."

Annie waited for Joy's response. The seriousness of her, that stoicism—her quiet felt reassuring in and of itself.

"Look," Joy finally said. "Here's my thought: I think there's nothing wrong with approaching her as long as you don't put pressure on her. Maybe she just needs to feel supported and with your support she'll feel comfortable coming forward. Maybe she just needs to feel her personhood is valued."

"But I feel like Erin is a strong person. Wouldn't she already know that it is?"

"I think something you have to remember is that people bring everything with them to work and they try to hold everything away. It's a place where intimacy is not acceptable. No one can be hurt or in pain. But everyone's pain is there all the time. Sometimes you just need acknowledgment, you know, humanity. And that's what HR is, that's what it should be anyway."

Annie had rarely heard Joy speak like this about her work, but she knew Joy was great at her job. Joy had once told Annie how she'd walked someone's paycheck over to their house and left it for them in their mailbox. "It's a week until the holidays. People need money right now," Joy had said. Annie felt entranced by the image of her friend walking herself through the cold. Carrying value straight to someone's door.

"Do you know what he did?" Joy asked.

"My boss?"

"Yeah."

"No."

"Well, fuck him," Joy said.

"Fuck him," Annie said back.

Annie took Joy's advice and got Erin's email address from Beth, who had invited her to the wedding.

"She hasn't RSVP'd," Beth texted after sending the address. "I don't think she's coming."

Annie wrote out a few drafts of the email. She hadn't spent this much time writing something in years, really not since her novel in grad school, to be totally honest. It felt surprisingly natural to think so hard about the ways words could construct meaning. She had worried that she'd forgotten how to do it, how to sculpt layers into as little language as possible, but here it was, still there.

Dear Erin,

I hope you are well. I want to start off by thanking you for giving me the letter regarding Arly's behavior. I am very concerned by it, and I want you to know that I'm doing everything in my power to make sure all the proper action is taken. Unfortunately, HR will not pursue anything unless I have a person who is willing to come forward about their experiences with Arly. I feel very upset by this because I do believe whoever wrote that letter did so in earnest, and I believe you gave me that letter in earnest as well. I would never ask you to do anything you don't feel comfortable doing, but if you feel you can come forward about your own experiences, it would be tremendously helpful in moving this forward. I want our work environment to be safe for all of us, and I'm going to do whatever I can to make that happen. Thank you again for bringing this letter to my attention.

My best,
Annie

She reread it one last time and pressed send.

Two days passed and still there was no response. It was the day of Beth's wedding. Annie had been dreading it for many reasons: she hated Beth, she didn't have a dress she felt like wearing, Jason didn't want to go, she really hated Beth. But more than anything she was jealous as hell. At first she tried to tell herself that the nonengagement didn't bother her that much. She thought she'd moved on. But as time marched forward she felt increasingly bad about things, and anything marriage or wedding related made her so incredibly angry that the best thing she could do was shut herself down and not think about it. She'd even stopped using most of her social media accounts, deleting every app from her phone just to avoid it. Annie didn't consider herself a person who easily unraveled, but when she saw the picture of a perfectly placed diamond on the finger of a hand that was not her own, she was really ready for violence.

But she'd said yes to Beth's wedding months ago, so there was no backing out now. More than anything it was Patrice's insistence that was making her go.

"If you don't go, I will kill you," Patrice said when Annie hinted at possibly backing out at the last minute.

"What if I'm sick?" Annie said.

"Better sick than dead," Patrice said.

Annie wore a light blue dress that she was pretty certain she'd worn to another co-worker's wedding, but it was better than the dress she'd hastily ordered for the occasion, which looked cheaply made and flattened her chest. She also hated her hair. She'd had her hair cut by a new stylist because her stylist was moving to Portugal after her husband got a new job.

"You should go with Glen. He's the most experienced one here," her stylist said before she left.

Annie was instantly sorry she went with Glen. He didn't listen to anything she said, and he made her feel bad about her few gray hairs.

"You should do highlights. It would hide the gray," he said. "It ages you."

Annie felt compelled to give a million reasons why she'd not dyed it yet, but she stopped herself. The man who was getting a cut before her had a bald patch and a receding hairline. Did Glen mention that? Did he say, "You should get a wig so that women still want to sleep with you and don't call you Grandpa"? No, he did not. So she sat there angry for the rest of the cut. And as she watched big chunks of her hair fall to the floor, her reflection looking less like the woman she had been walking in and more like the woman Glen wanted her to be, she felt so angry and so sad that she thought she might cry or scream. But rather than cry or scream or do or say anything expressive, she just sat there. Not only did she sit there, but she also tried to make sure to keep a neutral enough expression on her face so that Glen might not suspect how she was actually feeling. When he finished she said with a smile, "I love it!" Glen would go on in his merry misogynistic way, and she would be left with her hair in shambles. She cried that night and Jason said, "You look beautiful, don't worry." But it was more than the bad haircut. Why had she not said anything? Why did she feel the need to make Glen feel okay about his work? She couldn't shake the experience, and every time she looked in the mirror she saw herself back in the chair fighting tears and forcing a smile. For the wedding she pulled it back in the only braids she knew how to do. It looked pretty bad, but at least it felt more like herself.

Jason was in the worst mood she'd seen him in in a while. He was never great about weddings, but he seemed to be a special kind of miserable that morning.

"Why the hell do we have to go to the wedding of someone you hate?" he'd asked her as she handed him his cuff links, a pair she'd bought for him for a different wedding he hadn't wanted to go to.

"That's just what you do," Annie said.

"No, that's what *you* do."

Beth had asked Patrice and Annie to come join her as she got ready before the ceremony.

"She feels bad she didn't ask us to be bridesmaids, but she already has like seventeen bridesmaids," Patrice said.

"She couldn't possibly think we're close enough to be bridesmaids?" Annie said.

Patrice shrugged. "I just think she likes to feel loved."

When they got to the wedding, Jason stayed in the car.

"You don't have to wait in the car," Annie said.

"I don't want to sit around with a bunch of strangers while you do your dumb girl thing," Jason said. "Text me when you're done."

Patrice and she went up to the suite, where at least two dozen women fawned over Beth, who was standing in a cloud of tulle and sparkle. They stood on the outskirts of the pack waiting for whatever they were supposed to be waiting for. Annie watched as one of Beth's bridesmaids held up a small compact and contoured her nose using some kind of highlighter. Her nose went from normal nose to small bright elfin nose within mere seconds. *What a world this is we all live in,* Annie thought, and she took a swig of champagne.

After a while Beth finally took notice of Annie and Patrice standing uncomfortably to the side.

"Oh my god, hi!!" She ran up and gave them each a hug.

"You look unbelievable," Patrice said. "I cannot believe this dress!"

"Thank you! I can't either honestly."

"Picture perfect," Annie said. She didn't really think so, but it was hard to parse her true assessment of this dress from all the rage-filled jealousy she was feeling.

Beth went back to getting ready, and Patrice and Annie continued to stand there out of place.

"We're early," a bridesmaid said. "The ceremony doesn't start for another half hour."

"Early?" Beth said. "Who is early for their own wedding?"

A few women made jokes about Beth being so punctual.

"You are so lucky, Beth," a bridesmaid said loudly. "I am so tired of being single."

"Luck?" Beth shook her head. "No, I decided it was time and I went on a bunch of terrible dates, and then I met Benny. And I love Benny, but I will say this, was Benny the kind of guy I thought I was going to marry? No. But we work."

"But don't you think it works because you love each other?" another bridesmaid said. "I mean that's the key, isn't it? And that's the luck."

"I know this doesn't fit into the narrative we're all fed, but I think love is a choice. It's about compromising on what you can and can't tolerate in a relationship and making it work. Do I wish I was still single looking for some picture-perfect scenario with Prince Charming? No, I'd much rather be here in this gorgeous dress with you all, marrying a great guy who is here. That's the key, *he's here*."

Annie couldn't believe the Beth she was seeing. The Beth who had spent every waking hour intensifying every moment of her life to make it seem stunning and luminous and so much better than anyone else's was essentially saying, *You should settle because I settled*. Without even thinking, Annie said loudly, "Why?"

Beth turned to Annie. "Why what?"

"Why would we all want to find someone?"

And then all the women looked over at Annie, and she felt the moment very real and vivid, and she was instantly sorry she'd said anything.

"I guess, when you meet the right person, you know," Beth said, and even though that answer didn't make sense in relation to what Annie had asked, all the women, including Annie, nodded and cooed in agreement.

The ceremony was exactly as expected. Beth walked down the aisle after her army of female friends dressed identically in lilac chiffon. Benny acted inappropriately and made a bunch of obtuse jokes that everyone politely indulged. They read each other vows, which included Benny saying, "I promise to let you buy any shoes you want as long as you leave me alone to watch football. Go, Pats," and Beth saying, tearfully, "You are my rock, my dream, my Prince Charming. I love you more than words can possibly express." They kissed a short kiss and danced down the aisle together, which came off as desperate, and so incredibly banal.

The reception area was covered in succulents and mason jars. Across the walls "BB" was projected in a purply glow.

"Yikes, too much Pinterest," Patrice said.

Annie laughed, but she was too preoccupied with Jason to really respond. Usually at weddings or other social events like this, he'd have gotten his mood under control, and no one but she would know how miserable he was. It would be her alone dealing with the trauma during the car ride home. For whatever reason, though, he wasn't keeping it between their couplehood like usual. He sat with his arms crossed the whole ceremony. When they walked over to the reception hall, he walked two paces behind her and Patrice. And worst of all, when Patrice asked him if he wanted a drink, he rudely shook his head and didn't even look in her direction. Annie felt frantic. This was her worst nightmare. She was always worried people might pick up on something, sense a sadness, a tension, or maybe they would just feel some kind of loss that existed with them or with her. Now it wasn't a question of whether or not they'd notice, it was a question of how much they would judge her. And there was no one in her life whose judgment she was more afraid of than Patrice. She could just imagine what Monday would be like.

"Wow, your boyfriend is a cunt," she could hear Patrice say. "Why don't you just dump that loser?"

Something had to be done. They took their seats, and even

though the place card had Jason sitting next to Patrice, Annie insisted on switching.

"Sorry, Jason, I guess I'm the popular one," Patrice said.

Jason said nothing, and it stayed like that for all of dinner. He hardly ate, refused to drink anything but water. He was sulking for the intangible reason Jason sulked. Annie knew better than to ask why. Instead she just laughed a lot and made as many jokes as possible. She told the table an embarrassing story from the summer camp she'd attended as a preteen.

"And I had no idea what that even was!" she said, laughing loudly.

There was dancing, but Jason wouldn't dance so she danced with Patrice and the other group of single women that had formed on the dance floor.

"Jason doesn't dance?" Patrice asked over the booming music.

"He hurt his foot," Annie said, and even though she had worked out what to say ahead of time just in case anyone asked, it still sounded completely made up as she said it.

They ate cake and Patrice asked Jason how work was going. Annie felt like she was going to throw up as Jason slowly answered, "It's pretty good."

Patrice asked him a few more questions before Beth mercifully took the mic to announce the bouquet toss.

Annie didn't want to do it, but Patrice grabbed her hand and they headed over to the small swarm of women. Some were in their early twenties, or possibly late teens, Annie could hardly tell anymore when she saw young people who was young and who was really young. She thought briefly of the teenage girls from Instagram. They were buoyant and happy. She thought of herself and the feeling of stepping out of a bathtub. Her knees, she'd noticed, were looking worse and older and less like she wanted them to with every shower. The bouquet was in the air and some woman, her hand indistinguishable from any other hand reaching upwards, caught it and pulled it down into the mass of the crowd.

"Damn, I thought it was going to be me," Patrice said.

The night was winding down. Annie told Jason they were going. "I just want to go say goodbye to Beth quickly." She made her way over to the corner of the dance floor where Beth stood with Benny by her side chatting with a few people who were likely also leaving. As she got closer she saw Benny lean down and fix the part of Beth's train that had gotten caught on her heel. Something about the tenderness with which he leaned, the gentleness with which he handled Beth's dress—certainly a thing in Beth's life that meant something to her and could not easily be extricated from her dreams for herself—it was so incredibly touching. Annie stopped herself and turned back around. She couldn't face it, and she didn't even try to make excuses about it to herself as to why.

Patrice walked out with them. This time Jason was two paces ahead of them instead of behind. Annie didn't chat or make jokes; she wasn't trying to hide anything anymore. It was too late. She waited for Patrice to make some kind of nasty remark, to say something snarky and true.

As they got to the parking lot, Annie turned to Patrice while Jason kept walking.

"Well, we're just down that way. It was great seeing you—"

Patrice grabbed hold of Annie and pulled her into an embrace. She hugged her and hugged her and hugged her. Annie could feel what it was, and what it was was love.

After a moment the women parted. "Take care of yourself, Annie," Patrice said, looking hard into her eyes. Not too much later Annie would be walking off to catch up with Jason.

When they got in the car there was no question in her mind that she was going to say something.

"What was that?"

"What?" Jason said.

"You were in a horrible mood all night. It was so embarrassing."

"I was miserable."

"You were miserable? *You* were miserable?"

Just then Annie got a push notification on her phone.

"I think Arly should lose his job for all the disgusting things he put me through, but I'm not able to come forward at this time since it would mean I would never work in radio again. I'm sorry to have left all of this on you. I hope you understand."

Annie read it a few times over. She did understand, and she felt like she could cry.

SONG

These days Celine only ever saw Myriel on Instagram. And what an Instagram it was: She was followed by twenty-two thousand people. She was always looking beautiful or was doing beautiful things or was eating something beautiful. Everything was bright and vibrant and healthy. Celine didn't care much for Instagram or social media in general. Even so she had quite a number of followers from the few dozen photos she'd posted. Half of them were selfies she'd taken in the car. Every so often a guy would send her a message, usually saying something to the effect of "You're gorgeous are you single?" Celine responded a few times saying she was not single, but whenever she did, it just led down a rabbit hole, which usually ended in being sent a picture of a penis. She reported it to Instagram once. She even emailed about it. "This guy sent me an unsolicited picture of his genitals," she'd written. They never responded.

She texted Myriel and asked about getting together. It was strange to ask to get together so out of the blue like that, she knew it, but she was hoping Myriel would respond in the warm way she remembered Myriel responding to everything. Luckily she was right. Seconds after she'd hit send she felt her phone buzz beside her.

"HELL YES," Myriel wrote. "When are you free??"

Celine offered to drive out to meet Myriel at her apartment, which was in the most difficult part of the city to get to. Years before Celine would have taken the subway. She used to have patience for long-drawn-out commutes to childish places, but the older she got the more she avoided both childish places and long commutes on public transportation. Really if she'd had more money she thought she'd live in the suburbs at this point. The city had lost so much of its charm. It was dirty, dangerous, exhausting, hard to move around in. She was catcalled so much less in the suburbs too. There were too many young men around in the city. Too many deranged men. Rape felt constant and present. The older she got the less tolerance she had for the violence of men to be seeping in all around her. A friend of hers in college was dating a guy who regularly punched holes in walls.

"He has a bad temper," her friend said.

"How many holes has he punched?" she remembered asking.

"Only two," her friend said.

Only two? Celine thought. Somewhere along the line, her friend had lost sight of what was a normal number of holes to punch, which was zero. Before they graduated he punched a third hole, and now nearly ten years later they were married and had a baby named Fynix.

Celine had bumped into them once at a donut shop. The guy seemed calm, quieter. He was carrying their poorly named baby around his torso in a sling. Her friend looked charmed by all of it. Celine tried not to seem skeptical as they chitchatted and she cooed at the baby. It was not her prerogative to make judgments about the domestic vision before her and what bliss may or may not have been present, but even so, her friend must have worried because only a few hours after they ran into each other, she got a text.

"So nice seeing you today! Can't believe how long it's been! Also, I know Chase was kind of a jerk when you knew him in college, but he's really changed. He never has his outbursts anymore. I just wanted you to know that."

Celine felt sorry for her friend and wrote back a reassuring message. She didn't doubt that Chase was probably calmer now, probably less quick to punch a hole in a wall. In her experience there were many men who matured out of violence, but what she did wonder was what had her friend matured to? Her friend was never punching holes in things. No woman she knew was. They weren't fighting or flexing or posturing. Instead her friend had been cleaning up her boyfriend's messes in college and she was cleaning them up now. It felt unfair and maybe worse than unfair, it felt immobile.

"Thanks so much <3," her friend texted.

Celine sent a smiley face emoji and then added, "Your daughter is beautiful by the way."

To which her friend wrote, "Fynix is a boy but thank you!"

As Celine drove the last few blocks towards Myriel's apartment, she thought about what to expect. She'd run a few imaginary scenarios through her head, thought about how she was going to bring up the video and how she'd felt. Something that bothered her most as she looked back on things was how she had never told Myriel how upset the whole thing had made her. She would think back to that night in Paris when she'd started to but hadn't had the courage and she was hoping that if she could somehow verbalize the trauma to her friend, she'd feel a sense of relief from the whole thing. Maybe it could be the start of fully healing.

In reality her biggest fear about the impending interaction was that Myriel would bring up the matching tattoos they'd gotten one summer. They'd been at the beach all day bonding over a mutual girlfriend who they both hated.

"She's such a bitch," Myriel had said as she turned over onto her stomach to sun her back.

"I hate her," Celine had said.

It was a perfect summer day on so many levels. The weather was gorgeous, they were both nearly naked and feeling young and vibrant. They walked down the boardwalk and got lemon ices together and flirted with two guys who bought them frozen drinks. By nighttime it was still warm so they ate dinner alfresco and they walked the boardwalk once more before heading home.

"Oh my god," Myriel said as they came upon a tattoo shop that was open late, "we should get matching tattoos."

"What?" Celine said. "No way, I don't want a tattoo."

"Why not? We'll get something little. Let's just go look."

They walked around the tattoo shop and Celine felt more and more confident about going along with the whole thing.

"A music note," Myriel said, pointing to a drawing on the wall. "It's supercute. We'll get it on our ankles."

Celine agreed, and not a half hour later, her body was permanently scarred by a music note.

For a long time she didn't mind the tattoo. She loved music and it made her feel sexy and young. Myriel and she bonded over it and they'd put their ankles side by side whenever both their ankles were bare. It was fun. It felt like what Celine imagined having a sister might feel like. As the next couple of years passed, they saw each other less and less and Celine hardly even thought of it in relation to Myriel. It was just her tattoo, present in her life mostly during showers or on the beach or if ever a lover took notice.

And that was the way it was well into her twenties. But then one summer as she spread suntan lotion over her leg Celine realized that she was trying very hard not to look at her tattoo. And when she realized she was doing that, saw how quickly she rubbed the cream over her ankle, blinking a few times to keep the dark shape as undefined as possible, she suddenly allowed herself this truth: *I hate my tattoo.* And relentlessly she had this next thought, *I no longer care about music.* The thought rattled her. Years of her teenagehood and then young adulthood were spent with her heart pressed up to sound. She loved music with so much depth and clarity. Lyrics, all the cute boys from bands she had crushes on, concerts, all of it had felt so intrinsic to who she was and what she thought life was. But she'd gotten older and what she'd thought was so solid, so intrinsic, actually wasn't. She rarely sought out new music anymore and old music she'd once loved no longer pulsated through her in the same way it had. She didn't cry when she heard sad songs. She felt too tired to dance most of the time. On a rare occasion a song would make her feel nostalgic, but it wasn't a good feeling. It made her sad and lonely and there was a sense of loss for something she never knew she'd had enough of to ever know she'd miss it. *If I could tell her she wouldn't believe it,* she thought, remembering herself as a girl, then a young woman, finding meaning in the underbelly of so much sound. Was she happier back then? She wasn't sure, but she was less old, and in so many ways that seemed to be happiness by default. A few months later she'd have the tattoo removed.

She was hoping Myriel wouldn't notice or bring it up. It didn't seem like it would come across as anything but neurotic or somewhat offensive in the context of whatever it was meant to be between them. "I'm just not a tattoo person," she imagined herself saying if Myriel asked. It seemed like the best answer to give, all things considered.

She parked three blocks away from Myriel's apartment. It was in a hip part of the city that was now barely affordable for anyone but rich people. Celine walked fast with her arms folded over her body. She hadn't worn a warm enough coat. A guy who looked to be in his midtwenties stopped dead in his tracks to stare at her as she passed him. It happened a lot, but she would never be used to it. Partly it flattered her. Stopping men statue still, how could that be seen as anything but power, and how could that feel like anything but wonderful? But it did. *Power begets power,* a phrase her mom would say, and sometimes, mercilessly, she'd think, *What if there is no power to begin with? What begets what then?*

She texted Myriel as she got to her building. There was no buzzer. The front door was badly chipped and one of the glass panes was missing, the empty space taped over. She took the minute waiting for Myriel to really look around the street. It looked run-down and raw; someone was throwing an empty flower box away. A homeless man was lumbering down the block with a bag of cans. *So expensive and yet so crappy,* she vaguely thought.

"Babe!" Myriel said as she opened the door. "You look gorgeous!" She hugged Celine hard against her body. The frenzy with which she moved, everything about it seemed to be so much of the woman that Celine had remembered. It was instantly reassuring, hypnotizing almost, but she noticed something in the embrace. The faint smell of cigarettes off Myriel's clothes. *Myriel smokes?* she thought. She'd never known her friend to be a smoker. It was startling and broke her free from her stupor.

"I can't believe how long it's been," Myriel said as she led Celine towards a staircase. "I'm on the third floor."

Celine walked behind Myriel and without meaning to she

noticed how her friend's body had aged. Myriel was a few years older than she was. *Thirty-three? Thirty-four?* She tried to remember as she looked at Myriel's butt move step by step ahead of her. It looked smaller, like it had deflated over the years. *Or maybe it was never as round as I remembered it being?* Celine thought. She wondered what Myriel might think of her butt these days or of the lines etched onto the sides of her eyes whenever she smiled. *We're both* . . . and then she let the thought go before she could finish it.

Myriel opened the door to her apartment. "We're in luck," she said. "My disgusting roommate is gone for the weekend."

The apartment was small. It was much smaller than what would seem reasonable for two people to live in.

"I love your place," Celine said to be polite.

"Yuck, why? I hate it here. I'm trying to get out of the lease, but my roommate is a bitch and won't let me. She goes to law school and thinks she's like Judge Judy or something." Myriel sat down on the couch, which was badly stained almost all over. Celine hesitated before she sat down on some kind of dry white patch.

"Will you stay in this neighborhood?" she asked.

"Oh god no, I'm moving in with my parents after this. I'm sick of begging them for money constantly. I make money on Instagram, but I need to find something more stable."

"Oh wow, that's awesome that you make money from Instagram though." Celine tried to think of what she thought Myriel did for a living. For some reason she'd imagined Myriel had been the facilitator of this beautiful life of hers, with traveling and the very expensive grains and legumes she seemed to be continuously eating, but now, hearing it, of course it made sense that this wasn't the case.

"It's good money for doing nothing, but it's not good

money." Myriel tucked her feet up under herself. The bottoms of them looked dirty, as if she'd been walking around barefoot all day. "And you? Are you still working at that same job?"

"Yeah, pretty much. I've been promoted so that's good."

"That's awesome." It was silent for a moment. Celine was surprised that things weren't easier between them. Their friendship had always felt so breezy.

"Oh wait, I'm so rude, can I get you something to drink? Water, tea?" Myriel got up and started walking to the small kitchen that was pressed into the corner of the living room. "I'd offer you something better, but the only alcohol in the house is my roommate's and she'd have a stroke if I touched any of it."

"No rosé?" Celine said playfully.

"No, I quit drinking. I was having issues with it and my therapist suggested I quit and I pretty much do whatever my therapist tells me." Myriel was fixing tea for both of them even though Celine hadn't asked for it. She carried over two mismatched mugs and plopped them both down on the shaky fiberboard coffee table. Celine's mug had faded little flowers and Myriel's said WHORE BAG in big bold print.

"I like your mug," Celine said as she gingerly picked up the tea.

"Oh yeah," Myriel scoffed. "An ex-boyfriend gave this to me—you didn't know Rivers, right?"

Celine shook her head.

"Yeah, he left it for me after we broke up. It wasn't a joke. He was being a dick." Myriel took a sip of her tea. "I thought it was funny though so I kept it. To be fair, I did cheat on him a lot. I used to do that back then. Cheat on guys all the time."

Celine wasn't sure what to say. "Relationships are complicated," she offered.

"It's not relationships. It's really me. I have a lot of issues with sex. I had a rough childhood, you know? I don't know if I ever told you, but I was abused when I was little, you know, sexually. It's really affected how I've lived my life in a big way. I've just always been messed up with guys because of it."

Celine felt her stomach turn. She wanted to hug Myriel, but then she thought maybe she shouldn't. "I'm so sorry. I had no idea," she said.

"Yeah, well, I didn't used to talk about it hardly at all or ever really. Sorry, I know we haven't talked in forever and this is a lot to dump on you!"

"Oh no, please, don't even worry about that."

"It's just I've found lately that the more I open up to people, you know, good friends, people I love . . ."

The word *love* felt good, like it always did when someone said it towards you, but Celine had a hard time believing that Myriel loved her considering how little they'd spoken in the last few years.

"I'm getting a lot of help now. I am not the girl you used to know, that I can tell you." Myriel laughed a little as she said it, like she was remembering something absurd. She licked her WHORE BAG mug where a drop of tea was dripping down the side. "I was a mess back then," she said.

"You always seemed—to me anyway—like you had it together," Celine said. She probably shouldn't have said that right after Myriel had been so candid, was she really going to argue with her friend about who she was? But Myriel, at least the Myriel of yesteryear, was the most put-together person Celine had ever known. Whenever she thought of effortlessness she'd think of Myriel walking down a city sidewalk in a long red dress with a big summer hat.

"I think I just seemed that way because I was so skinny then, to be totally honest," Myriel said.

Celine took a second and just stared. She wasn't sure what she had expected when she saw her friend. In her mind she'd envisioned a person who hadn't aged and lived life in a full, ephemeral way, but hadn't she just envisioned that off Instagram? She knew Myriel as someone flesh and blood yet here she was at this juncture conjuring up a pixilated vision of her.

"You're still skinny," Celine offered, as a courtesy.

"Ha, tell that to my jeans!" Myriel said. "No, honestly, it wasn't healthy. I was doing a lot of drugs. I hardly ever ate either. I honestly had a borderline eating disorder."

"I'm so sorry," Celine said. "I wish I'd known you were in so much pain back then. I wish I could have been a better friend to you."

"Why?" Myriel said. "I was a horrible friend to you. Do you remember that toothbrushing video?"

Celine felt like every bit of earth and gravity had been ripped from under her.

"I do," she said weakly.

"How fucked up was that? I shouldn't have told you to do that. It was disgusting."

Celine hesitated. She wanted to say what she'd come there to say, but everything felt like it was tumbling around her. The confession she had envisioned, it seemed silly now. Pathetic really.

"Do you know how many of those videos I made?" Myriel asked. "Dozens of them. I felt disgusting after every one of them, but I was never brave enough to tell myself that I felt that way. Bravery, you know, people used to talk about bravery all the time. Do you watch *Game of Thrones*?"

Celine shook her head.

"Well, it's a made-up world, so it's not a good example, but I think our generation never talks about bravery anymore. I was afraid of so many things. That's why I made those videos and had sex with all those guys in bars. I finally stopped when Zee, that was the guy—you know, the guy who I made the tooth-brushing videos for—asked me to do one topless. I actually filmed it and sent it to him. I felt so bad and so sick that I actually threw up all over myself. I called him and begged him not to send it on to whoever he sent those on to, and he told me he wouldn't, but then like ten days later I got a check in the mail, and I know he felt guilty not sending me the check so he did, but it was awful because as soon as I saw it, I knew he'd sent the video on. I cried my eyes out that night." Myriel paused and the two of them sat in silence side by side. "Bravery, man, that's what we need."

"Zee?" Celine said, "Was that his name? I never knew."

"Yeah, Zee. He was a sleazeball."

"Where did you meet him?"

"At some ritzy party. I used to go to them a lot. I thought I was hot shit because men were giving me attention. That's all it took back then. A man would talk to me a little extra, and suddenly I felt like I was somebody. It was pathetic."

Celine thought briefly of herself with Theo. It was hard in that moment to extricate herself and her relationship from the woman that Myriel was talking about.

"Myriel," Celine finally said.

"Yeah?"

"I just want you to know that when I did that video, I also felt—"

"Oh, my, god!!!" Myriel screeched at the absolute top of her lungs. She jumped up onto the couch as she screamed it. "A rat!"

"What??" Celine swung around and there was a big fat rat in Myriel's tiny corner kitchen.

"What do we do?!!" Myriel screamed.

"I don't know! I don't know!" Celine screamed back.

And the two of them stayed there standing on the couch until the rat finally took off and disappeared under the oven.

"Holy fucking shit, I am not sleeping here tonight," Myriel said. And as she slid herself off the couch with her attention fixated on the oven, Celine caught sight of the musical note tattoo on her ankle. It was there plain as day, but the shape was different. It looked like there was script written over the top.

"Your tattoo," Celine said. "You changed it."

"Oh yeah, I did. I was sick of it."

"What does it say?" Celine asked.

"It says, 'I'm a lot like you.' You know, that Neil Young song?"

"Oh nice," Celine said. They were both walking towards the door.

"What about your tattoo?" Myriel asked.

"I got rid of it," Celine said. "I burned it off."

On the car ride home Celine thought of very little. Sometimes detachment and exhaustion could be healthy. But she couldn't shake the feeling of that rat being there. Her skin felt bumpy and knotty, like something would rub up against it at any minute. As she waited at a long stoplight, she looked at her phone. Myriel had posted another Instagram post; this time she was standing in the sunlight blowing a big gum bubble. "#Bubbleyum" she wrote. She looked beautiful, and put together, and sexy, and as skinny as ever. Celine wondered what was really different about her friend. Where bravery ended and starvation began. There were a lot of healthy grain bowls in this woman's life and who was to say what their true meaning was.

As the stoplight turned green, Celine turned on the radio. A song came on that she had loved in college. It was from an indie band she'd seen at an outdoor concert where the moon was big and above her, and she felt young and vibrant as the music in all its glory vibrated through her rib cage. She started singing with all her heart, but when she got to the chorus she had to stop because she was getting the words wrong. She'd remembered the line as *There's nothing I won't do.* She remembered it so strongly and so surely that she sang it like the words were coming from that same gravity that only minutes before had been ripped away from her. But that was not the line, not at all. The line was this: *There's nothing I can do.* And when she realized that was the case, when she realized the difference, she felt herself start to cry. It felt good: moonshine, a tattoo, and a big sun hat that never was.

THREESOME

It had been a few months now, and Joy was busier and more invested in taking care of the household than she'd ever been. She kept on top of the cooking, and the cleaning, and the washing. She'd even put up a small dry-erase board where she wrote daily to-do lists. Theo was home more by himself, but he was also home more with Celine. At first it hurt just as it had the first time and the second time and every time she'd seen Celine by Theo's side, but she worked hard to stop herself from feeling panicked. There wasn't anything she actively did in her mind, no saying she said to herself, or promise she made. It was slower and more methodical than that. Like turning a gauge or pulling a needle through a soft fabric. Preciously and precisely she put up the barriers necessary to lie to the most vulnerable places of herself. *Joy,* she would say, *you're fine*. And just like that, she was cooking dinners for Celine too.

Oddly it was when Theo was not home that she felt the best about their relationship. Cleaning up for him, prepping for meals, there was a sense of accomplishment in every little challenge. She loved the feeling of herself moving around their space together. She was folding *their* laundry and scrubbing *their* toilet, and chopping *their* broccoli. She knew all the cracks and crevices. She knew where the faucet dripped below the sink and which window was warped shut. Her body and mind could feel calm as she felt a palm on a cool doorknob or a bare foot push off a newly vacuumed rug.

Over time, Theo had asked her to do more and more of his room. It started with Joy offering to clean his windows or dust behind his dresser.

"I'm doing the dusting anyway," she'd say.

He'd pause and then cautiously relent. "Okay, sure, thanks, Joy."

Then one day he asked her to organize his closet. He'd been hanging out in her room and he saw her beautifully stacked closet, which she'd recently organized, and he said, "Wow, what I wouldn't give to have my closet look like that." And then he paused and said, "Joy, would you consider helping me organize my closet?" And after a few days the whole thing evolved into her just doing it on her own because it would be faster if she just did it on her own, or at least that's how Joy justified it to herself in the convoluted mess of logic that brought her to folding his socks in neat little squares. Soon after that, his entire room was as much a part of her cleaning routine as her own room had been, and it was because of this that she found the porn.

Joy never snooped through Theo's things. She had all kinds of very strong belief systems based on the idea that women had no right to go through men's belongings, or text messages, or even the pictures on their phones.

"I think trust is key," she'd said to a friend in college who had asked for advice on the matter.

"But I know his passwords and he's cheated on me before," her friend had said.

And Joy, with stoicism and firm resolve, said, "I still think trust is key."

And so it was not Joy clicking through the history on Theo's laptop, not at first anyway. At first it was just a DVD that she'd found in a box of old sneakers.

Three Is More Fun! it said on the cover with a picture of a few porned-up women bending over and making salacious faces. Her stomach jumped. She felt like she was both seeing something she shouldn't and also seeing something he shouldn't be doing. It was rooted somewhere in jealousy, although it wasn't exactly that; it was a feeling any girlfriend might feel if she stumbled on a boyfriend's porn, but she wasn't his girlfriend so she quickly sifted through that reaction, and her next reaction was to laugh. It was silly. The women, the DVD, the ridiculous description: "Hot threesomes of horny sluts who are ready and can't get enough." She took the DVD and tucked it back in the box where she found it.

Days passed, but she kept thinking about it. It wasn't so much that she was bothered as it was that she was curious. In so many ways this was as close to his sexuality as she'd ever gotten. What she couldn't understand was why he had a DVD. Most men watched porn online for free. Who would bother buying something like that? She slowly and meticulously began convincing herself that the DVD must have been given to him as a joke. A gag at a bachelor party, a goofy friend from college who thought he was clever, maybe his younger brother who was pursuing stand-up comedy. She told herself that she was telling herself this not because she was bothered by him watching porn, but because it had to be true. *No one would hang on to a DVD like that,* she'd think as she'd watch him pour cereal in a bowl or as she'd load his wet sheets into the dryer.

A few weeks later she was cleaning his room again and noticed he'd left his computer out on his bed. The screen saver was still on, bright lights that changed into geometric shapes. She felt a thud and a thump in her chest as she had the impulse. It wasn't so much that she was curious about his habits, it was more that she wanted to prove to herself that the DVD had been a gift. This was how she'd splice and dice the whole thing through her mind. *It's not about the porn,* she'd tell herself as she sat down and went to search his history. At first there was not much. After all, most people, and likely Theo, would be sure to search with a private browser. She scrolled a few months' worth and then went to the search bar. "Threesome" she typed out.

Six links came up. All from Pornhub. Her heart pounded hard again. She knew better than to click the links though. Instead, she grabbed a Post-it that was sitting on the desk and manually jotted down all six URLs. Her hand hurt as she got to the last couple of links. She hadn't thought of it, but she hadn't written in free hand like that in years. Really high school was the last time she'd taken notes by hand, maybe once or twice in college. Her handwriting was looking sloppy and a lot like how she remembered her mom's handwriting looking. For whatever reason that thought made her sad. It was the same feeling as looking in the mirror and realizing your face was aging into your mother's. It wasn't so much that she didn't want to look like her mom as it was the realization of how she was little more than some genes stranded together. Her mom likely looked like her grandmother and her grandmother likely looked like her mom before her too. *And here I am thinking I'm someone special,* she thought as she tucked the Post-it away. *Really I'm some woman somewhere who is long dead.*

She quickly finished up in Theo's room while the links burned brightly in her pocket. She didn't need to finish cleaning first. He certainly wouldn't have cared, or noticed for that matter, but her thinking was the same as it had been when she told herself she was looking through his internet history to prove the DVD was a joke. She twisted and turned and groomed her own mind so she could cower and hide herself away from herself. It felt easier to say, *You are not excited to look at what he looked at. You are not already gone.*

Joy went back to her room and sat at her desk with her laptop open. It didn't feel quite right though, and so she took it and went to her bed. Joy had never in her life watched porn. She knew that was strange, but something about it really bothered her. She found it disturbing and inescapably exploitive.

"I can't believe you've never watched porn," a friend from college had said to her once when she mentioned it.

"Why?" Joy asked.

"You've never even seen it at all? Aren't you curious? I mean even if you don't want to watch it, aren't you at least curious about it?"

"I mean . . ." Joy tried to choose her words in a way that wouldn't sound judgmental because really that's not what it was. "I just find that people say prostitution is bad, but then with porn they're okay with it, and I don't understand that."

"I don't. I think all of it's fine," her friend said.

"But is it healthy?" Joy said. "Can you honestly say it is healthy for the people doing it?"

And to that her friend paused. She blinked hard as sunshine fell on her face from a nearby window. "I don't know," she said. But Joy felt like she did know.

Despite her convictions, Joy didn't begrudge people watching porn. It seemed that even if a person could not argue that something was moral, it didn't mean that it wouldn't still happen. To Joy it seemed naïve to expect morality to factor into everything that human beings took part in. So, she gave people a pass and hoped for something better in the next world or the next life or whatever it was that kept humanity marching forward into darkness. But for herself, in her own quiet space, she just didn't care to watch it, and so it was a big deal to type out each letter and number of that Pornhub link. It meant something as little as it meant anything.

The first link was a threesome at a doctor's office.

The next was a threesome with two cheerleaders and their coach.

Then some kind of dungeon house.

A beach.

Another doctor's office.

And then some kind of scenario that Joy couldn't quite figure out, something to do with a landlord maybe?

She didn't watch each one more than a few seconds, but it was clear that the consistent thread through all of them was that they were all threesomes. It was disappointing because now it felt like that DVD wasn't a joke and even though the significance that could be drawn from the DVD being real or a joke was at this point nearly impossible to untangle from all the convoluted thinking that it had taken to get her to this point, Joy did not feel satisfied. She got up and walked back to his room and opened his computer's search history again. This time she searched every sexual word she could think of besides "threesome," but nothing came up.

Her heart went thud and thump in her chest again. But now it was at something else. Theo took on a new dimension in her mind, and she felt completely distant from it and from herself. It was glaringly obvious how she was not a part of his sexuality on any level. She was just a pathetic roommate with a crush. Tears welled up in her eyes and she went to go shut his computer but stopped herself. She paused a moment and went up to the search icon in the corner of the screen.

"Joy" she typed out.

A few things came up that were unrelated, but then there was this: a photo album. "Joy and Me" it was called, and she clicked through each photo with absolute ruthless wonder. There were many silly selfies the two of them had taken and a few pictures she remembered he'd snapped of her as they goofed off when they'd badly burned a homemade pizza. Then there was this, a picture of her standing at the sink and looking out their kitchen window. Her face looked calm and happy. Her expression longing, as if she were seeing something exciting and far away. Theo had filtered it in black and white with deep shadows and bright whites. It was one of the best pictures of herself she'd ever seen. But here is where it was, here is what mattered, he'd captioned it with this: "Joy looking like joy <3"

It wasn't healthy, but she couldn't help but feel bliss. Not everything is moral.

BOSSED

Annie had resolved that the only thing left to do was to talk to Kathy about Arly. It was Kathy's show, and at the end of the day no matter how big a fixture Arly was to the network or to anyone who had fawned over him, Kathy was the one who would be able to put a stop to things, to change course, to say *no*.

Annie had had only one conversation with Kathy that wasn't 100 percent related to the show and 100 percent necessary. They'd been in the elevator together. Kathy had sunglasses on and what looked like a very expensive coat.

After giving each other a small smile and nod, it was silent for three floors' worth of time. Annie felt sick over it. She felt like she should say something or make some attempt to break the silence between them, and yet, it never felt right to talk to Kathy. She talked to you. You didn't talk to her. And so she just stood there searching for an answer to the rhetorical question that was this woman's presence. Finally moments before their floor, Kathy said, "Cold out today." And Annie responded, "It's freezing." And that was it. The most personal and intimate exchange they had ever had.

It wouldn't be easy to walk into that room and stand in front of that woman and call out the only person that Annie was directly connected to who was also directly connected to Kathy. Arly was that thread, and Annie wondered where it would leave her if she severed it. But as scared as Annie was, she also wasn't scared. Her mom used to say, "Bad women run, good women fight." As a child, she'd imagined the bad women would look like witches. Big long faces, distorted by evil. Now she knew bad women looked like anyone.

She'd emailed Kathy's assistant to set up the meeting. She figured it would be a few days until Kathy would have time to sit down with her, but surprisingly her assistant emailed that she had time the next day. Annie wasn't entirely sure what she was going to say in the meeting, but she knew Kathy as a smart, and very aware, woman. Just a few months before she'd interviewed a congressman and grilled him sharply about recent sexual misconduct allegations.

"But what is in it for these accusers to come forward?" Kathy had said as the congressman stumbled over his response. It felt like if anyone would hear her and get it, it would be Kathy.

The door to Kathy's office was open and Annie hesitated in the doorway wondering how to get Kathy's attention, but luckily Kathy saw her and waved her in.

"Annie, hi, come on in," she said.

The office, unlike Arly's, was very neat and chic. Everything had its rightful place and was set up with purpose. The only personal artifact was a framed photo of Kathy's granddaughter smiling a wide smile as she ate a slice of cantaloupe.

"Take a seat," Kathy said. Kathy herself was standing and moving some papers around. "I was just—" she said and then picked up a paper and read it for a moment. She didn't finish her thought, but it felt intentional, as if she was too busy to even finish a thought. "Hmm," she said in response to what she read.

She put the paper down and took a seat opposite Annie. She smiled and looked up, finally meeting Annie's stare.

"What can I do?" Kathy said.

"Yeah, umm . . ." Annie's mind was racing. "First of all, thanks, for meeting with me so soon."

"Of course," Kathy said.

"Well, I wanted to meet with you because I received a letter that was, umm, very concerning to me. It appears to have been written by one of Arly's former assistants, although it does not indicate who, but, in it, this person accused Arly of sexual misconduct."

Kathy raised her eyebrows ever so slightly and that, as little of a change in expression as it was, felt incredibly reassuring to Annie. Kathy typically bore no expression at all, so this felt like the green light.

"I went to HR first of course, but unfortunately because the accusation was made anonymously, nothing could be done. My hands feel very tied, and yet, I just feel that whoever wrote this letter did so in earnest, and I don't feel it would be right of me not to come forward and do everything in my power to be sure that this matter is handled properly, and that these claims are given the proper attention." Annie took a deep breath. She felt like she had been clear and forceful in how she worded it. She felt like she was doing everything right.

Kathy took a second. She too took a breath. "Have you ever known Arly to act inappropriately? I mean, firsthand?" she asked.

"No, not firsthand."

"And has he ever acted inappropriately with you?"

"No, I honestly have only had good experiences with Arly," Annie said.

Kathy nodded. "I've only had good experiences as well. Arly has only ever been kind, thoughtful, brilliant."

Annie felt the word *brilliant*. It felt brittle. It hit hard.

"I think whoever wrote this letter and whoever gave it to you is mistaken," Kathy said.

"You do?"

"I do. People get angry when certain job prospects don't work out. They act vengeful."

Annie felt like her insides had tightened. She looked down at the picture of Kathy's granddaughter and thought about rape.

"I don't think you're right," she said. "I think he did it."

Kathy stared at her, gobsmacked. Annie didn't care. Something about everything had reached a tipping point. She didn't feel scared. There was a child eating cantaloupe beside her framed on a desk. Who would stand up for her? It wasn't going to be this bad woman.

"I don't have any other evidence to prove it's true, but we know he loses assistants left and right. The person who gave me this letter wanted me to protect her anonymity, so I will, but I believe she was hurt by him as well, and I don't think whoever wrote this letter did so because a job prospect didn't work out, I actually think she wrote this letter for one reason and one reason only, and that was to protect other women. She said she went to HR and nothing happened, and I believe her about that because nothing happened when I went to HR either. And now I'm here with you, and it's looking like you're going to protect Arly instead of women."

"I understand your frustration, but I can only go off of the facts I know and the facts I know are twenty-plus years of working with Arly," Kathy said. She had regained control of her face and no longer looked gobsmacked.

Annie thought about the feeling of jumping off a swing as a child, or the chill of an ice cube in her hand. Sometimes life felt like many things at once and there didn't seem to be a way up or down or in or out. A person could feel completely stagnant. They could feel like they had roots that ripped through the earth, leaving them tied to the place they were growing out of. Suddenly Kathy seemed very real all at once to Annie. She looked at a wrinkle that went from Kathy's nose to her mouth. Annie had no such wrinkle yet, but she would one day. Life was arbitrary like that. Lines would emerge on your face to show the world that your body was dying away. It was used up, old. Annie wondered what difference there was between death and watching other women's bodies be misused by men. And then she knew what to do.

"You're making a mistake, Kathy," Annie said, and she turned and left the room without bothering to look back.

Now she was walking to Arly's office. Now she was at his door. It was open just a bit, and she knocked, but didn't wait for him to say it was okay to come in. It was all one fluid motion, moving her body from the hallway into his office with the sound of her knuckles as a small hollow scream in the middle of it. An interlude between where she had been and where she was going.

"Arly," Annie said.

"Annie, hi, what can I do for you?" Arly said. He looked surprised but warm.

"I want to let you know that I'm quitting this job. I'm leaving right now." Annie took a breath. It would feel like the deepest breath of her life. Oxygen all over, into her brain, where so much had to happen to keep her alive and so much more had to happen to keep her kind. "I want you to know that I know what you do to women. I *know* what you do."

Arly's face turned bright red, but he didn't say anything. If

Annie hadn't been so ready to leave, so rolled up in the moment and her rage, she might have seen this man, who she knew to be a demigod, totally and utterly disarmed by her. She turned to leave, but as she got to the door she stopped and said this: "I can't do anything to stop you. I tried. If there is anything inside of you that is decent, you'll treat every person like a person." And then she added, "Humanity, I hope you know it."

Annie was packing up her desk. No one was around. There was the big weekly meeting. A meeting she'd never missed in all her time at the station. She once sat through it with pneumonia. She once sat through it minutes after she'd heard her grandmother died. Now all of it seemed silly. Success and what she had envisioned for herself, it was as paper-thin as much as it was anything. *Real success is being brave,* she thought as she tucked away the picture of Jason holding Simon that she kept on her desk. Despite herself, she felt like she was going to cry.

As she walked down the hallway, Reid was walking opposite her. He was running late to the meeting, as was often the case. He stopped dead as he saw her carrying the box of her desk packed away.

"What's going on?" he said. "You're not leaving, are you?"

She didn't answer but shrugged as she kept walking.

"You're leaving," he said. His voice cracked as he said it.

She kept walking and passed by him.

"Annie," he called after her.

Annie stopped and turned around.

Reid was standing there. His face, his body. He looked like himself in the way she knew him to be, as little as she did know him.

"Yes," she said.

"I just want you to know that . . . I'm not a bad man," he said.

And even though she didn't really know, she answered back, "I know you're not."

It felt good. It felt human.

MIRRORED

Celine took up yoga. She'd been meaning to for a long time. It was the thing she turned to whenever she felt like she ought to make a change. *I should take a yoga class,* she'd think whenever she felt in a funk or had the false impression that she'd gained weight.

She liked it more than she thought she would, and with absentminded intensity she found herself taking classes multiple times a week. Part of it had been a distraction from every horrible thought that had occurred to her the last few months as she'd confronted herself about the toothbrushing video, and part of it was that she wanted to have an excuse to get away from Theo.

She cared about Theo, he was her boyfriend after all, and they spent a lot of time together, but the boredom she'd felt those first few dates had not subsided and now was not so much boredom anymore but detachment. Not every time they were together but most of the time, she felt herself feeling more and more distant from not only him but also herself.

"I can't eat okra," he'd say as they sat at dinner.

"Let's go for a day trip somewhere fun," he'd say as they lay in bed.

"I love you," he'd say many times in many places.

And every time she'd feel like she was floating, empty, lonely. It was draining, but she felt more than anything immobilized by it.

Her fourth week of yoga Celine left work early so she could take a four o'clock class rather than the six o'clock she usually did. The truth was she did feel a little under the weather and had plans to go home after yoga and cuddle up and watch bad TV with a bowl of mac and cheese. It was such a motivating thought, and she was so preoccupied by it, that she nearly missed seeing him when she walked into the room. He was far off in the corner. A blur nearly, his body, his hair, his skin, the tangled way he moved. She was instantly shocked by him, rattled by his presence, and yet moments after the shock, seconds really, she felt surprised at how disappointing he seemed. *Derk!* she thought, and then, *Derk?*

She situated herself a few rows behind him so she'd be out of his line of sight.

Class began and she followed closely and with attentiveness to the instructor as she usually did, but she also followed closely with attentiveness to Derk fumbling through the movements. He seemed shorter and skinnier than she'd remembered him. His skin looked less bright and vibrant too, which really she just attributed to him aging. She'd made it a point to unfollow all of his social media accounts, so she'd really not kept up with where he was or what he was doing. It was hard to picture him having his life together in any capacity as he slipped on the mat or his knee shook during downward dog. She could make out the shape of his testicles through his thin exercise shorts as he leaned over, and it was gross. How that part of his anatomy had ever been near her face she really wasn't sure. He was just an aging man trying very poorly to do yoga, and as soon as she had that realization, she knew she was no longer in love with him. And then she had this thought, *Was it ever really love or was it wanting to be wanted by someone who was so impossibly difficult?*

Class came to an end, and she made a point of walking up to him. In the past she might have skirted out the side of the room to avoid having an uncomfortable conversation, but she felt refreshed. She felt miles away from the girl who had once stayed up till 4:00 A.M. waiting for his text message.

"Derk," she called out.

He turned around. He looked puzzled, and then instantly he looked overwhelmed at the sight of her.

"Celine, hi."

They came together for a distant embrace. His back was sweaty and cold.

"You look, amazing," he said.

She smiled. "How are you?"

"I'm good. I'm good." He folded his arms and began to sway in place. "I'm still, you know, doing the whole project manager thing."

Celine watched his mouth move as he talked. She remembered how he wouldn't go down on her and said she had to "wax first."

"That's great," she said. "Sounds like things are good."

"Oh yeah, and I'm living downtown now, which I love."

She thought of the time he'd left her waiting for him in a downpour. He'd been two hours late and hadn't texted.

"That's great," she said.

"How are you doing?" he asked, and all she could think of was herself back then and the feeling of wishing with her whole heart for this man to wrap himself up in her as much as she was wrapping herself up in him. Standing there now she felt alive, and powerful, and sexy. She would have at one time mistaken that for happiness. Now she saw herself mirrored through him and he was an image of her insides, what she would settle for, how little she thought she deserved. *I don't love you,* she thought. *I never did.*

"I'm good," she said to him. "I'm happy."

After that she headed home. She got in her car and felt good driving and felt good when she unlocked her front door and felt good as she jumped in the shower and let her hair fill with water. There was peace in feeling like she didn't love him and never had. On some level it felt like triumph. But then she opened an email from one of the grad school programs she'd applied to and read the rejection, "We're sorry, but we're not able to offer you a place at this time." She thought, *Have I ever loved any man?* And then even more mercilessly, *Has any man ever loved me? Is that love? Is that really love?* Her hand shook and she mindlessly grabbed a pen that was lying on her desk, and she started scribbling on a notepad. First a heart, then a star—it was a nervous habit of hers to draw the same few things. She drew an eye, then a flower, but when she went to draw a house, she could not remember how to draw a cube and the feeling of that—*trapped,* she thought. She opened her phone and looked at a picture of herself in a bikini from five years before. She looked thinner to herself. Really she looked like a child. *So many people wanted to sleep with me back when I looked like a child.* She felt like she might crawl right out of her own body and climb back in time to another place, *another person,* she thought.

Just then she got a text from Theo: "Pizza night with me and Joy?" She thought of herself staying home with mac and cheese, her rejection letter, and the house she couldn't draw, and suddenly it seemed less like what she wanted. Her life may have been split open, mirrored back, but the heart wants what the heart wants and what she wanted was to be with her boyfriend.

Celine had sunk her hands into the mess, squeezed it through her fingers, and felt every gory part of her insides slip through her palms, and here she was not too much later, reaching for something else, something stupid.

"I'll be there," she texted back.

That night Joy would hand her a slice of pizza and they'd talk about work, something they talked about more than most other things. Theo was in the kitchen getting another beer for himself. Celine thought about mentioning Derk. She even brought up her yoga class once or twice, but she couldn't bring herself to say anything. Instead, Joy told her a story about her friend Annie and a boss that was harassing women at work. Celine listened and thought about many things. Herself mostly. Places she'd been and men in her life who had either been there in a big way or merely brushed up against her in one way or another, a catcall, a hand on her lower back, an invitation to a wildly inappropriate date.

"Hellscape," Celine said as Joy got to the end of the story. And then added, "And you know it makes me think of that line in *Lolita* where she says something like 'The thing about dying is, you do it alone.' I love that line."

"Why do you love that line?" Theo asked as he came back in the room.

"Because it's true," Celine said, but she wished that she didn't have to answer him at all. She wished he knew what she was saying without her having to explain it. *Loneliness,* she thought. *It's more than that, but it's that too.*

BODY

When Celine sat opposite Joy and chewed a piece of pizza, Joy was mostly amazed at the way in which Celine was able to cross her legs. Her leg didn't just cross over her knee, she was able to tuck her ankle behind her other ankle. It was a double crossing of sorts. Joy certainly could not double-cross her legs. She was able to cross one leg over the top of the other, but even that leg was still sticking up some. It didn't lie flat, and it certainly didn't lie flat enough that she could tuck it behind her other ankle. Joy couldn't keep her eyes off Celine sitting there like that. Many times she had obsessed about Celine's body in relation to her own, but this was different. It was the first time she fully considered the implications of her body and what it meant for her life. Of course she'd always thought about pretty and not pretty and how someone as gorgeous as Celine lived differently than she did, but this was outside of pretty. This was about the way her body swerved and folded and lumped and lay. It was about its limitations in how she moved or slept or even breathed. *Maybe,* she thought, *I would be a totally different person if I was able to cross my legs twice.*

Three nights later Joy had a dream about her stomach talking to her.

"You're a dumb whore," her stomach said.

"No, I'm not," she said.

"Yes, you are. I want pizza."

"I can't give you pizza, it's the middle of the night."

"Who are all these cunty friends of yours?"

"What friends?"

"All of them. Why are they here?"

"Do you mean Celine?"

"Who is Celine?"

"She's Theo's girlfriend."

"Who is Theo?"

"Theo is Theo, you know Theo."

"No, I don't. I'm hungry."

"You just ate. You're always eating."

"You're always starving me, you whore."

"Please stop."

"One day I'm going to eat you too."

"You already do. My whole life is ruled by you."

"Your life is ruled by nothing."

"What does that mean?"

"Please feed me."

"If I feed you then what? When will it end?"

"That's right, when?"

"What does that mean?"

"You're a whore."

"Stop it!"

"Pizza."

And then she woke up. She thought about it for a second and in the light of day it seemed funny and absurd. She brushed it off and didn't think of it again all day, but the next night she had the same dream.

"Why do you wear Spanx?" her stomach said.

"Because I can never look thin in dresses without them. You're too big."

"It hurts me, you cunt."

"What the hell, don't say that."

"Why not?"

"It's a horrible word."

"What does it mean?"

"Vagina."

"What's so horrible about that?"

"I don't want to *just* be a vagina."

"Nobody thinks that about you. You wish someone would."

And then she woke up.

The next night and the next night she had that same dream.

"What about law school?" her stomach said.

"Law school?"

"Didn't you want to go to law school at one time? What is stopping you?"

"I did, but I no longer want to. I like my job."

"It's not about that."

"What's it about?"

"Please, stop wearing jeans. They hurt me."

She tried to ignore it, figuring the dreams would surely stop at some point. But weeks went by and they kept coming.

"He doesn't love you," her stomach said.

"Stop."

"He doesn't love you."

"I'm serious, stop it!"

"I love you and you treat me like this. I'm your body."

"Please stop! Please!"

"He's the reason you hate me, and he doesn't love you."

Every night she had so much anxiety about the nightmares that she didn't want to go to bed. She'd stay up late, sometimes drinking wine, hoping it would put her into a deeper sleep. She even took an over-the-counter sleeping pill. It worked briefly. A few nights passed where she didn't have the dreams, but as soon as she'd stop drinking, or not take a pill, the nightmares would come back, each time more vicious than the last. She googled "recurring dreams" but nothing helpful came up. Then out of desperation, she googled "dreams about talking stomachs."

"Whale Dreams and What They Mean" was the most relevant result.

"Whale dreams are sacred and shouldn't be feared," the blog post said. "They mean you aren't afraid to go after your wildest dreams."

I think I need therapy, Joy thought.

The nightmares were the start of it, but two more things happened that led to her writing the email.

She and Theo were getting ready for work in the morning. She'd made homemade blueberry muffins the night before, so they were having those muffins. Theo was talking, but Joy was distracted, thinking about the sugar glaze and how she didn't think it was quite right. She pushed the chewed muffin through her mouth and as she scooped a piece of wedged muffin out of her molar with the tip of her tongue she heard Theo say,

". . . when Celine and I move in together."

"What?" she said. She probably looked more alarmed than she would have liked to. "You're moving in together?"

"No, I mean we don't have any plans to yet or anything," Theo said. "But, you know, it's where things are going."

Where things are going. The words seemed so powerful to her little life. Where were things going for her? She was sitting around worried about sugar glaze.

"Don't worry though," Theo added. "I would give you plenty of notice so you could find another roommate."

The next thing happened that weekend. Usually Saturdays Theo was out with Celine, but apparently she was sick or had yoga or something. Joy had planned on going out and running some errands, but when she saw that Theo was staying home, she decided to hang out for a bit. They sat in the living room talking about high school in a vague way. Joy rarely thought about high school anymore. She had thought about it all the time when she was in college, and now that college was over, she found herself thinking about college all the time. *What will I think about after this?* she thought. *Sitting in the apartment and paying my cellphone bill?*

"Were you popular in high school?" Theo asked.

"Are you kidding?" Joy said. "Have you met me?"

Theo laughed. "Well, it's rude to assume."

"I bet you were popular," Joy said.

"Nah. I mean, I had a few popular friends and kind of bounced around groups, but I wasn't actually one of the popular kids."

"Well, I didn't bounce around groups, that's for sure. I had my three good girlfriends, and let me tell you we were wild. We once got frozen yogurt *twice* in one night!"

Theo laughed. "Hey, I wasn't going to a bunch of ragers myself. I collected coins in my spare time. That's not a lie. I had a lot of coins."

"You know what I hated about high school?" Joy said. "How everyone greeted each other by saying, 'What's up?' I never had, nor will ever have, a good answer to that question."

"You're just supposed to say 'Nothing.'"

"I know, but it's stupid," Joy said.

"I hated how much hugging there was."

"What do you mean?"

"Everyone in the halls, everywhere, we were constantly hugging each other hello."

"I literally don't know what you're talking about."

"The girls would usually do it. I think it made them feel good to have the guys give them attention like that or something."

"That sounds like something popular kids would do. Nerds don't hug hello."

"It was always this kind of hug where, like, you'd hug the person low down."

"Hug the person low down?"

"Stand up, I'll show you."

Joy stood up and Theo walked over. He draped his arms around her waist. She was nestled into his body. It was, by its very nature, an incredibly intimate hug even without any connotation Joy might have given to it in the context of her life and love.

"Isn't this, like, way too much to say hello with? I mean, who does that? I think it was a way to feel grown-up even though no adult would ever hug like this."

He let go and she was left just standing there. She felt dizzy. Her body felt like it was wavering. She felt like if she took a step forward she might shatter.

That night she'd lie in bed and think about the feeling of this man that she loved draped around her. A few hours later she'd be asleep and talking to her stomach as it chastised her. In the morning she'd wake up and think of what Theo had said about moving out and living with Celine. Celine's body would come to mind. The way she could double-cross her legs and absolutely everything else she would and could do that Joy could not. Joy was a flicker and Celine was the flame. Joy was an afterthought and Celine was the epiphany. Everywhere and everyone in the lives of these two women would look at their bodies and decide so many things about them, and on top of it, one woman would fold her legs over and over while the other would not.

Jenny Craig, maybe? every day, all day really, and so here is the email Joy sent Theo at 3:00 A.M. two nights after the hug.

> "Hey, this may sound crazy but have you and Celine ever wanted to explore having a threesome? It's been something I've been thinking of a lot lately. I think it could be fun. Think on it and let me know.—Joy"

Most important of all is this: Joy did not want to have a threesome.

PART SIX

ANNIE AND JOY

It was Annie's birthday and Joy was meeting her for dinner. Annie had asked her explicitly about going out for dinner because Jason was away on a work trip and she didn't want to be alone on her birthday.

"You don't want to go to your parents'?" Joy had asked.

"No," Annie said. "My mom won't understand that Jason had to work. She'd complain about it all night."

Joy did not understand why Jason had to work either. He was never good in general on Annie's birthday, but couldn't he have asked to skip this trip? Sometimes a person has to do things for work and sometimes a person doesn't *have* to so much as chooses not to bother making sure their girlfriend isn't alone on her birthday. Joy feared with Jason it was the latter. What she was sure of was that Annie was sad and hurt and of course angry, and Joy was not looking forward to dinner with her. On top of it she'd been a nervous wreck ever since she sent that threesome email to Theo. The second she sent it she regretted it. She spent two hours afterwards googling how to delete a sent email, but there was absolutely nothing she could do apart from sneak into his room and delete the email from his computer, which of course was impossible (though she seriously considered it). She did not sleep for one second that night. Not one second was her mind quiet enough to allow her respite from herself and the depths of her own terror. Despite it—the terror, the fear, the restlessness—there was an ever so slight part of her that was looking forward to what Theo would do. It was the first time she'd ever indicated to him that their relationship move in any direction that wasn't entirely platonic. She couldn't help but feel an inherent thrill about that. But unfortunately, the very next day Theo left to go visit his parents in South Carolina, a trip she'd known about for nearly two months, had marked on her calendar, and had written on her dry-erase board. And yet, as she sat there writing that absolutely deranged email, she had totally forgotten about. Luckily he'd be home tonight. They'd texted a little while he was away, but she figured this wasn't the kind of conversation he would address in text. Needless to say, that didn't stop her from checking her phone and her email eight thousand times a day. Basically what it came down to was, on the drive over to meet Annie, Joy was about as frenzied as she'd ever been.

Annie was pissed. It wasn't because of work. Work she felt good about. She thought she might feel scared or sad about quitting, but really she had felt such resolve over her decision.

"I just couldn't live with myself if I stayed," she'd emailed to Patrice.

"You're my hero," Patrice emailed back.

What she was pissed about was Jason. She'd known about the work trip for a while now and Jason had offered, "We'll celebrate the weekend after." But when she woke up the morning of her birthday to nothing—no card, no flowers, certainly no gift—she felt a long sense of emptiness. Her mom had called her first thing and had sent her a gift the week before, a new jewelry box with a bracelet inside that had her name engraved on it. It made her happy, but it also made her sad. Was her mom the only one who really loved her? Her mom gave her Christmas gifts and birthday gifts. Of course they were from both her and her dad, but it was her mom who lovingly picked everything out. It was her mom who wanted her to feel special and loved and to give her memories and physical things to remember those memories by. Jason never gave gifts. Early in their relationship he'd gone off about how he found holidays overcommercialized, and so he would just give her a card here or there or some odd joke gift that he found ironic or funny. She'd told herself she was okay with that, holiday after holiday, year after year, but when she woke up alone that morning, she didn't feel as complacent about living a life free of commercialization. Freedom and money seemed tied together, and so she texted Joy about meeting up for dinner. It felt pathetic considering how little time they'd spent together lately. Their friendship now was the rare text here or there, but of all her friends, Joy was the only one she knew who wouldn't judge her neediness, and so as angry as she was, as exhausted as she felt, she was grateful and happy and could not wait to see her dear Joy.

Joy had been waiting for Annie for fifteen minutes, but she wasn't surprised, because Annie was typically always late. She was actually glad to some degree, because the wait gave her a little more time to obsess and check her email fourteen times. When Annie finally did get there, Joy was in the middle of re-

reading her threesome email and cringing to herself. *What the hell is wrong with you, Joy?* she thought, and then she saw Annie winding her way past table after table to get to her.

"Hey!" Joy said, standing up. "Happy birthday!"

The women embraced before Annie sat down. "Thanks. And thanks for meeting me on such short notice."

Annie seemed sad to her.

"Of course!" Joy said, and then offered again, "Happy birthday," not sure what else to say.

Annie smiled slightly in response. "Did you order anything? I need a drink."

"No, I was waiting for you. I didn't know if you wanted to get a bottle of wine. Or champagne maybe?"

"Let's do cocktails," Annie said. "I need something overpriced and fruity."

They ordered drinks and a few appetizers. Annie seemed restless as she talked about jobs she was applying for. Joy was listening, but she kept her phone in her lap in case Theo texted. He'd said Celine was going to pick him up at the airport, but she vaguely hoped that wouldn't work out, and he'd be asking her for a ride instead. It was complex and absurd and stupidly hopeful, but she was clinging to it tight as she bit into a jalapeño popper and listened to Annie say "good health insurance" and "401(k)."

Annie was trying not to be miserable. She was trying not to think of Jason not being there or how she'd felt so alone that morning waking up to the dry sound of an empty home. She was trying not to think of herself as pathetic and alone, but most of all, she was trying not to think of the fact that Joy was not paying attention to anything she was saying and it was pissing her off. Finally, as she watched her friend check her phone under the table for the tenth time, she'd had enough of it.

"What are you doing?" she said.

"Oh, nothing, sorry."

"Who are you texting?"

"No one."

"Theo."

"No, not Theo." Joy sounded defensive already, which further pissed Annie off.

"I know it's Theo."

"Well, who cares if it is?"

"No one. I don't care if you text Theo, I just wondered why you're so distracted."

"I'm sorry. He's just getting home from a big trip visiting his parents, and I made him lasagna this afternoon, and I just wanted to be sure he knows how to heat it up."

"What?" Annie tried to pull apart each one of the words that Joy was saying. "You made him lasagna? But I called you this morning. Didn't you know you wouldn't be home to eat with him?"

"Oh, I did. I just made it for him because I knew he'd probably be starving when he got off the plane."

"So you're cooking food for your roommate in case he's hungry and, what, can't feed himself?"

"I was just trying to do something considerate for him."

Annie looked hard at Joy. Her face looked vacant in a way it hadn't in all the time she'd known her. Annie had been annoyed by but tolerant of Joy's love for Theo for a long time, but here now, with Joy sitting with a cellphone in hand talking about lasagna, she could see it was more. She could see it for what it was, and what it was was vile.

"You are being considerate of *him*? Joy, he should be considerate of *you*," Annie said. "He is *using* you."

Joy sat back in her seat still clutching her phone. She shook her head. "No."

"Yes," Annie said. "This whole thing is out of hand. You're in love with him and he knows it."

Joy's face grew red with embarrassment. "Annie." She shook her head again.

"No, he does. He knows you're in love with him. Believe me, he knows. And he's just living there with you getting all of this stuff out of you, the cooking, the cleaning, the nice home, the companionship—a wife, that's what he's getting, a wife—meanwhile he's sleeping with someone else and getting a girlfriend on the side. And what do you get? You get *nothing*."

"That's not true," Joy said.

"Then tell me what you get."

"I get him," Joy stammered. "I get a life together with him."

"Joy." Annie sat up and leaned in close to her friend. "Do you hear yourself? Do you even hear yourself? You get *him*? You deserve more than him. You deserve all of it: love, sex, a person who doesn't use you for his own disgusting selfishness; you certainly deserve respect. You deserve to be happy."

Joy shook her head again. "You don't know what's going on."

"I know exactly what's going on. You don't have any self-esteem. You are accepting this garbage because you don't believe you deserve better. But guess what?" She leaned in even closer. "You do."

"I have self-esteem," Joy protested.

"Then, why, tell me, why on earth are you doing this? Do you hope that he's magically going to start being your boyfriend? You know what, even if that would happen, it would be bad. You deserve better than Theo. You deserve someone who would never ever think of using you for even one second. You deserve someone who would take one look at you and know that they can't live without you, not some guy who is dicking you around while he's sleeping with Beyoncé."

"You don't get it."

"Oh no, I do get it. You're hurting yourself for some stupid useless man. You're afraid to speak up for yourself and say what you want. You're acting desperate and pathetic." Annie paused as she tried to find the right words. "You're acting like you are worth less than he is," she said.

"Well, well, what about you?"

"What about me?"

"Jason."

Annie pulled herself back.

"What about Jason?"

"Why isn't he here on your birthday?" Joy asked.

"He had to work."

"Did he?"

"Yes, he did."

There was more resolve in her voice, but Joy could still see the fear in Annie's eyes. Normally Joy would have backed down, but the hurt she'd felt at what Annie had said was flipping her insides. She was reaching out now, grabbing for more hurt in the room. And of course she knew Annie had plenty to give.

"He couldn't have done this trip some other time? He couldn't have made sure you weren't alone on your birthday?"

Annie was quiet for a second. "What's your point?"

"He does this stuff all the time."

"Wow, so all of a sudden you don't like Jason? And you waited till now to tell me?"

"It's not about Jason. It's about you. You're not happy."

"What are you talking about? I'm absolutely happy." Annie grabbed hold of her drink and shakily took a sip.

"I just want you to have what you want."

"And what does that mean exactly?"

"You're afraid to tell Jason what you want. You're afraid to ask anything of him because you're so afraid to lose him, and I can't believe, Annie, that you're afraid of anything. You're the bravest person I know."

Annie just looked at her.

"I don't want to live in a world where you're afraid. What kind of an awful world is that?" Joy said.

Annie shook her head.

"You found out about your boss and you did everything you could to do the right thing. You fought for this woman you didn't even know and now you're just letting yourself, you're letting yourself be treated, just terribly. It doesn't make sense to me. It doesn't make sense to who you are."

"It's not the same," Annie said.

"It is the same and you know it is." Joy took a breath in. "You deserve better than to be with someone who hurts you all the time."

"He doesn't hurt me all the time," Annie said.

"Then why are you so mad?"

The two women stared at each other in silence for a second. Their eyes were the same then, cold, lonely, angry, devastated. Somewhere far away in there were both of their mothers and somewhere even further was every other woman who sat silently staring at her own reflection. Suddenly Annie got up.

"You know what?" she said. "I don't need this. It's my birthday and I'm leaving."

She tossed a twenty-dollar bill onto the table and walked off. Joy stood up and thought to go after her, but instead, as she watched Annie moving farther and farther away, she called out to her:

"Annie!"

Annie was already by the door. One more step and she would have been outside. She stopped and turned around. Joy was back at the table, still standing. The restaurant was loud and busy in the stretch that separated them. They met each other's stares and then Joy said as loud as she could so that Annie would hear:

"He isn't kind."

There was electricity in the space between them, though silent and distant. A rumble, a friendship, love.

Annie turned and left. Joy watched her go.

JOYOUS

Joy went off birth control. She'd started to notice pain in her left breast months before, and although her gynecologist assured her it could not under any circumstance be the result of the hormones she'd been on since she was thirteen years old, Joy insisted.

"Are you sure?" her doctor said. "It's hard for your body to adjust to going on and off hormones like that."

"I'm sure," Joy said. But what she was thinking was *Who is to say I will ever go back on?*

After Joy left the dinner with Annie, she was in too much of a frenzy to get home in time to see Theo to seriously consider anything Annie had said. She still felt angry and hurt. Little phrases from the night would sail through her mind; *sleeping with Beyoncé* was on repeat, but really she kept her focus on Theo and what he would say about the email. *Just get home,* she told herself. *Just get home.*

But when she got home Theo was already there. He was standing at the kitchen counter eating the lasagna cold, straight out of the tray.

"You're home," Joy said. "I thought your flight didn't get in till eleven."

"No, sorry. Nine-thirty. I was confused."

"Oh, okay," Joy said. She didn't feel as nervous as she'd thought she would. Maybe she was already too drained from the fight with Annie.

"How's the lasagna?"

"Delicious," Theo said. "I don't know how you do it."

She searched his face for any signs of her email and the weight it bore, but he seemed like he did any other night. It was that same Theo she'd seen a million times by now.

"It would be better if you heated it up," she offered.

"No, it's great like this," Theo said.

"How was your trip?" Joy asked. It was the best thing she could think to say that might somehow segue into things.

"Great, great weather too."

"And your parents? They're good?"

"Yeah, they're great. Same as ever."

After that she watched him chew some more lasagna before giving up for the night. *He's probably just tired,* she thought. *He'll bring it up tomorrow.*

But tomorrow came and he was the same. The next day came too and the day after that. Every time she saw him she expected he would say something. She'd feel herself nervous with anticipation, but then nothing would happen. It was just like any other day. Slowly she convinced herself that somehow he'd not seen the email. But as soon as she had the chance to sneak in and check his laptop she did, and saw that he had opened it. *You read it,* she thought whenever she'd see him after that. *You did read it.*

And once she realized this, everything Annie had said to her that night as they ripped each other apart stood out to her. Now *sleeping with Beyoncé* didn't make her sad, it made her angry. And so when the doctor said, "It's hard for your body to adjust to going on and off of hormones like that," she knew that sex and love, whatever it might be, was the last thing she gave a damn about. Her breast hurt. Her body was talking, and as things stood, she was going to listen.

This was the point when many things would come together for Joy. Only days, maybe hours really, of her cycle not being suppressed, her sense of smell changed. She'd be able to smell lemons more strongly, if she smelled lemons, and flowers would smell sweeter and more raw, but she didn't smell lemons and she didn't smell flowers, what she did smell was Theo, and suddenly that small shift in her hormones changed the way she pulled in his pheromones, and, very quickly, he seemed less attractive to her. He'd peel an orange or open a door, and she would see his body and his face, and rather than be delighted, she felt disgusted. The stories he told about work or his friends or what he thought about the world no longer seemed charming or entertaining but rambling and self-obsessed.

"I think air-conditioning is overrated," she'd hear him say, and she'd think, *Overrated? Takes one to know one, Theo.*

But the pheromones were only part of it. Joy could not let herself think her way around the reality that with that frantic, desperate, pathetic 3:00 A.M. email, Theo had to have *seen* her. He had to have *seen* her need, her love, at least some of her suffering. No person who was decent would have read that and ignored it. No person would have continued on with the dinners and the cookies, and the laundry. He was allowing things to be the same because he was *using her.* Joy said it over and over again to herself in her head. *Using you,* she'd think as he ate the last bagel or neglected to wipe his toothpaste smear out of the bathroom sink. *Using you,* she'd think as she lay in bed and felt her mind fall on the tender moments between them, of which there were many. *Using you,* she'd think as he dared breathe beside her all the while knowing that she had offered her body up like that to him because she was so hopeful that somehow, some way, his favor would fall on her and a fantasy that she'd built, and he'd kept, would come true.

Joy knew it was over. Now she just needed a plan.

Thursday was movie night. "What's for dinner?" Theo said. "Are we doing pizza or do you want to cook something?"

"I'm not hungry," she answered. "I'm going to bed, actually."

"What's wrong? Don't you feel good?" he said.

"I'm just tired," Joy said, which was a simple way of putting it. Theo stood there a little longer, but soon he left for his room and she left for hers. The second she shut the door behind herself, she ordered a pizza for delivery. She wasn't worried about the doorbell ringing and Theo coming out and seeing her take a whole pizza to her room to eat by herself just after she'd told him she was not interested in sharing it with him. She felt calm and she didn't care. Theo didn't come out of his room when the pizza arrived though, and she took it easily and happily to her room, where she ate slice after slice while looking up apartments.

The truth was that she could not afford to get her own apartment. The smart thing would have been to move out and find another situation with roommates, but she wasn't going to do that. She needed to be on her own. She needed her own space. And so, she was reckless. She applied for a small loan. It would get her enough to put the money down for a deposit, and after that, she'd be able to swing rent. She wrote it all out: rent, student loans, food. There would be no savings or extra money, but there really wasn't much of that now anyway. She had to have faith in her life working out somehow. She had to jump blindly into everything she couldn't see.

That weekend she looked at three apartments and found one that was sunny and had a small wood-burning stove. The bed was pressed up next to the kitchen, and it was no home someone wading into their thirties would be proud of in any context, but Joy was not in any context, she was in her own. And so she felt proud when she filled out that application. And she felt proud when she signed for that loan. *Twenty-two point three percent interest, freedom isn't cheap,* she'd think as her hand spelled, in swooping letters, J-O-Y.

Now it was time to give notice. She had worked out what she was going to say to Theo. "I just need a change" was the phrase she'd clung to when she imagined he'd look at her the way she knew he would look at her when she told him. It was morning. The first of the month. She hadn't felt nervous as she went to bed the night before or woke up that morning. Even as she saw him in the kitchen pouring himself a bowl of cereal.

"Theo," she said.

"Yes, Joyous," he said as he swung around.

And that was it really, *Joyous,* and she could feel the weight in her heart. Every little thread she'd tied together was unraveling at breakneck speed.

"I, I, I," she stammered, "I have to tell you something."

"What?" Theo said.

"I, I'm, I'm, I'm giving you my notice. I'm, I'm moving out."

"What are you talking about?"

"I'm, I'm, I'm, I need a change."

"What?"

"No, I—" Joy didn't think and she didn't search herself or stop herself. She was there with her body and her mind and every little bit of her life and she said: "I can't live here anymore because I'm in love with you, and I don't think it's healthy for me to be around you. And I know you saw that email I wrote. And I know you probably don't know why I wrote that email—I didn't really want a threesome with you and Celine. Obviously that would have been a very bad idea for me—and I think what it was was that I felt really desperate for you to be affectionate with me in the way that I felt like I needed, and I couldn't think of any other way of having that happen. I'm very mad at myself for sending that. And I'm very mad at myself that I've not had the strength to tell you that this, all of it, it's been hurting me, and so I'm moving out, which is something I should have done a long time ago."

Joy took a large breath in and let it sit inside her body before she finally exhaled.

"I don't know what to say." Theo leaned against the counter with his hands reaching back to support himself. Joy paid close attention to the way his fingertips lightened as he gripped tight. Her mind felt empty then, flushed.

"Why, why didn't you tell me?" he asked her.

"Which part?"

"Well, I mean all of it really."

"I guess, I was afraid."

"Of me?"

"Of losing you. Of losing this whole thing." She motioned broadly to their little kitchen. A pile of dishes was behind him. Beside her a cup half full of coffee that was growing cold. It was Theo's, though it could have just as easily been hers. Their intimacy seemed ever-present in the kitchen. *Or is that just what I want to feel?* Joy thought. She tried to think of intimacy in its most literal sense, and she couldn't help but feel foolish the second she did.

"I should get going. I just wanted to give you notice as soon as I could," she said.

"Wait, can we talk about this?"

"Talk about what?"

"You leaving. I'm shocked."

"That's the shocking part? I just told you I loved you." Joy felt oddly calm. As soon as the words had left her mouth and every moment after that, it was like something was slowly leaving her body. She may have felt too exhausted by all of it to feel powerful, but really that's what it was.

"That too." Theo looked away. Joy thought he looked both younger and older then. A strange division of being thirty-something. It was vexing and maybe a little boring? She tried to find clarity, but she kept her stare focused on his face so long that she wasn't sure what it was.

"Well," she finally said. "What do you think about it?"

"I don't know what to think. I'm—I guess, I'm . . ."

"You must have known I felt something for you?"

"I wouldn't say I knew." He started shaking his leg a little as he spoke. "I mean, I thought you and I had—have—a good thing going. We're . . . best friends."

"Friends? Is that what this was?"

"I mean, isn't that what it was?"

"Not for me."

It was quiet for a moment. The apartment hummed the low sound it always did. Its insides hard at work to keep itself a home.

"Theo," she finally said. Not because she was calling him or expecting anything from him, but because she felt like saying his name out loud.

He looked over at her.

"I do love you, Joy. I do."

She felt the word singularly and true. It was warm and cool

all at once. More than exhilaration though, she felt a sense of relief. *I know that,* she thought.

"But . . . that's where it ends, isn't it?" she asked him.

Joy saw tears in Theo's eyes. "I don't want you to leave. Please don't leave."

"I can't think of even one reason to stay," she said. She could feel herself start to cry too.

Theo took a step forward like he might have gone to hug her. But she didn't feel like being hugged and as if he sensed that he stopped himself.

"And my email? You ignored it."

"I didn't know what to say . . ."

But she didn't feel like that was true at all.

"I felt humiliated." She stopped crying.

"I'm sorry," he said.

"You aren't really though," she said, and she knew those words were true, at least to the extent that it mattered.

"Please let's just talk this through. You don't have to move out at all. You don't."

But Joy was no longer listening. She just wanted to leave, to take her body as far away from his as she could. Suddenly she felt protective of herself, a feeling that felt so new and strange that it was almost startling. And yet she thought if he walked over to her and kissed her she'd want that as well.

"I need to go," Joy said. And that's exactly what she did.

Theo would text her at work. She'd read the messages and text back, but days later she'd start packing and weeks later she'd be moving her life out of their little home. A coffee cup they'd shared, a lamp they'd bought together, things that would lose their meaning as soon as she moved them to a space that was her own.

BRIDE

It was a Friday. All day long Simon wasn't himself. He didn't eat breakfast and he didn't lie in the sunshine like he usually did in the mornings. Around noon Annie tried giving him some of his favorite cat treats, but he wouldn't come out from under the bed.

"I think Simon is sick. I'm really worried," she texted Jason.

"It's probably nothing," Jason texted back.

She called the vet and the vet said to wait and keep an eye on him. She tried to busy herself the rest of the afternoon. At four-thirty she had a phone screening for a job.

"And it looks like you have an MFA," she could hear the man interviewing say. "That's great. I'm a former film major myself."

All that time Simon stayed in the same spot under the bed. Finally just after five, she heard him meowing loudly. She ran over to find him throwing up. When she looked close she could see there was blood in his vomit.

She grabbed the cat carrier and texted Jason.

"I'm taking Simon in to the emergency vet. He threw up blood."

Simon meowed the whole way in the car. They weren't normal meows; they were low and guttural. Annie felt herself start to panic. She wanted to cry, but instead she just sang the little song she always sang to him. "You're my love, my angel, my boy." She'd made it up when she first adopted him, and she'd sung it to him the whole car ride home after they'd had to have his eye removed. Since then she always worried about his health more than she had with any other pet she'd ever had. Something about him had always seemed fragile.

There were a lot of people in the waiting room at the vet's, which meant they likely had a long wait ahead. The lady at the desk took her name and wrote down "Stomach problems," which annoyed Annie because it certainly didn't characterize the severity of the situation.

"What do I do if he throws up blood again?" she asked, hoping to impress upon the woman how bad things were.

"Definitely let us know," the woman said.

Annie took a seat with Simon in the far corner of the waiting area. A dog with a limp was being walked by. Just in front of her was a woman with another cat carrier. Annie took out her phone. Nothing back from Jason yet, but she figured he might be driving. A TV was silently playing *Sleeping Beauty* in the background. Annie couldn't remember the last time she'd seen the movie, but she remembered the song from it vividly. *I know you. I walked with you once upon a dream.* The lyrics moved through her mind and seconds later they'd replay themselves. Simon had quieted down. She stuck a finger through the door of his carrier and tried to scratch his nose, but he was just out of reach.

"It's okay, buddy," she said to him quietly.

A half an hour passed. She texted Joy, and she texted her mom. Her mom called her, and they spoke briefly.

"Please, keep me posted," her mom said.

Joy sent a dozen or so very concerned texts. She loved Simon, but the truth was that even if she hadn't known him, she likely would have sent that many texts. Joy was good like that. They hadn't talked much since the fight. The day after, they'd both sent apology texts, but Annie knew they were both still angry and sad and reeling from that night. Now though they just went back and forth about Simon. *That's what love is,* Annie thought as she briefly put her hand over her heart.

Jason still hadn't texted and Annie began to worry. She called him, but he didn't answer. Twenty minutes later she got the text: "On my way home."

"Could you meet me at the vet's? I'm really scared," she texted.

It wasn't often that Annie asked for something from Jason like this. In fact she tried to think of another text that was this expressive and nothing came to mind. Sure Jason would be supportive if she had a bad day or was mad about something at work or was frustrated by a friend, but she'd never had to ask him outright to go somewhere, do something, make any bit of real effort. It struck her then how strange that was. She felt in so many ways like she was living with the least trustworthy person in her life.

"I'm really tired," Jason texted back. "Are you guys finishing up?"

"No, he hasn't even been seen yet," Annie wrote. She could feel her anger rise as she punched out the words "It's a long wait, and I don't want to be alone."

"Ok," he texted back.

Another half hour passed and finally Jason came in the door. He scanned the waiting room looking for them. She waved a big wave so that he would see her, which was unnecessary, but she couldn't help it. She was really glad he'd turned up. He walked over and sat beside them.

"Hi," she said. "Thanks for coming."

"It's fine," Jason said. "How's he doing?"

"I don't know. I think he's okay right now, but it was so scary when I saw all that blood. I've never seen an animal throw up blood at all. I was freaking out."

Jason nodded. "I hope the vet sees him soon."

Even though he was answering her, and even though he'd shown up for her, Annie could see that Jason was in a bad mood. No one else in the room would probably be able to tell, maybe no one who even knew him, but she could see it. She could see it in his eyes, in his hands, in the way he moved an eyebrow and the angle he leaned back in his seat. She knew his body so well. She knew his heart in some ways better than she knew her own. *Is that love?* she wondered as she watched a silent princess prick her finger on the spindle of a spinning wheel.

Finally a technician called out, "Simon."

Annie got up and grabbed the carrier.

"I'll wait out here," Jason said.

"Are you sure?" Annie asked.

He shrugged and followed dutifully behind.

The vet examined Simon and listened to all the details Annie gave. She was quiet and meditative and took her time. Annie searched the woman's face for answers about how serious this was, but there was nothing. Finally the vet said, contemplatively, "I want to do an ultrasound. I think this could be a blockage or possibly some kind of growth."

Annie's heart beat hard at each word. None of that sounded good. None of that sounded hopeful. *Simon,* she thought. Her hands reached forward, but she wasn't sure to what.

"Of course," she said. "Whatever you think he needs."

They went back out to the waiting room without Simon.

"Poor Simon," Jason said. "How much do you think this will all cost?"

The question bothered Annie. For one, the last thing she wanted to think about was where in the hell she was going to get the money for this. She had about four hundred dollars to her name at the moment. But more important, why on earth did Jason act like he gave a damn about the cost? He wasn't going to offer to pay. This she felt like she could bet her life on. For a second she thought about sitting across the room from him rather than beside him. *Maybe he wouldn't even notice I was gone,* she thought.

They sat there for a while in silence. Annie thought to call her mom again but decided to wait. She kept thinking back to her mom on the phone the day that Simon lost his eye.

"They have to take his eye," Annie had said.

"They do?" her mom had said, but the way she said it was with so much mourning and sadness. It tapped into Annie's own pain, as if between them ran that same long stitch of misery and hopelessness.

"Stop, Mom!" Annie had said. She was trying to keep herself from crying or screaming. Really more than anything she was wishing that her cat, who was, in many ways, her dearest friend, didn't have to face loss, didn't have to live with trauma. "He'll be fine," Annie said to her mom. "It's nothing to freak out about."

Annie felt this was what her mom should have been saying to her instead of that concerned "They do?" Her mom was supposed to be her sanctuary, but Annie had noticed the older she'd gotten, the less she could depend on her mom to ease the blows of pain in her life. Very often she was left with the thought that *if my mom is scared, then what hope is there?*

"Can I go to the car?" Jason asked.

Annie snapped her head around to look at him. She knew he was miserable, but she figured he'd at least stay and wait with her.

"I'm tired. I'd like to take a nap," he said.

At first Annie tried to think of what to say that would make him stay. Normally, she would have thought of a perfectly crafted response that would be distant enough so she wouldn't seem needy while still hopefully achieving whatever desired goal she had. But this time she didn't want to do that. She searched herself for the willpower, but the willpower wasn't there. Instead there was something else, a flicker, a spark.

"I think," she said, "you should do whatever you *want* to do." She didn't say it with anger or frustration. She didn't even sound sad or disappointed. She meant it as clear as day.

Jason paused. She looked at his eyes, which were bright and the same as they ever were. "Okay, I'll just take a quick nap and be back. Wake me up if you need me." He got up and walked out the door and that was that.

At first Annie felt an urge to run after him. *Tell me you care about me!* she'd scream. But something weighed her down. The panic, the emptiness, it wasn't enough to get her to change course. That flicker, that spark was still there. *He didn't want to sit here with you, Annie,* she thought. *He didn't.*

Just then she heard the door open again and then the jingle of a collar, the lumbering movements of a dog, manic panting. Then she heard "Oh hell no," and she instantly recognized the voice. It was Benny. Beth was beside him. They were walking a large yellow Lab over to the receptionist.

"Annie!" Beth caught sight of her right away and waved. Not too much later they were both sitting beside her.

"This is Duke," Benny said. "He's Duke of our house. That's for sure." He was leaned over, scratching Duke's chest.

"Is he okay?" Annie asked.

"He was just neutered, and he looked like he was getting really irritated near his sutures so we thought to bring him in," Beth said.

"Ball issues," Benny said. "Or lack thereof."

Annie laughed politely. They all talked like that for a half hour before Benny decided to take Duke outside.

When he was gone Beth swung around to face Annie.

"We got the dog because I can't get pregnant," she said. "We started trying before the wedding. It's been almost a year now."

"What?" Annie was completely taken aback. Beth had never been so forthright about anything like this.

"Sorry, I just got my period today, so I'm just really feeling it. I already cried twice," Beth said. Her face looked panicked. She looked around the room as if Benny would magically appear and continue on in his oblivious obnoxiousness. "Nobody knows we've been trying to get pregnant. I haven't even told my mom, and thank god I didn't because I can't imagine how depressing it would be each month having to be, like, 'Nope, not this month.'" Beth reached up and tucked the hair behind her ears. She looked like she hadn't washed it in a while. Usually her hair was perfect, silky, fluffy, doll-like. "I thought it would happen right away. I thought as long as you had sex the day you were supposed to that, that was it. But that's not it. It's much harder than that."

"It is?" Annie said. Her whole life people had told her to do everything in her power to prevent accidental pregnancy. The sudden terror in Beth's face as she was telling her otherwise was jarring.

"I've wanted to be a mother more than anything else in my life ever."

"I'm sure you'll be a mother," Annie said.

"Are you sure? Because I've had sex while I was ovulating a million times now. All that money I wasted on birth control for years. I always thought that it would just happen for me, but it's not like that. It's like magic. You need luck. I've never been lucky, Annie."

Annie didn't know what to say. Somewhere close by Simon's stomach was on a screen. Somewhere close by Jason was asleep.

"Do you want children?" Beth asked her.

"Well . . . I—" Annie had never been asked this before by anyone. It was strange to think of, but either people assumed she did want children (like her parents) or they never cared enough what she wanted to ask. She tried to remember if maybe Joy had ever said something to her, but nothing was coming to mind. "I do want children," Annie said.

"Then do it now," Beth said. "Don't wait. I hope you're lucky. Luckier than me."

Right then Benny came back, loud and insufferable, with Duke dragging him through the waiting area. Not too much later the vet would call them in and Annie would be sitting alone again, waiting for whatever was going to happen to her.

She felt dizzy, pinpricked. She couldn't help but think hard about what Beth had just said and the terror in her eyes. Annie had never seen someone look quite like that. Like something precious had been ripped away from them, something irrecoverable and sacred. Annie hadn't thought about how children factored into her life with Jason. She knew she wanted them and Jason had once or twice said he wanted them too, but when he would come around to being ready she had absolutely no idea. She was thirty-one now. In the back of her mind she'd always thought she had time, but did she? What if Beth was right and it wasn't easy? And then she had this thought: *Even if it is easier than Beth said, when is it that I want children?* Me, *what do* I *want?* And really when she thought of that, she knew the answer was if she had her way she'd already be married and trying.

She looked back up at the TV. The movie was over and the credits were silently rolling. She'd missed Sleeping Beauty waking up. Somewhere she could hear a cat was meowing loudly. She was pretty certain it wasn't Simon, but it was still unnerving. Annie stood up and went to get a drink from the watercooler even though she wasn't thirsty. When she sat back down she took out her phone and thumbed through her email. Then she took in a deep breath and then she took another sip of water. The movie had started up again. It was on a loop. The meowing was louder than it had been before. *Don't,* she thought to herself, but it was no use. Unrelentingly, she couldn't stop thinking about her imaginary baby. And really here was where so much came together for Annie. There was that spark from before, those burning embers, Beth's terror, and then Joy standing in the restaurant calling out to her, "He isn't kind." She envisioned a child growing up with Jason's mood swings and his selfishness and what would that child's life be? *What would that do to my baby's heart?* she thought. And then as quickly as she'd thought about her baby, she thought about herself. *And my heart? What has this all done to my heart?* She could argue to herself so much about Jason and love and every bit of him that she carried around and felt close to, but that word, *kind,* she could not think her way around that. Jason was not kind. He wouldn't be kind to their baby. And he wasn't kind to her.

She thought about her mother waiting on her father. She thought about Beth tolerating Benny. She thought about Joy baking for Theo. Then that woman from the letter. And she thought about herself, her pathetic self, being hurt over and over by the person who should be hurting her the least. Who should be hurting her never at all.

Her hands were shaking, her breath was catching, but when she carried Simon out to the car, she'd wake Jason up with a hard thud against the window.

"Get up," she'd say. "I'm going home."

EXALTED

When Theo told Celine about the email he was laughing. It was a Saturday afternoon. He had been gone visiting his parents and this had been the first day they'd spent together in a while. They were lying on his bed. Celine was eating dried mango slices. She'd just taken a bite of something bitter when he first said it.

"So I got quite the interesting email from Joy."

"An email?" She couldn't have begun to guess what a roommate would email to another roommate.

"Yeah." Theo laughed. "She offered to have a threesome with us."

"What?" Celine sat up. She tried to picture Joy as she was. Celine liked Joy. She thought she was pretty and smart. At this point they'd spent a good deal of time together, but oddly she didn't feel she knew her well. Whenever she was around her, Celine felt as if Joy was holding in a breath.

"She did," Theo said. "It was bizarre."

"Where is it?" Celine asked. "I want to read it."

Theo pulled it up on his phone. Celine followed each word

carefully. The tone, the way it came together, it was very intimate, unlike anything she associated with Joy.

"Well," Celine said. "What did you say?"

"I didn't say anything," Theo said.

"What do you mean?"

"I thought it would be awkward if I said anything so I didn't."

"Doesn't that make it even more awkward?"

"No, I don't think so."

"How has she acted?"

"The same, I guess."

"I literally am in shock. Aren't you in shock?"

Theo shrugged. Celine watched that shrug and the solid way his jaw moved as he took a breath in. *And what do I know of him really?* she thought. In the same way that the email had unearthed Joy to her as intimate, she felt suddenly aware that any person, a stranger, a lover, anyone at all, could be turned over, pulled apart, set upright and suddenly they'd be someone different. And so, she said this:

"Would you ever want to have sex with Joy?"

And Theo, with the indifference of a person who brushes a fallen leaf off their shoulder said, "No," and then, mercilessly, "She's ugly."

Celine's initial reaction was happiness. *Good, I'm prettier* was the vague thought behind it. Being prettiest. Being desired. Her childhood, her life, the world that ticked in her ears and under her feet all wanted that from her and for her. It was as much a part of her as the folds of her hands or the smooth turn of an artery. But when she had that thought, when she felt that good, rather than pocket that self-worth and move on with herself, as she had countless times in her life, she felt the slice, the sting, really the horror of what it all was. *No,* she thought. *No.* And this too she knew, Theo was lying. Maybe not about wanting to sleep with Joy—she didn't think he wanted a threesome with her—but his indifference was not honest. He and Joy were at the very least friends, and reading that email, it was hard for Celine not to feel there was something more. She'd only once suspected that Joy had a crush on Theo. It had been late at night and Theo had left his jacket on the chair by the front door rather than hang it on a hook. Celine had woken up to use the bathroom and as she made her way down the hall, she saw Joy was still awake and heading for bed, but as she walked past the chair she picked up his jacket and hung it on a hook. That was it. Nothing remarkable in the way she was moving or acting, just as there was nothing remarkable in the way Celine was moving or acting. Just two women awake in the night in the same home maneuvering around this man's space and this man's stuff. *She's in love with him,* Celine had thought. But she shook the thought away and by the next morning she'd virtually forgotten it. Celine had always taken note of how well Joy and Theo got along, but now she could see it was more and his brutality became clear. *Threesome,* she thought, and then, *Theo, I'm going to break up with you.*

And for a moment it felt impossible that she'd ever felt like she needed a man, needed love to buoy herself. For a moment she thought of everything in her life as her own and of her doing. *I'm proud,* she thought. *I'm worthy,* she thought. Joy had been coming all along. Joy was here.

PART SEVEN

CELINE

At first it felt great breaking up with Theo. I felt excited. Empowered even. I was relieved that things were over. But the next morning when I woke up and didn't get that "good morning" text I felt, well, I felt empty, and scared. All day I'd check my phone hoping he'd reach out. And he did, he texted "thinking of you" at around 3:00 P.M., and when I got that text, I felt completely elated. I felt wanted, or maybe it isn't just wanted, maybe it's needed too, and I hope it's loved, but I'm not sure that it is. But it *is* wanted. That's why I was with Theo, that's why just a few days later I was on a dating app hoping to meet someone else. I can see the problem, I can touch, and feel, and know the problem, but it's one thing to know the problem and it's another to fix it. It's been so long of this. My whole life really. When I was twelve years old hoping for a boy to choose me, when I was fighting for the love of a horrible man, when I stood in that bathroom making that video even. It was there. Always, it was there. And I know now that it's ruined my life. That's a strong word, *ruined*. People don't like to say it because people like to feel hope, but this feeling of needing men to approve of me, it's ruined my life so far. I want it to stop because I can see myself just hurting myself like this over and over. I don't want to feel happier than he feels by the idea of saying "I love you" or getting an apartment together or marriage. One time I went to a wedding and the bride, when she walked down the aisle, tears were streaming down her face. She looked beautiful and she looked so in love, and I looked at him and he looked happy of course, but it wasn't the same. She was living big and full because of the wedding, and he probably didn't need to feel big and full because of a wedding or because of her. He probably already felt big and full just by being who he was. And who am I when I'm alone? I couldn't begin to explain it to myself because I know that I feel the most powerful when I have a man standing at my side, and I know that's true for a lot of women. Actually, I haven't met one straight woman yet who hasn't gotten self-worth from having a man in her life. It's true. I've tried hard to think of it, but even my mom, I know she's the same. It makes me so angry and scared, and I feel empty too. But at least now I see it, and at least now I'm not with anyone, and I've started therapy. I need it to come to terms with my feelings about the video, and I'm hopeful I'll get more out of it than just that. I'm hoping one day soon I won't search for someone for any reason different than the reason he searches for me.

"Boundaries," I told my therapist. "I'm trying to define mine."

And I'll say this too, yesterday I went to my mom's house. I went in her closet. I used to spend so much time there so I knew exactly what to do. I dug through the back, where she keeps all her old bags that she doesn't use anymore. At one time I know these bags were like all her newer bags. Perfect, and pretty, and important. She's held on to these old bags for sentimental reasons, but she can't use them anymore. Some of them are damaged. Some of them are out of style. I dug and I dug and I dug until I found it: the Celine bag I was named after. It's completely crushed at this point. It holds no shape and hardly resembles a bag at all. I haven't seen it in years, but when I held it in my hands, I felt calm and I felt, in a way, thrilled. I asked my mom if I could keep it. She hesitated at first. I know this bag means a lot to her still. But then she said okay, and now I carry it on my arm. I like how it looks. It holds a lot, this bag. I can carry everything with me.

ANNIE

First of all, Simon was fine. He had a bacterial infection, and after two weeks of antibiotics he was back to being his sweet wonderful self. I waited until he was better to move out. I even gave it a couple of extra weeks, which was hard and strange to be living with Jason when it was over, but I didn't want Simon to be stressed by a move when he was still recovering. Luckily, I was able to move in with Joy for a while. She got a nice little place for herself, and it was like old times with the two of us living there. We'd watch movies. We'd laugh. It was calm and peaceful and Simon seemed very happy to spend time with her again. I was hoping I'd be able to save up enough to get my own place once my new job started, but it didn't work out. I took a job at a tech startup. It's really not what I want to be doing, but it's paying the bills. In the end I did have to move back in with my parents. It's definitely not my first choice of where to be living as a thirty-one-year-old woman, but it's not as bad as it could be, and mostly that's because of Sam.

I wasn't looking for anyone when I met him. Obviously since Jason and I had just broken up I wanted to take some time and be single. People say you meet someone when you aren't looking. You hear that so much that it's cliché at this point. But I met Sam randomly at a friend's engagement party, and we hit it off right away. Our first date was at a coffee shop. We talked for five hours. At the end of it I remember thinking, *This is the man I'm going to spend the rest of my life with.* That whole idea of love at first sight, I can't say that it was love exactly, but it was comfort Comfort at first sight, which really is almost as good, I think. I feel around Sam like I can be myself. The funny thing is if you'd asked me back when I was with Jason if that's how I felt around him, I would have lied and said yes. I did a lot of lying back then. I'd lie to my friends about how happy I was and how great things were. I certainly lied to my family. But mostly, I lied to myself. That's the part I can't get over. Why was I trying so hard to make it work? To be fair, I was in love with him, god knows I was. When we first broke up I cried for weeks. Everything reminded me of him and of us and of what we could have been. It was like I had a shadow everywhere I went. *Jason would love this,* I would think all the time about everything. I just really loved him. And I do believe he loved me too, and at the time I thought that was enough, but love really isn't enough. Love is the first step, the starting-off point. But it isn't enough.

The most incredible thing about being with Sam is that he treats me exactly how I treat him. I am kind to him, and he's kind to me back. I know that sounds like it should be obvious, but it's completely revelatory in my life. I was constantly kind to Jason when he was terrible back to me. And everything is so easy now. I'm never afraid to send Sam a text message out of the blue or to ask for anything from him. Back when I was with Jason, the word *needy* was truly and utterly the worst thing I could ever imagine being called. It was insane how much I fought not to seem like I needed anything from him. Well guess what, I am needy and so is Sam. And so was Jason! The whole point of finding someone to love is that you can need things from them and they can need things back. I need love and affirmation and commitment and affection and a best friend to spend my life with, *and so does he*. At one time I used to say that I was low-maintenance. Is that a way to describe yourself? Is that something a person should be proud of? And here's the other part of it. Sex is actually good now. I didn't know it, but until now I'd really never had good sex. I certainly wasn't having orgasms, and for whatever reason, I thought that was acceptable. I think at one point I'd said something to myself like *It's harder for women to have orgasms than it is for men.* What kind of bullshit was that? I think the truth was I was never comfortable with Jason or any of the other guys I ever slept with. I was always thinking about how I looked or if my boobs looked too small or god knows what else. Sex was something I was performing. It was like I wasn't even there. It was for them and them alone. When I think of myself using my body like that, it makes me feel sick. It makes me feel like I'm going crazy. But it's no wonder I would hurt myself like that because look at what I tolerated in that relationship. I just allowed everything. A thousand little wounds all day every day while I clung to what exactly? I look back on the woman who sat in that apartment with Jason and I just keep asking myself over and over again, *What was I getting out of that?* What was that? Who was that woman? It wasn't the same woman who learned to read at four years old. And it wasn't the same woman who stood up to Arly. It was a part of myself that is desperate, and raw, and almost unhuman. When I think of it, it scares me mostly because of this: I met Sam and he's wonderful and now I have this best friend and equal partnership. Now I have kindness in my life. Now I have love and pleasure and happiness that is based on who I am rather than some sick need to feel like I have a complicated, terrified man who deigns to be with me. But is that because I'm so brave? Did I make that choice? Or did I just luck into Sam being in my life? If I'd never met him would I have just fallen back into another relationship with another terrible guy? If Sam suddenly left me, would I be able to find another good man? Would I be strong enough to find one or would I just reach for that feeling again of being loved by someone? And why are there so few men like that out there? Why are there so many women who are kind and decent and where are the men to stand beside them? These thoughts keep me up at night when I try to reconcile that time I brought soup up to Jason after he'd asked me to text him less. I don't want to ever be a woman who carries soup up to a man. But I was that woman, and to believe she's gone out of me, been dug out, peeled from my skin, just because I can see what goodness there is, I think that's naïve. So for now I'm just reveling in what is and hoping for what might be.

And I'll tell you this too, just the other day it was dark and hot and when I opened a window in my old childhood bedroom I suddenly felt this rush inside myself. I went over to my bookshelf and pulled out one of my old journals where I used to write poems and stories as a child. I sat there on the floor and moonlight broke over me through those same branches that had been outside my window for so many years and I read my old writing. What struck me was not only how sure I was but also how calm and in control. I guess you can feel like that when you have faith in yourself and in a world that you're too young to understand. And here's the main point, rather than put those journals back where they were, rather than think of the past as the past and the future as the future, I felt hot and bothered at myself and at my mind. I felt like suddenly I had so much to give. I could hardly contain myself in my body. I felt like jumping or flying. I felt like screaming, but not from anger, from vividness and exaltation. And so I opened up a fresh page of that journal, and I started to write again. It felt like the kindest thing I had done for myself in ages. It felt like moving through life, even if it is just towards death, really won't be that bad. I'll say this, I just think I'm happy.

JOY

My favorite thing about living alone is the sound of the ice maker dropping ice cubes in the freezer. I couldn't tell you why exactly, but there's just something so lovely about it. When Annie was staying here with Simon for a few weeks she first pointed it out to me. She said, "Joy, do you hear that?" And it took me a few seconds to really think of what that sound could be, but then it occurred to me. That's *my* ice maker. I know that sounds little, but I take ownership of that sound. I take ownership of my space and water being turned to ice.

I'm very broke these days. I'll probably never be able to afford another vacation, or god knows I'll never be able to save up to buy a house, but I really love living alone. I love how at night I can walk around in my underwear and feel totally safe and secure. I'll even eat ice cream standing up by the counter sometimes. Really, I'll get a late-night craving and hop out of bed and eat a few spoonfuls and just completely indulge. *Fuck Jenny Craig.*

I always thought living alone would make me feel lonely. I thought it would point out every deficit in my life, but it's been the total opposite of that. I feel more complete than I ever have as an adult before. I don't feel frantic like I did. I don't feel desperate.

That isn't to say that I haven't had to seriously consider what happened in that apartment with Theo. I think about it all the time. I have nightmares about it too. Not talking to my stomach anymore, no. Those stopped. It's different nightmares now. Most of the time it's the same one. I'll hear Theo laughing in another room and I'll be trying to find him, but I can't. Then there was one where he was in bed with me and was crying about something he did as a child. When I woke up from that one I had the strongest feeling that I wanted to call him and tell him about it. I wanted to ask him what happened when he was a child that made him so sad, but obviously I didn't. I stopped myself from even thinking like that because why is there such a tenderness in me to want to take care of someone, to help stop the pain of someone who caused me so much pain? It's like some kind of sick mothering is built into me. A few days after I moved out I was at a café. I was feeling very sorry for myself. I think I'd cried all morning thinking about Theo, missing him and our home together. I was waiting in line to order and the man in front of me was in a suit on his way to work. He was in his fifties, with a square jaw. He looked like a dad, not my dad, but somebody's, everybody's. And I remember the kid who was serving him, he had to have been twenty-two at the very oldest, he was just so reactive to this man's presence. He was hopping to, making the coffee as fast as he could. He was polite and sharp. It certainly was different from how he'd treated the older lady who was in line before the man or how he treated me. Not that he was rude to either of us or anything. It was just that he so wanted this man's approval.

And then I thought, *Maybe we're all just reacting to the world like we react to our families. Soaking up our mothers' love. Being fearful of our fathers' disconnect.* Certainly our society is built around this dynamic. All the men in the world making decisions. All the women in the world fretting over those men. And I thought of myself in that apartment. The silent way I lived. The silent way I loved. I'm ashamed of it. Completely and utterly ashamed. But I did make myself tell my mom about it. I called her up and I said:

"Mom, I've moved out of the apartment with Theo."

And she said: "Oh really."

And I said: "Yes, I was in love with him and he wasn't in love with me and it was unhealthy."

And I remember my mom talking delicately, trying hard to find a way to soften my fall, but I know more than anything that as I went into detail about how things were being there in that home with my crush, it scared her. I'm sure she thought of her sister living in the woods. I'm sure she thought about the loneliness of what it means to be a person who loves someone without any reciprocation. She said, "But you know it's a learning experience," and I think that was just her trying to find her own peace with it. Trying to feel like her daughter wasn't someone who once handwashed a shit stain out of a pair of underwear that belonged to a person whose body she'd hardly ever touched.

The funny thing is I didn't try to tell her how Theo had loved me back. I couldn't tell her about the way he'd laughed beside me or saved me the last donut and put it with a little note that said, "Joyous, a donut for you." Our "love" will never be explicable. And I'm also not a fool. I only use the word *love* because there's no other way to describe it, but I know Theo didn't love me. Not in a real way. It's painful to say that, but I do say that to myself very often because as painful as it is, it's also freedom.

I see my aunt more these days too. I don't think of her the same way anymore. Maybe she doesn't have everything she's ever wanted and maybe much of her life isn't what she wanted it to be, but I never think of her as someone who settled. I think of her as someone who likes her choices and likes her life. She's a good person too, and that means more than anything. To tell the truth, my mom knows that about her and maybe what she's grieving is less about my aunt and more about the arbitrary way life can sometimes happen to you. My aunt, she got bees like she wanted. She sends me honey all the time.

And so I'm going to say this: I may not be happy yet, not in the way I hope to be, but I'm not living scared anymore. In fact I saw Theo out one day. He was walking across the street from me. At first I wanted to run the other way. But I made myself keep walking in the direction I would have been going if he hadn't been there. Then, I was struck by how he looked so much smaller than I remembered him. He almost seemed like half the man I had ever imagined him to be. Then he saw me and I know he did because he stopped dead in his tracks. I could have walked across the street to go talk to him, but I figured if it was important enough to him he would come over himself. I, on the other hand, had already said anything I needed to say. So I waved to him and he waved back. That was it. Which made me angry and it made me sad. I wanted him to come over and tell me he loved me. Who doesn't want that? From an old lover, from a former crush.

But then I went home and I took a long bath and the ice machine came on and I could hear it in my home and in my space. It was loud as it ricocheted off my walls and over my floor. My heart was also beating in the bath, though I wouldn't hear that. Then I stood up and caught sight of myself in the mirror, naked, dripping. My same round belly. My same aging face. Freedom, yes. I was ready.

ACKNOWLEDGMENTS

A huge thank-you to everyone at Dial, and especially to Whitney Frick, my ever enthusiastic, brilliant editor whose care and keeping of my novel has made me feel like the writer I've always wanted to be. A thank-you to Dorian Karchmar, who is genuinely a genius. To my friends and family, especially my parents, for always loving and supporting me. And to my husband, Jacob, whose talent, kindness, and love inspire me every day.

ABOUT THE AUTHOR

JANA CASALE is the author of *The Girl Who Never Read Noam Chomsky*. She has a BFA in fiction from Emerson College and an MSt in creative writing from Oxford. She currently resides outside Boston, Massachusetts, with her husband.

janacasale.com

ABOUT THE TYPE

This book was set in Bembo, a typeface based on an old-style Roman face that was used for Cardinal Pietro Bembo's tract *De Aetna* in 1495. Bembo was cut by Francesco Griffo (1450–1518) in the early sixteenth century for Italian Renaissance printer and publisher Aldus Manutius (1449–1515). The Lanston Monotype Company of Philadelphia brought the well-proportioned letterforms of Bembo to the United States in the 1930s.